The Asgard Saga

The Spinners Tale

Rochelle Tattersall

ROCHELLE TATTERSALL

First published in the United Kingdom.

ISBN: 9798880286683
Imprint: Independently published

Cover design by: Rochelle Tattersall
Printed and bound in the United Kingdom
www.rtattauthor.com

For Lily,
May you always find the strength to be yourself.

Preface

"Beware of the defenders, with power untold,
Their force shall end a world of old,
When time comes, a soul unites, to save all beings, from endless night.
The warrior, the protector, light and dark, a bond creates an eternal
spark,
This spark ignites a raging fire, to burn all evil upon a pyre,"
- Unknown Author, Prophecy, 963AD –

I would like to think there is good in all beings, that we are all capable of bringing light into the world. But my life so far makes these ideals hard to hold onto.

Three centuries ago, I was an ordinary spinner, a near-immortal witch, sent to Earth to maintain the balance between good and evil. I lived in Asgard - a world hidden from non-magical beings - with my birth parents, blissfully unaware of the battles they faced.

As with most spinners, we had a good life. My father was a healer at the royal court and my mother a teacher. My childhood was spent learning and exploring, as children do.

I was ignorant of the plight of the other creatures who walk the earth along with spinners.

In 1770, my life changed forever when my parents were murdered and I learned of a curse that had been placed upon my family by The Witches of Endor hoping, to steal our powers.

"With the ties that bind, the clock begins, to drain these spinners for their sins, as they fall, we hear their cries and witches of the world will rise."

- Nimune, Witch of Endor, 1322 –

My Gran warned me of the curse, after my parents' death, hoping to save me from their fate.

Spinners, like many other magical creatures, mate for life once we find our 'twin flame.' It is the joining of two powerful souls, created as one. They are said to be destined to reunite on the earthly plane once they have learned the lessons of their past lives. Together they can move mountains.

After watching my mother and father, I don't doubt that. I will never forget watching them together. My early magic allowed me to see auras, and theirs appeared as one shining so brightly, it was hard to look at.

Beyond that, their love seemed eternal. My parents truly believed they could break the curse, but it was not to be. They tragically died trying.

The curse means once my mate and I unite we will both die. My parents might have failed to break the curse, but I have a plan. Gran and I are the last surviving Beaumont's, when we have gone, when we eventually die, the curse will die with us.

I just have to ensure, my mate, doesn't find me first.

Chapter 1

Alexis

The full moon shines brightly onto a clearing in the forest. There's not a cloud in the sky and the stars sparkle like tiny diamonds on a black canvas. The tall trees surrounding the clearing have started to shed their leaves, which fall to the ground, spinning in the breeze like red and orange confetti.

The scene would be serene were it not for the figures at the centre of the clearing.

Illuminated only by the moon's rays, a woman bends over a man, tears streaming down her face. She has a burst of fiery red hair, which shines like a beacon in the moon's light. The man's hair is darker, and he is dressed in fine clothes and furs, lying pale and motionless on the damp grass.

"No, no, no. Please hold on," the woman cries. She places her hands over the man's heart, a white ethereal light emitting from them. "You can't leave me; I won't let you" the woman pleads. Tears stream down her face, splashing onto the man's chest, but the woman knows her tears are falling on deaf ears.

The man is gone.

No longer an observer, I am the woman, her tears are mine as I realise the man lying cold beneath my sobbing form is my father.

My hands stroke his handsome face as I plead to the heavens to bring him back to me. Closing my eyes, I turn my face up to the full moon, silently begging her to spare him.

When I open them again, the man in my arms is no longer my father but a beautiful raven-haired man. He looks peaceful in his slumber, but still, I am unable to wake him.

I bring my lips to his, fresh tears streaming down my face as the grief hits me anew. I am not sure who this new man is, but I know he is everything to me and I must save him from the fate of my father.

The air around me suddenly begins to swirl and I'm surrounded by dense fog. When it clears, I am stood by an open grave. People all around me are dressed in black, faces wet from the tears they shed. I see two coffins being lowered into the ground. My head is bowed as if weighed down by grief.

The feeling of someone looking at me, makes me look up.

My own eyes meet the most vivid blue eyes I have ever seen. A recognition stirs within me, and a jolt of electricity runs through my body.

This beautiful man is my mate, my twin flame.

I see the recognition appear on his face, as he too knows what I am to him.

He is the most beautiful creature I have ever seen, with those piercing blue eyes that seem to touch my very soul, with a head of long, thick almost jet-black hair, elaborately braided back from his face.

His symmetrical features seem to fit his face perfectly and I long to run my hands through the beard her wears, which is as dark as his hair. Even from here, I can tell he is a warrior, muscles ripple through his mourning tunic. His shoulders are covered by a dark fur, held together at the front by a beautiful golden chain (only a fool would go against him in a fight). He can't seem to take his eyes away from mine.

Panic seizes my being. This cannot be happening. The funeral isn't over yet, there are still many customs to be followed. The tribute I have chosen to send my parents into the afterlife with is still clutched in my frozen palm, but I know I can't stay another minute. A loss even greater than the one I have already endured will follow and I don't think I can survive it.

My mate is stood between the king and queen, and I see the war inside him, he wants – no needs – to comfort me, but he stays where he is, respecting my grief.

I take a final look at my parents' wicker coffins as they are lowered into the ground and offer a silent apology. Opening my hand I release the comb within, letting it fall to the ground by my feet.

I take a final look at my parents' coffins being lowered into the grave, then to my mate before I turn on my heel to run, as fast as my legs will carry me.

I wake with a start. *It was just a dream*; I tell myself firmly. It has been almost 250 years since those fateful days, but it feels like only yesterday to me. The grief of losing my parents never abates, the dream has been a constant reminder of my inability to save them.

Running away from my mate, left a void in my heart that has – and will – never heal. But what choice did I have? I couldn't let him suffer with me.

Of course, I like every other of my kind, I know the spinners tale – the reuniting of a soul split in two.

Spinners are the most powerful beings on earth. So powerful that before we are born, our soul divides in two. According to the story we are told as children, if we are lucky, learn to use our power for good and not be tempted by the dark, we will be reunited with the other half of our soul. Once the souls find each other the flame cannot be extinguished, they are bonded for all eternity.

I had seen people in Asgard who found their mates, and it was a magical sight to see them together. Like the most beautifully choreographed dance, each so in tune with the other they appear to move as one. But rather than becoming the same person, each illuminates the essence of the other.

My mother and father were true mates, twin flames and their light shone brighter than I could ever describe.

My mother, Selene Beaumont, had beauty and power like no other – rivalled only by my Gran, Mormor Frayer. I share her vivid red hair – a testament to our quick tempers – and emerald-green eyes but that is where the comparisons end. She had the grace and elegance of an angel.

Selene worked at the most prestigious school in Asgard. She would spend her days teaching fledgling spinners how to control their magic.

When she wasn't in class, she could be found in the library, surrounded by her precious books. Returning home, my mother perpetually smelled of old books, ink, cedar, and henbane. I could always tell when she'd had a particularly trying day, her hair would be full of static and often slightly singed on the ends.

As a child, I would watch on in delight as she directed everyday objects around our grand home. Selene was the conductor of a magnificent orchestra, making everything sparkle in her wake. Even when doing housework, she seemed to glow.

My mother would sit before bed, patiently trying to tame my wild red hair with a beautiful comb, she claimed was a gift from a mermaid, she'd met on one of her many adventures.

It was this I planned to give as a tribute at her funeral. It might seem worthless to others, but for me the comb was priceless.

As she worked on my unruly hair, she would enchant me with stories of her adventures with my father. The object held some of my happiest memories and seemed a fitting tribute to the people who raised me - I can only hope someone placed it on her coffin as it was lowered into the ground.

After her stories, my mother would create tiny orbs of light to sit on my ceiling, a perfect representation of the stars in the heavens looking down on us. *"To chase away the monsters in dark corners, Alexis,"* she would say, before kissing me goodnight.

I can only imagine what her magic could do outside the house. Not that she or my father would ever allow me to see. I hated it when they left. I always had fun at Gran's house, where we would bake delicious treats and tell tales of fearsome gods and giants, elves, and fairies. Still, I wanted to be out having adventures with them.

They would leave full of excitement and hope for their trip ahead, only to return weeks later despondent. My mother would return to the library and bury herself in ancient texts and my father to his practice at the palace.

I always worried they would be disappointed to return to me and our dull lives. Gran assured me they weren't, just that their trip hadn't gone as planned.

No one ever told me where they went or what happened on their journeys.

I am more like my father, Saul. He was a quiet and reserved man, always preferring to shine a light on others – my mother in particular – over himself.

He spent long hours at the palace, often coming home after I was in bed. Every night though, he would come to give me a kiss goodnight.

Some nights the smell of eucalyptus and pine trees lingering on his clothes would be so strong, that it would wake me, and I would get to hear a story from his day before he sent me back off to sleep.

I always believed that there was nothing my parents could not overcome.

A momentary smile finds my lips as I think about watching them together when they thought no one was looking. The way they looked at each other, with pure unconditional love was the envy of every couple they met.

The smile fades as their loss hits me anew. As the daughter of the royal court's chief healer, I should have been able to save my parents. I should have been powerful enough. I come from a long line of supremely powerful spinners.

My father's family had been healers in at the court for millennia and though I know little about my mother's family (my Gran would never discuss where she came from), I know they were very powerful. Even more so than the royals and elders themselves, or so my Gran said. In the confines of her small cottage, she let her magic run free and there was never a doubt in my mind.

Mormor Freya - my maternal grandmother - could have been my mother's twin, they looked so alike, but unlike Selene, she hid her power. Freya was an expert in reigning it in.

I'd hear her arguing with my mother when they thought I was asleep. *"Selene, my child you must be more careful with your power,"* she would say. *"It makes others envious."*

In the company of outsiders, Freya could hide who she truly was, she taught me to do the same and it's a trait I perfected in the years following my parents' death – not that I have anywhere near the kind of ability she or my mother had. Gran has more magic in her little finger than I have in my entire body. No, the Beaumont family power did not pass to me. Had I stayed in Asgard, I'd have been the laughing stock of the city by now.

I will not share the fate of my parents. I am sure our Goddess had good intentions when she split a soul, to have them reunite here on earth but I will not be controlled by destiny.

I create my own life and that does not involve being magically tied to a man I don't know the first thing about. When my time comes to die, I will do so alone and put an end to the curse.

I lay for hours staring at the ceiling, tracing the grain of the wood with my eyes. I miss my parents and Gran every day. Why did they keep so much from me? Maybe I could have helped.

As the years passed, I came to terms with their untimely death but made a promise never to follow in their footsteps. I've found a comfortable and somewhat happy existence in my new home; with people I care for greatly.

I don't need to slay dragons or whatever it was my parents did on their trips. I might never experience the love they had, but my life here is enough.

Tossing and turning, I watch as the sun slowly rises over the Pacific Ocean. I feel my losses all over again and eventually drift back into a restless sleep.

When I wake again, the sun is streaming through a gap in the sheer white curtain. I lay for a moment, watching it blow around in the gentle sea breeze.

Dust motes sparkle where the sun hits them, making them look more like tiny diamonds than shed skin and dirt. It's amazing how the sun can transform even the dreariest of objects into something more…something magical even.

My body is drenched in sweat from my fitful night, the breeze cools it on my skin as I untangle my limbs from the sheet and come to sit on the edge of the bed.

The small cabin is a world away from the grand house I lived in with my parents in Asgard. It's humble and unassuming. Matias, my adoptive father built it for me, when I first mentioned having a place of my own by the sea.

It's relatively sturdy, considering its age and structure. Dad used the driftwood he collected around the island. The wood has taken on blueish-silver and white tones from its years at the mercy of the salty sea air.

The main room holds my bed, a small, battered sofa and a Victorian writing desk. None of it matches per se, but it's always felt more comfortable than the longhouse I grew up in. There I was afraid to touch anything, for fear of breaking it. It was more museum than home.

The only other rooms in the house are the bathroom and a tiny kitchen. The latter isn't particularly well equipped – it doesn't need to be. I don't eat here often, preferring to dine in town with Mum and Dad or friends. The cupboards predominantly contain tea – hundreds of varieties. Everyone on the island knows of my love for the stuff. I look forward to special occasions, where I usually receive more as a gift.

French doors lead to a small deck, beyond which lies the sea. At high tide, I can sit on the edge of the deck and let the water wash over my feet.

Heading to my tiny kitchen, I hunt down a clean cup to make myself some tea. The tea here isn't the same as it was back in Asgard, but it's grown on me over the years.

Waiting for the water to boil – something my mother and gran never had to do – I stare out at the ocean. There isn't a window in the cabin, that doesn't look out over the sea. It seems to soothe my aching soul. I breathe in deeply through my nose and sigh, letting the tension out as I do so.

Stepping out into the air, I embrace the breeze, allowing it to blow away the cobwebs left by another sleepless night. I slowly walk down the beach to the shore. The white sand is soft underfoot and not yet, too hot to walk on barefoot. I reach the sea and stand looking out, while gentle waves wash over my feet. The sun is already high in the sky, shining down on the crystal-clear ocean.

It doesn't take long for the sun to warm me, filling every pore with its healing light. I often wonder what my kind was thinking, when they made their home in one of the coldest places on earth.

Why live in eternal the coldness of the Arctic Circle when you could live here?

This island - my home - is paradise. My cabin sits at the edge of a long white sandy beach with a spectacular view over the Pacific Ocean.

Thick forest covers most of it. Passing boats wouldn't know it was inhabited, even were it not enchanted to look that way. There is just one dirt path leading inland to the small town, where a few hundred other disillusioned souls live.

For a long while I lived inland with my adoptive parents, Brighid, and Matias. The ocean always called to me though, so when I felt strong enough, I moved out here on my own. Even when I lived in Asgard, I loved the water. I'd spend hours playing in the shallows of the fjords as Gran watched on.

The ocean represents freedom to me. She is wild and untameable. The calm exterior hiding the truth within. In some ways, she reminds me of myself. Only the ocean, has real power to unleash when she needs it.

I sometimes wish I had her strength.

Serenity Island is the one place on earth I don't need power - other than to heal the sick, which I do with traditional herbs and folk magik, and not a spinners gift. We are so cut off from the rest of the world, we have never had to worry about threats from other creatures, so it's all we need.

This small island paradise exists in a way the rest of the world can't understand. We function as a commonwealth. Power is shared by a group of leaders, there is no king or other single authority.

The creatures here have found a way to live together in harmony, appreciating each other for our individual strengths. We aren't constantly battling for supremacy. Importantly, spinners don't feel the need to rule over anyone else - we are all equal. I shudder to think what life is like for the rest of the earth's population. It is a world based on segregation, prejudice, and fear.

That is why I am here and not back in Asgard with my mate. I know it seems foolish to live my life alone, without someone to share it with. I would rather be here living in peace, without him though, in the knowledge he is safe than in Asgard in constant fear for our lives.

Does that make me weak and selfish? Possibly. Maybe I could have returned when I saw what was possible and shown the court a better way to live. Being my parents' daughter and the crown prince's mate would give me some sway.

I know better though. There would be no changing the minds of The Elders. 'This is how we have always existed, how the heavens intended it,' I can almost hear them saying in their condescending tone.

Gran told me The Elders always refer to gods never the Goddess – she always hated their unwillingness to admit our creator is a woman. In fact, she didn't think very highly of them. She said they were scared, weak men, who used fear to hold on to their limited power. *"One day soon, they will get what's coming to them, Alexis,"* she would say.

The Elders have been around since the beginning of time, or so we're told. Most spinners believe they were sent by the gods. They are guardians that reside in a realm between Earth and Vanaheim – acting as a vessel for the gods' will. And The Elder's word is final. Some of us were raised to believe in the Goddess, not gods and it's she we look to here in Serenity. My relationship with her is somewhat strained, however.

Coming out of my thoughts, I take in a deep breath letting the scent of salty sea air and wild jasmine fill my nostrils.

Placing my now empty cup in the sand, I quickly strip out of my clothes and walk into the sea. It's still cool at this time of day, helping to wash away the vestiges of sleep still clouding my mind. I focus on the repetitive movement, letting everything else fall away. My body slips easily through the water, and I can't resist a peek below the surface.

The ocean floor teems with life, and I lose track of time and place, mesmerised by the show. Tiny fish swim by in bursts of impossibly bright colour. A crab watches on, perched artfully on a rock. It appears to be posing, but I know it's waiting for an early morning snack to swim by. Other creatures, I can't name come and go. I could stay here all day watching the underwater world go by.

Eventually, though, I need to breathe. I resurface and swim back to where I left my clothes.

When I arrive home, my best friend Ginny, is at the door. She opens it, popping her head inside. "Wakey wakey, rise and shine, sleepy head," she says with a huge smile.

Her good humour is infectious, and I respond with a smile of my own.

She has arrived at my small house with the same greeting every day for longer than I care to remember. Every day, I am grateful to have such a wonderful friend.

See, who needs a mate when I have such amazing people around? Not me!

Ginny is a head shorter than me, with stunning golden hair, that suits her now sun-kissed complexion perfectly. She is the kind of person who looks good in anything, with curves in all the right places.

Her spinners marks are like an intricate tapestry weaving up her body. Small creatures - butterflies, ladybirds, bees, and other tiny creatures give away her affinity to nature.

Every single man on the island has asked her out at one time or another. I've lost count of the number of men she has dated. They don't keep her interest long. Ginny is a spinner like me, she is waiting for her twin flame and no one else will cut it.

This is the one downside of living on an island, cut off from the rest of the world. You're not likely to run into your twin flame whilst wandering in the forest – unless the other half of your soul happens to reside in a wild boar.

Perfect for me. Not so much for other creatures who wish, and have yet to, find their mate.

I have been on Serenity Island since I ran away from Asgard, after my parents' funeral and I shudder to imagine where I would be without it.

Mated to the crown prince or dead, more likely, I think to myself.

I make a fresh pot of tea and we sit quietly enjoying the view. I opt for the green variety, needing an extra hit of caffeine after my sleepless night. It does its job seeping into my blood, bringing me back to life.

I sigh contentedly. "Good morning," I say eventually. "It's a beautiful day." Ginny smiles, she loves the sun as much as I do. It was a rarity in Asgard. "It is, I've been up since five," Ginny replies.

Then a shadow crosses her face, and she looks sternly at me. "You were dreaming again last night." It's not a question. "Do you want to talk about it?" I sigh, I don't really want to talk about it. We have discussed this dream countless times over the centuries - well most of it. I've never told another soul about leaving my mate at my parents' graveside. She knows there is more to it, but never pushes me. "It was just the usual," I say.

"There is more to it, Lex. Even after all this time, you are still trapped there." She is smiling and I know she isn't angry with me, just frustrated with the way I deal with my past. I sigh, not knowing what to say and decide to get a shower, rather than discuss the dream further.

I am still thinking about it as I turn on the shower. Slipping out of my shorts and vest, I put it out of my mind and focus on plans for the day ahead.

Stepping into the hot shower I let the water work out the knots that have formed in my back. It feels wonderful running over my skin. As I start to relax, I feel an intense heat that begins in my foot and travels all the way up my body. I gasp and look down to see my spinners marks faintly glowing. I am mesmerised by the glow and the heat making me feel truly alive, for the first time in a very long time.

I've always loved my marks. Beautiful flowers and herbs - roses, lavender, peonies, and daisies - on vines weaving around my left leg, up across my tummy, breast, neck and back down my left arm. A spinner's marks are meant to represent our powers. Seen as I have little power by spinner standards, I take mine to align with my father's healing abilities and my affinity for helping the sick. I'm more like a forest witch, using the gifts of the earth to ease the suffering and sick.

They have never glowed or felt like this, and my long-ignored intuition tingles. I feel the heat spread to my whole body and gasp in surprise, feeling the urge to run my hands down my marks. The sensation intensifies as my hands slide over my wet body making my legs shake. I am intoxicated, but as fast as it starts it stops, I look down and the glow has gone. Taking a minute to recover, I turn the temperature of the water down and gather my thoughts.

I step out of the shower and slowly dry off. A nagging feeling begins to creep into my mind. I can't put it into words, but something is telling me what just happened in the shower is a sign and I'm not sure it's a good one - even though it felt... wonderful for just a moment. Like my power had been there all along and it was starting to wake from a long nap.

Back on the beach outside the cabin, Ginny is waiting for me. We take the small dirt track into town, the tree canopy above, offering some relief from the blazing sun. *Just another scorching day in paradise,* I think to myself with a smile.

Ginny talks animatedly about her garden and the new herbs she is growing. She has loved mixing with creatures from other cultures and learning about different types of plants and medicine, some she sells in her small shop, but most she gives me to use at the hospital.

She has clearly decided to save her dream analysis for later. I am grateful for the time to gather my thoughts.

Others say good morning as we pass by them. Our little paradise island is a haven for all creatures. The commonwealth was established before I arrived and has flourished over the centuries. It's the only place on earth where nonmagical beings knowingly live alongside magical ones.

Ginny and I sit on the leadership council which is responsible for the wellbeing of the Serenity's inhabitants.

My magic - the little I have - comes in the form of caring for others. Like my father. For a long time after my parents' death, I wouldn't use magic at all. My parents had been killed for theirs and I wasn't about to follow in their footsteps.

The healing power gave him dominion over the forces of life and death. Most healing spinners use their magic to care for others. There are of course those who use it to gain power over others.

Then, other species seek our power to cause harm. Some, like the Witches of Endor, are drawn to evil, and dark magic calls loudest to them.

Eventually, Ginny and Mum convinced me to start a healing practice, of sorts, on the island and I now run the small hospital - like my father but on a less grand scale.

Entering the town's main square, it is already a hive of activity. I smile as everyone buzzes around hanging colourful decorations, in preparation for visitors.

When settlers first came to Serenity, they lived a very simple life, but since the council was formed, we have thrived. We are completely self-sufficient, with an impressive infrastructure including a hospital, school, power station, farms, shops, bars, and restaurants. We produce all our food and energy. The town is peppered with stores selling everything you could ever need – clothing, shoes, books, the latest tech, food, you name it.

Most people never leave the island. Some of the children go to explore other parts of the world, but they usually come back, bringing new knowledge and experience with them.

Occasionally others seek refuge here, they are always welcomed with open arms. Our strength is in our diversity. Unfortunately, this way of life is unique to Serenity. The world outside our small island is segregated by species.

I beam with pride as I watch everyone prepare for the week's events.

Along one side of the quadrangle, sits the council hall. A modest obsidian building, highlighting the island's volcanic heritage. The hall is nothing like the magnificent white palace of Asgard, with its enormous turrets and stained-glass windows, but it's still impressive in its own understated way and I love it.

On the steps leading inside, Brighid waits with her partner and my adoptive father, Matias, by her side, as always. "Buenos Dias, Alexis, Ginny," Matias greets us as we approach. "Buenos Dias," we reply in unison, with smiles spreading across our faces. Solid arms enfold me in a cold, yet comforting hug. "Morning, Dad," I say, breathing in his black pepper and grapefruit scent.

My Dad is a vampire. An odd match, you might think, for a warm-blooded empath like Mum, but they are perfect together. Myths about magical creatures have a lot to answer for.

Dad, while having inhuman speed and strength, isn't interested in draining the blood of the warm bloods on the island. He gets by just fine on rare steaks and the odd bag of donated A negative.

Pulling away from Dad, my smile falters as I see the look on Mum's face. She lets Dad and Ginny walk in ahead of us and rounds on me. "You're exhausted," she says. She is an empath, and nothing gets past her.

"I'm fine," I quip back, rolling my eyes. She narrows hers at me. "You are not fine, don't even try that line with me, little cherry. You need rest."

Mum and Dad gave me the nickname "cherry blossom" on account of my red hair, when I first came to the island, and they became my parents. I'd never had a pet name before, and it made me feel like I belonged. It is rarely used now, other than when they are really worried about me and when it is used, it's shortened to cherry. Their other name for me is Firefly – something to do with my fiery temper.

I am forever grateful for their generosity. When I first arrived in Serenity, they took me into their home, never having children of their own. Though I was technically an adult by the time I arrived, I was vulnerable and needed their love and care.

Neither pried about my life before, and I was grateful for that. Mum sensed I had been through hell, and I needed them to take on the role of parents.

"You work too hard and need to learn to let others take care of you as well."

I just nod. There is no point in arguing with her. "I will try," I say. She scoffs but lets it go as we enter the council chamber.

The other dozen members of the council are already seated. Mum and I take our seats between Dad and Ginny. The chatter stops and all eyes fall on Mum. "Good morning, all," she says with a smile, before running through the plan for today.

In a few short hours, ambassadors from the Spinners Court in Asgard will arrive on the island. In the more than two hundred years I have lived here, it is the first time this has happened.

It isn't that sending ambassadors to visit other lands is uncommon. As a matter of fact, the crown – or more accurately The Elders – like to keep a close eye on every community. We have simply been missed before now.

As I ran away from my home and life at court, I was always grateful for the oversite. However, I knew this day would eventually come. Thankfully, there doesn't appear to be anyone on the guest list who either I or anyone else know.

We finish the meeting and head back out onto the square, which has been transformed from its usually humble appearance into a truly dazzling spectacle.

Adults stand around the edges talking animatedly and having a well-earned drink, while children run around the whole square laughing and squealing.

The sight fills me with such joy, for a moment I forget about the void in my heart.

Just before lunch, Mum and Dad make their way to our small port to meet the 'royal ambassadors'. They want me to go with them, but I remain in the square with the others, delaying the time I must face the spinner's court again.

I wonder what might be going through the ambassadors' minds coming to our island, where spinners, werewolves, empaths, vampires, faes and many other kinds of creature live peacefully together.

I imagine they are wary, to say the least. Spinners are very traditional and our way of life... well it isn't exactly traditional.

I remain in the square with the other council members, to await the arrival of the visitors. "Will you please stop fidgeting," Ginny says to me.

I hadn't realised I was until she said it, but for the past five minutes, I have been oddly on edge. "Sorry," I mumble.

"Why are you so nervous all of a sudden?" she asks. "We've been planning for weeks, everything is perfect." Not knowing of my connection with it, Ginny doesn't fully understand my reluctance to have anyone from the court of Asgard here.

I try to calm my nerves and focus on my breathing. It works, but as I see a group of people turning into the town square my blood runs cold and then hot as my marks begin to tingle. A wave of panic hits me and I think I might actually vomit.

The group approaches and I see him look up startled at my sudden proximity. His eyes search the square and land on mine. A feeling I haven't encountered for 250 years hits me as my mate's strange blue and amber eyes look straight into my own.

I see a million emotions flash across his face before he lands on confusion. Mum feels it too, she looks quizzically between him and me but says nothing.

I want to run, but his eyes hold me firmly in place. I feel so nauseous, I think I must be green. Ginny glances at me and takes hold of my hand. I can't imagine what my face is telling her, but it must be bad. I am grateful for her hand, holding me in place. If it wasn't for her anchoring, I might well be laid out on the floor.

I look at our hands and then back to Mum's confused face. She sees the panic in mine, and I immediately feel a wave of peace wash over me as she uses her empathic power to calm me. The nausea immediately fades, and I am no longer at risk of passing out where I stand. Ginny feels it too and gives my hand a tight squeeze before letting me go.

Mum begins making introductions and my mate approaches me. Despite the terror I feel, my eyes rake hungrily over his entire body. The prince is as striking as I remembered, the passage of time has done nothing to change him - the only difference being the absence of a beard and his now-cropped hair.

He is easily well over six feet tall. Broad shoulders, narrow to well-defined abs and long muscular legs. He looks straight at me through a row of long, dark eyelashes. High distinct cheekbones sit in direct contrast to the gentle curve of his nose.

Finally, my eyes land on his soft full lips. My teeth find my own and gently bite down, as a longing to taste them runs through me.

The terror returns with force, and I again have to fight back the bile rising in my throat.

He leans in kissing my cheek. My skin burns from the heat of his proximity. "Hello, my love, I think you and I need to talk," he breathes before pulling away.

Chapter 2

Henri

I stare out at the vast ocean surrounding me, wondering where the hell we are. We apparated to Cairns in Australia, but the island, the Asgard ambassadors and I are visiting, is protected from apparition, so we complete the journey by boat.

It's hard to believe that less than an hour ago, I was surrounded by icy fjords and now, I'm basking in the tropical sunshine of the Pacific Ocean. It will be another hour or two until we reach our destination - Serenity Island.

None of us really know what to expect when we arrive. Oddly, the island has been off the spinner's radar until recently. I've been told it is likely to be primitive, simple even, given how cut off it is from civilised society. While I know, the words used to describe my destination are meant as a slur, I can't wait to see how another society lives. From the day I came of age and could leave Asgard without a guardian, I loved to explore.

I have climbed mountains with giants in Nepal, visited vampires in Romania, and even swam with mermaids in Mexico. If I am to be king one day, I want to know and understand all the people I rule over – not just Asgardian spinners.

Initially, I had no intention of accompanying the ambassadors on this trip, preferring to explore without watchful eyes. However, I was left with little choice following my latest *disgrace*.

I think back to the conversation with my father. Although he was furious, I think his disappointment is what hurt most. He and my mother have served long enough. I owe it to them, to take over the family business. I just can't bring myself to commit to a woman who isn't *her* - even if it would allow them to step down so I could take the throne.

Ed approaches me, telling me we will dock just before eleven. "You OK, Hen?" He asks. Am I? I'm not sure, so I nod non-committaly. "You did the right thing, you know," he adds. We have been able to read each other's thoughts since we were kids, so he knows what I'm thinking.

"I know," I say. "I just can't help feeling like I am letting everyone down. At the same time, I just couldn't tie myself to someone who isn't *her.*" I refuse to even think of her name, the mate I lost before I even knew her, the pain it evokes is too much to bear.

That pain has driven me to do terrible things. My thoughts turn dark as I remember the heinous acts I have committed. While I believe, they have made the earth a better place for all creatures, I have no doubt, that I face a fate far worse than death when my judgement day arrives. Every individual act has already cost a part of my soul.

Ed can see the way my thoughts have gone and is there to pull me back, as always. "Maybe if you explained to your parents, they would understand. They might even convince the Elders to change the law," he says. His heart is in the right place, but we both know they wouldn't. Our traditions are too deeply rooted. *'This is how it has always been done,'* I can almost hear the Elders telling my father.

"We both know that would never happen, Ed. They would just find another *eligible* spinner to tie me to, instead. If they knew my true mate was dead, I wouldn't have an excuse." The words cut me to the bone, just as painful, now as the day I found out, over a century ago. Ed winces as he feels my pain and drops the subject.

We are quiet for the rest of the journey and Ed, doesn't comment on my thoughts again - he has either tuned out or conceded.

I can just see the outline of land on the horizon. From here it doesn't look big enough to be inhabited, but I know from the pearly hue surrounding it, that this is Serenity Island. I can feel the magic, protecting it from prying eyes. Whoever cast the protection is powerful, that much is clear even from this distance.

As we draw closer, we pass through the protective barrier, and I am surprised to find the island doesn't look any more conspicuous than it did before. It's small, I can see only a few miles in each direction, before the land curls round on itself.

We head into a dock, that houses just a couple of speed boats and a run-down yacht. A group of half a dozen *people* are at the dockside awaiting our arrival.

I double-take when I realise that among the group I can see a werewolf, a vampire, and a *human.* I almost laugh out loud when I realise it's like the beginning of a sad dad joke. Ed snorts hearing my thought. "A werewolf, vampire and human walk into a bar..." he says quietly shaking with mirth. Fortunately, no one else hears.

Boat safely moored, I jump onto the jetty, before anyone can help me and take in my surroundings. The island is so beautiful it takes my breath away. Beyond the dock are miles of soft white sand, which gives way to the perfect turquoise sea beyond. A few hundred feet from the dock, there is a tiny cabin looking out onto the sea. I am mesmerised by it. What would it be like to live there and awaken to that view every morning? I'm not even close enough to see through the windows, but for reasons beyond my understanding, looking at the cabin feels like coming home.

Eventually, I turn to look inland, but the dense forest blocks the town from view. There is just one dusty track leading towards the centre of the island, where I imagine most of its inhabitants live.

I smile at the group of people waiting to greet us. A striking woman with straight, jet-black hair and caramel skin stands front centre with her hand outstretched. I struggle to place what she is. Not a species I recognise, but I instantly like her.

None of this group of people look 'primitive' as I'd been told to expect. They are wearing the latest fashions and one of them is looking at a mobile phone. I'd say they are far more advanced than those back in Asgard, with their traditional dress and total lack of tech.

I have a feeling that this island is going to be full of surprises and as I take the woman's hand in mine, I feel excited to explore, for the first time in a very long time.

Alexis

His voice has a hint of an order to it, which instead of repulsing me – which it definitely should – sends a shiver of excitement through my very core.

He moves to greet other members of the council and I mumble mine to the other ambassadors, still feeling his gaze upon me. My mind is racing. I can't understand what he is doing here, I would have recognised the prince's name on the list.

I don't want or need a mate; my life is great as it is. I've never been interested in a romantic relationship, especially with my twin flame. I mean who wants to be with someone because destiny says so? Does free will mean nothing to the Goddess?

Romantic relationships are more trouble than they are worth. No matter how drawn to this arrogant ass I am, I need to get away, now! No good can come from his presence in my life.

People begin buzzing around and both Ginny and Mum make a beeline straight for me. I shake my head, silently begging them to act normal. "Not now," I mouth. I'm not sure how much longer I can keep up the calm act. I need to get away. There is a loud buzzing in my ears and my last cup of tea is still threatening to make a reappearance.

As soon as the welcomes are over and everyone is seated, I excuse myself, walking as calmly as I can out of sight. Rounding the corner, I break into a sprint in the direction of my cove. I sense more than hear his sigh, as the crown prince excuses himself and takes off after me.

I know if I move quickly enough, he won't be able to find me, and I can make a plan. "Alexis, stop," his angry voice echoes through the trees and I almost stop. There is a command there, I fight the urge to obey. His mere presence is throwing me off. It has been a long time since I'd heard a royal command, but it's there in his voice.

The boulders protecting my cove come into view and I almost sigh in relief. As I cross them, the rest of the island fades away and I know, I'm free – for now. I look up to the clear blue sky for help. "Is this your idea of a joke?" I ask no one in particular. It has been a long time since I tried to communicate with the Goddess and she clearly has no intention of helping, as usual.

I drop onto my hands and knees in the white sand as my entire being is wracked with grief. "Is it not enough to you that I was driven from my first home and family, and now you drive me from the one I chose?" I am talking to the Goddess again. Something I vowed never to do.

She was never there for me. Gran told me the Goddess never makes mistakes, but she certainly made one when she made me. A spinner with no real power and who cannot be with her mate. She cursed me to live for eternity with only half a soul. That is either a huge mistake or a cruel joke. Either way, she has never been there for me. I am on my own. Again.

After a few deep breaths, I push myself up and sit on the warm soft sand with my back resting on a rock. What am I going to do? I need to get off the island, but as soon as I leave the cove, he will be able to find me. I can only imagine the reception I will get. Not to mention, I will have to face Mum, Dad, and Gin.

The only option is to run. There won't be time for explanations. If the prince catches me there will be no escaping a second time.

I wait until darkness has fallen before getting up to leave. I spent the entire afternoon, looking out at the ocean attempting to work out a plan that didn't involve me leaving my home. I came up short again and again, resigning myself to the fact that I need to leave. I have no idea where I will go. My only plan so far is to get to the mainland where I will (hopefully) be able to apperate far enough away that the prince won't be able to find me again.

I carefully climb down the rocks leading out of the cove any mistake now and I will be found. When my feet hit firm ground, I run as fast as my legs can carry me.

Henri

As soon as I stepped foot on the island, I could sense something. I recognised it immediately but pushed it away. *It can't be possible, she died long ago*, I tell myself sternly.

Pushing the thought away, I smile approaching the island's leader. I've never been here before; I'd never even heard of the place until my father decided to send me with the ambassadors.

It is beautiful though; I feel the peace settling all around me. It's the first time I've felt anything like calm in a very long time.

As we head inland, Brighid, the chair of the island's council tells me about how the community has grown, with every kind of being imaginable living here and how they developed a thriving and prosperous community.

As we approach the town's small square and council building, the calm feeling I experienced only moments before evaporates. I sense her again and this time there is no pushing it aside. My marks begin tingling and I notice the ones on my hand glowing slightly.

Then I see *her*. The one who's name I still can't bring myself to think – my mate. It has been 250 years since I saw that face, but I would know it anywhere. When we lock eyes, I feel the jolt again. The one I felt stood by a graveside so many years ago.

I don't know how, but she is standing right in front of me, a look of abject terror marring her beautiful face. Her stance reminds me of a deer hunt. She senses the danger and is stuck between the desire to bolt and playing dead.

Her panic rises to a point that it makes my own hackles rise and I start to search for the danger she senses. The woman beside her takes hold of her hand, and they exchange a brief look. Her panic suddenly disappears, and I feel a wave of calm. This is one strange vision; I think to myself.

My eyes sweep over the mirage before me, with her full ruby lips, endless green eyes and vivid red hair shining like a beacon in the midday sun. I dare not even blink, knowing that the moment I close my eyes she will disappear. The closer I get though, the greater the pull and before I know it, I am stood close enough to kiss her.

Her panic returns in full force, it almost takes me off my feet. She is shaking and her breathing has hitched up – fast and shallow.

It takes every ounce of restraint I have not to pick her up and run into the forest surrounding the town and make her mine right now.

"Hello, my love, I think you and I need to talk," I say to her as I lean in to kiss her on the cheek.

Oh, her scent. She smells of a meadow in the height of summer when the flowers are the sweetest, Jasmine and Honeysuckle. The need I have to be close to her almost knocks me over.

She tenses but doesn't say a word as I make myself move on to the woman by her side. My eyes never leave her as I make my way around the remainder of the group.

I will never let her out of my sight again if I can help it. However, I get the feeling she isn't as pleased to see me, as I am her.

Brighid and the woman who had held Alexis' hand as I approached turn towards her, but she shakes her head, whispering "not now," a pleading look in her eyes. They immediately back away turning to other conversations. These women are important to Alexis and her them, I can see that already. They are her family.

Everyone begins to take their seats, around tables set out in the square. I take mine directly opposite Alexis, hardly able to tear my eyes away from her. She never looks at me, but I hear her make her excuses and walk away.

I sigh; she is running away from me *again*.

I hadn't followed her at her parents' funeral, trying to give her the space she needed to deal with finding me amongst her grief. That had been the biggest mistake of my very long life and one I am not going to make twice.

Before I know it, I am on my feet chasing her across the island. I hear gasps, as I sprint away. I understand my actions look more than a little odd, but nothing Ed can't smooth over.

She is faster than I thought possible, disappearing into the dense forest. I am quickly disorientated, shouting out her name in frustration. It's strange to feel her name on my lips. I have refused to speak it for so long. Old emotions begin to stir, as I realise, I am lost, and she has disappeared again.

27

She can't apperate from here though and there can't be many places to hide on this tiny island. I will find her.

After an hour of searching, I am almost consumed by rage. How did I let her escape again. Ed catches me off guard, as I run through the trees like a wild animal. "Hen, what the fuck are you doing?" He asks amused, worried, and furious at the same time.

I stop in my tracks and turn to face him. The tortured look on my face tells him more than my words could. "Are you sure it was her?" He asks. He thinks I have finally gone mad.

"It. Is. Her." I say, gritting my teeth. "If not, why would she run?" Ed simply nods.

"I'll help you look then," he says. We set off again into the trees. A while later we both realise this isn't getting us anywhere and head back to the town to start asking questions.

The dinner is still in full swing, but I can see the look of concern on the faces of Brighid, Matias, and the blond-haired woman. I head in their direction. They are the ones who will have answers. As I approach Brighid stands looking as furious as I do. "Where did she go?" I ask.

Her anger matches my own, and I can see she won't back down to my power or authority, this is her island, and she calls the shots. "I don't know and even if I did, I wouldn't be telling you. I have never seen my daughter look so afraid." I'm taken back by her words, and I feel the look of confusion that lands on my face.

"Your daughter? That's not possible. That woman is a spinner and her parents lived in Asgard before they were killed." It is Brighid's turn to be surprised.

"We adopted her when she arrived here," she says. "Your Highness, how do you know Alexis?" She asks, formality returning to her tone.

"Henri, please." I say, hating the formality of the address. "I wouldn't say I know her. I watched her from a distance growing up, her birth father worked at the palace. We only met properly once – the day of her parent's funeral to be exact. Brighid, Alexis is my twin flame, please tell me where she is. I need to talk to her."

I feel the shock of everyone around me. Matias – Alexis's Dad hasn't said a word and neither has the blond woman who I'd seen holding her hand. She is a spinner too. Her shocked expression tells me, Alexis has never shared this fact with them.

"Henri, we don't know where she is." Matias finally says. "But we do know that while ever she is hiding, you won't find her." My brows furrow, what could that mean? "When Alexis wants to be alone, she takes herself off and we can't find her. Usually, we just wait at her house until she eventually goes back there."

"Where does she live?" I ask, before he has even finished speaking.

"Henri, I'm not sure…"

"Matias, with all due respect, I will be the one to decide what is a good idea. I have been without Alexis for over two centuries. I can see that you all love and care for her dearly, but so help me Goddess, if someone doesn't tell me where my mate lives, I will tear this island apart looking for her."

"Henri," comes Ed's warning. He knows I am close to losing it. I look at him as my eyes flash to black and back to blue. He is wary but not backing down. I close my eyes and try to regain control.

"Matias, Henri won't hurt Alexis. You have my word," Ed says. "Where does she live?" Matias looks from me to Ed and seems to believe we mean no harm to his daughter. "She has a cabin on the beach, half a mile from the dock." Of course she does. It now makes sense why it felt like home.

"Thank you," I breathe, finally back in control. I turn away from the group and walk back towards the dock. Ed follows, catching me as I get to the edge of town.

"Hen," he says concern etched in his voice. I turn to look at him. "Can you do this?" he asks.

"Yes," I answer in a clipped tone. I don't have time for this, I need to get there before Alexis docs.

"You haven't seen her for a very long time, Hen. Be careful. If he takes over, he will make her yours – he won't give her a choice. That isn't how you want the bond to be. Don't let him make me regret my words to her dad. I know you could never hurt her physically, but please don't break her that way." I sigh letting his words sink in and I am ashamed to admit there is truth in it. It's the price you pay for selling your soul to the devil.

"Ed, I have no intention of hurting her. I just need to see her. Talk to her. He won't get a look in." Ed doesn't believe me but concedes, knowing the longer he keeps me away the less control I will have.

Alexis

I reach the cabin in record time and find a bag from under my bed. I don't have much time, so grab just a few essentials. I know it will break Mum and Dad's heart, just leaving like this, but what choice do I have? I figure, I can take the beach round to the port and use one of the speed boats to get to the mainland. I'm not sure where I will go from there, but one step at a time. I need to get off the island first.

Turning to take a final look at my home, I'm hit with a wave of grief and a sob escapes my mouth. It has been my sanctuary for so long. Another surge of nausea hits and I lurch toward the kitchen sink as the tea finally escapes my stomach. Tears spring into my eyes as the buzzing in my ears gets louder and black begins to creep into the edges of my vision.

"Pull it together, Alexis," I tell myself. I don't have time for emotions right now. Taking a few deep breaths, I hold the edge of the sink to steady myself before racing back out into the dark night, ready to make a run for the port.

I barely make it to the shoreline before I'm grabbed from behind. Strong arms hold me in place, and I feel him taking in my scent. He turns me to face him. I choose to look at the floor, rather than the mesmerising eyes that I can feel boring into me.

"Not so fast, me errant mate" he says, almost menacingly. He puts a finger under my chin forcing me to look up. "I thought you were dead," he breaths out, tone completely at odds with his earlier words. "I don't understand." He looks confused, but I can also see a spark in his eyes, something in him enjoyed chasing and catching me.

I still haven't said a word, I'm silently running through my options, which at this moment in time feel... limited. I need to get away from him. Every ounce of my conscious mind is telling me to get away. Without him, I am free. Letting this man into my life would be a mistake.

"Alexis, if you run again, I will catch you and I don't think you will like the consequences." The confident powerful demeanour I felt in the square is now coming off him in waves. His anger is palpable. There is more to it though. I can almost feel his grief.

Grief is something I understand well. It's been my constant companion for more than two centuries. The grief of losing my parents and leaving my home behind. I don't need any more. My response to his anger is what surprises me, though. It excites me.

The thought fills me with dread. "I can't... I can't do this," I stutter, turning to walk away. He reaches for my elbow, gently pulling me back to him. I look down at the hand holding my arm, then at his face. The look I give him convinces him to let me go.

"I am not your mate, your highness. You need to keep your hands off me and while you're at it stay away from me," I spit out at him. I was raised at court, I know full well my attitude could get me into a world of trouble, but I am beyond reason.

"I have spent a very long time thinking you were dead Alexis, and I am sent to some tiny island in the middle of the Pacific Ocean and find that you have been here alive and well all this time.

"I am your mate, the other half of you, so I will let your attitude slide. However, I will not, no, cannot let you run away from me again."

"Let my attitude slide? Who exactly do you think you are? I have a Dad, thank you. I don't need another." I am well aware I sound like a spoiled child, but this man has serious control issues.

"I am not your mate." I repeat, as he clearly didn't hear me the first time. He looks affronted by my words. Whether it's because he is the crown prince and people don't usually speak to him that way, or because spinners usually accept their mate at first sight, I'm not sure.

"You don't understand. I don't want or need a mate, so, please leave me alone." I go on, with as much venom as I can muster. I can feel the pull of the twin flame bond, my entire being yearns for him, but I will not give in to it. I am safer off on my own, hell, he is safer without me. The sooner the prince sees that, the better.

"No," he says, closing his eyes. "I will never leave you again." He is trying hard to stay in control, I can feel that even with my limited power.

"And you're damn right I don't understand, Alexis," his words linger over my name, like he is enjoying how it feels on his lips. "You never gave me the opportunity. I didn't follow you at the funeral thinking you needed some space to come to terms with your emotions, but then I tried to find you after, and you had disappeared without a trace, your grandmother too."

Not for the first time, I wonder what happened to Gran, after she helped me to run away. I knew she wouldn't remain in Asgard, but I never heard from her again. I did as she instructed and didn't reach out; too afraid I would be found.

Turning my attention back to the matter at hand, I put as much loathing into my words as I can. "Perhaps that should have given you an indication of how I felt." I can see and feel that my words sting - *Good!* Even so his resolve never wavers.

I can't let myself love again, only to lose him to the vindictive witch who stole my parents. We are both safer, better off apart. I just need to figure out how to get through to him.

I turn on my heal and stalk off towards my tiny house. I don't want to leave my home again, but what choice do I have? He can't watch me forever, when he leaves, I will try again.

The prince follows me, and I spin to face him again fury emanating from every pore. "Is there something else I can help you with?" I seethe.

He reaches out a hand to touch me but thinks better of it, letting it drop to his side.

"Why do you hate me so much, Alexis? What can I have possibly done to you?" I close my eyes, resisting the urge to comfort him. I don't hate him. The bond saw to that. I don't really know him, but I do know it's not safe for him to be around me. If it takes him believing I hate him to keep him safe, I can live with that.

"What else do you expect from me, your highness. How long had you known we were twin flames when you allowed our eyes to meet at my parents' funeral? I know how it works. You are royalty. You don't need to look into the eyes of your mate to know who they are. And yet, you chose to look into mine across the open grave of my dead parents."

I am being cruel, I know I am. He didn't mean for that to happen. But it is all I have to work with.

"Alexis, I…"

"You're what Henri? You're sorry? Good for you. That doesn't fix anything. I was broken. My whole life had fallen apart, but you didn't care about that did you?" Tears fall down my cheeks as the lies flow out of my mouth. I don't mean a word of it, but it's all I've got to make him leave.

"Alexis stop," he says. "Stop pushing me. I know what you are doing, and it won't work. It was stupid of me to choose that moment to look into your eyes, but I never wanted to hurt you. I wanted you to see, you weren't alone. That even though they were gone, I was here for you, and you would never need to suffer on your own again.

"I didn't want to take anything away from your loss. I wanted to hold your hand, hold you up at the side of the grave, so you didn't have to carry the weight of your grief alone."

"I didn't need you or anyone else to hold me up, Henri. I could then and still can hold myself up. I am happy – was happy – here. I have a good life and people who love me. Go back to Asgard and leave me to my peace." I say, deflated. All I ever wanted was to live in peace. Without the fear of losing loved ones, without the fear of losing him. If I allow him to stay that will happen. "Please, Henri," I plead.

"I am not leaving, Alexis," he says sounding as broken as me.

The look on his face, breaks through my anger and I feel the urge to soothe him. "My house is just over here," I gesture with my head in the direction of my cabin on the beach. "I'll make us a drink and we can talk."

He looks at me and nods. I start walking trying to put some space between us. He, however, has other ideas and moves close to my side. This isn't going to be easy, but what choice do I have?

In my tiny kitchen, I pour us both a cold drink and go to find him sat on the porch bench. He is staring out to the crescent moon hanging high above the water. He remains silent as I sit beside him and hand over a drink.

For the first time I allow myself to wonder what his life has been like since I left Asgard. Did anything change for him like it did for me, or did he just go on like he had before? From the way he has reacted to finding me, I can't imagine he just went on as though I never existed, like I'd always imagined. I want to ask but stop myself allowing the silence to stretch on.

Eventually it seems he can take it no more and he speaks first. "I never formally introduced myself. I'm Henri, by the way." I almost laugh. Of course, I already know this, he is the crown prince. Everyone on earth knows his name.

"Oh, I know who you are, prince" I respond, with a small chuckle. He turns to look at me and the smile that lights up his handsome face is dazzling. I can't help the one that creeps onto my own. Despite my protestations, the pull linking me to this man, is real.

"That is the first time I have seen you smile in a very long time," Henri says. I realise that the only time we met, I was consumed by grief. I wasn't aware of meeting the prince at another time. My smile falters and I look away. I need to be stronger than that.

"Did I say something wrong?" he asks.

"Yes and no," I reply.

"Please explain."

"I am truly sorry for what I put you though. My intention was never to hurt you. I... we weren't fully mated. I don't want a mate. I'm sorry, but I just don't buy into this whole destiny crap. We make our own lives, and this is the one I choose.

"I don't want a life at court in Asgard, I want to be here," I gesture to our surroundings with my open arms, "free to live my own life, on my own terms." It's not a complete lie, just not the whole truth. He can see I'm holding something back, but I keep my lips tightly closed, afraid to say too much.

I feel his eyes on me again, but I don't turn to look. My own are fixed on the sea. I will not allow this to happen. I have kept us safe for too long to fall now.

It is the reason both of my parents are dead. The kind of power they had attracts attention and envy. Some last longer than others but the curse eventually kicks in. My parents were lucky, they had 50 years and a child. They truly believed they would be the ones to break it.

But it wasn't to be.

Others were even less fortunate – or more, depending on your point of view. Dying much sooner. Before they could build a life together or have children.

If my parents couldn't find a way to break the curse with all their power, what chance did I have.

My parents' fate was horrific, but they at least had each other. Gran's fate was worse than death. She found her mate and he left her – while she was still with child. She hid it well, but for a spinner, to be betrayed by their twin flame is… I don't think the words for that kind of pain have been created.

I'd see Gran when my parents were away, and she thought I was sleeping. The pain on her face almost as unbearable as her pleas to the Goddess to bring him back, even all those years later. It didn't matter how much, he hurt her, the bond couldn't let her hate him. That's what the twin flame bond can do. It is that strong.

Neither path seemed particularly appealing.

"I'm sorry Alexis, I still don't think I understand."

I can hear the pain in Henri's voice, but I have to be strong. It is the only way I can protect him, and I've already said too much.

"What don't you understand Henri? I don't want a mate or a partner or any of it really." I say as matter of fact as I can.

Henri stiffens and I can feel his anger. "You're lying, Alexis. What aren't you saying?" he asks through gritted teeth. I again feel the order in his tone, it is only natural, I suppose. He was born to be king.

"You want to know the truth Henri? The truth is my parents both died and left me an orphan because of the damn bond and my Gran lived a life of misery because her mate betrayed her, and the bond wouldn't let her hate him or move on. I don't want that. I don't want you.

"Go back to Asgard and leave me be."

"You are still lying to me Alexis, I can feel it," he roars, jumping to his feet and knocking his drink to the ground. I can't be sure, but I think I see black in his eyes. I flinch feeling the raw power emitting from him. "What are you holding back?" his voice seems different, deeper, but the command is still there. It rubs on my mind, trying to force me to tell him. I fight back, pushing the command away.

When I don't answer, he pulls me to my feet and pushes me back against the wall hands trapping me there. His eyes are closed, and I can see he is fighting for control. I should be afraid, but I'm not. I relish his closeness.

"I am running out of patience, Alexis," he breathes, pressing his body against mine. "I have been without you for a very long time. Instinct is telling me to seal the bond and I am fighting very hard against it. I don't want it to be this way and I am sure you don't, so please tell me."

His plea is harder to ignore than the command. Mesmerising blue eyes bore into mine as Henri leans his head against me. He is so close I can hear his heartbeat and breathing. It takes a few moments for both to return to a normal speed. "Alexis," he breathes. "I am so sorry, please forgive me." Henri backs away giving me some space. I can't speak yet, so I simply nod. I don't blame him.

We stand looking into each other's eyes both lost in our thoughts for some time.

Eventually Henri breaks the silent stand-off. "I won't push you any further now. This has been a huge shock for us both. *But this is not over, and you will not run from me again, Alexis.*"

This time I feel the order in his words and fury ignites white and hot in my veins. "Oh yes and all happy relationships start with an order," I fume.

He at least has the grace to look ashamed. I almost believe the regret I see behind his eyes. Almost. "The last thing I want is to give orders, Alexis, least of all to you," he says, and I scoff. "But I won't lose you again, I don't think I could bare it."

The fight leaves me, and I close my eyes to fight back the tears I know are forming there. I feel Henri's lips lightly brush against my own and I gasp in surprise as a spark of electricity passes between us. Henri pulls away and I watch as he walks back up the beach, leaving me alone.

Henri

I wait for hours, watching the tiny hut, while hiding in the tree line. Eventually long after darkness has fallen, I hear her approach. She runs in the direction of her cabin, and I remain here, shrouded in darkness. I am close enough to feel her fear and pain as she franticly runs round the small cabin.

I realise she is packing! Oh no, my love you are not getting away from me again.

A sob from inside the house followed by several loud wretches, makes me want to run and comfort her, but I stand my ground. Eventually emerging from the cabin, Alexis turns in the direction of the shoreline, and I take the opportunity catch her.

When I reach her, I grab her waist pulling her body close to my own. I could stand this way holding her forever, just to keep her close. But I can feel her discomfort, so I drop my arms, spinning her to look at me.

It is difficult to speak at first, her proximity takes my breath away. "Not so fast, my errant mate," I choke out breathlessly.

She doesn't say anything. I need to hear her voice, so I speak in the hope that she will finally respond, when she doesn't, I say, "Please, say something Alexis, anything."

"I can't. I can't do this." Alexis, replies. "I am not your mate, your highness. You need to keep your hands off me and while you're at it stay away from me."

Anger roars in my veins as she tries to walk away again. I try desperately to gain control of it.

"I am not your mate," she repeats, like either of us have a choice in this.

"You don't understand. I don't want or need a mate," she says defiantly as if she heard my thought.

Being reunited with our twin flame is a spinners greatest gift in life – trust the person within whom the missing half of my soul resides, to deny the bond. The irony is not lost on me. I have caused so much destruction, it seems fair that I would now have to deal with this.

I might even laugh, if I wasn't trying so hard, to control the rage building with in me.

Why is Alexis so keen to walk the earth alone. She says she doesn't want a romantic relationship of any kind. It's odd, spinners aren't usually solitary creatures. We are always happier when we have our mates beside us.

Whether my mate is ready to admit it or not, I can feel the connection, she is drawn to me, and I do like a challenge.

Winning Alexis might just be my biggest challenge yet... but I never loose.

To my surprise, Alexis stands down and invites me to her house for a drink. I am not fool enough to think she is conceding, she is merely playing for time, before she makes her move.

As we walk, it occurs to me that Alexis might have been cut off from the world during her time here.

Does she not know that I searched for her for 100 years? That I learned of the curse that killed her parents? That I found the witch who cursed them? Of course, I killed her in a fit of rage when she told me Alexis had taken her own life, because she was weak.

The witch had been wrong though. Alexis is far from weak; she is stronger than anyone I have ever known – I can sense her power, even now, when she is almost overcome with fear.

Rage has become my constant companion since that day – my own curse to bare. I used it to keep me going, to rid the world of witches like the one who had ruined my life – and I have become good at it.

Alexis continues to push back though and the monster within me, roars to life. "Make her yours and put a stop to this now" he urges me. Before I know it, he is the one in control and I have Alexis trapped between me and the wall. "Do it," he says again. I could, it wouldn't be hard, and I can tell from Alexis's reaction she wouldn't even try to stop me. I know my eyes are close to black and I close them not wanting her to see the monster I have become.

"No" I tell the monster firmly. "Not like this, she might not stop me, but I would never forgive myself for taking her freedom. I take in a deep breath, allowing her sweet jasmine and honeysuckle scent to sooth the raging beast.

Now I have Alexis in my reach, my anger will only push her farther away. She doesn't strike me as the kind of woman to put up with that in her mate.

I consider telling her about the witch and the curse, I almost do. But again, it's not the right time. Even if I tell her, I'm not sure she would believe me. There is a good chance, she would think I was telling her what she wanted to hear.

I need to earn her trust and love first.

She said she doesn't buy into 'the twin flame thing' so maybe I have to make her fall in love with me. Not just be with me because destiny tied us together.

"Alexis I am so sorry, please forgive me." I retreat and give her some space.

Eventually I say, "I won't push you any further now. This has been a huge shock for us both. *But this is not over, and you will not run from me again, Alexis.*"

I do something I have never done before; I make a full royal command – one she can't just brush off. I don't want to, but I need her to stay, I can't risk her running from me again.

Chapter 3

Alexis

The kiss leaves my lips tingling as I sit stunned by today's events. Before long I hear Ginny and Mum talking as they walk down the beach.

They come to stand in front of me with narrowed eyes, trying to work out what the hell is going on.

"Well…" Mum says, sounding every bit a chiding mother expecting an answer.

"Well, what?" I reply.

"Really? You just ran out of the square and were followed by none other than His Royal Highness, The Crown Prince, the most stunning creature ever to walk the earth. You are gone all day; he comes to find us to tell us he is your mate and you have known about this for 250 years and never bothered to mention it. You think we are just going to let this go," Ginny quips. I sigh.

"No of course not," I say rolling my eyes "What do you want to know?"

"Everything," they say in unison.

Deciding I might need my allies in the near future, I take a deep breath and launch into an explanation of everything. "The prince – Henri – he is my mate, we met once before, at my parents' funeral. Well, when I say met, I mean our eyes locked over the grave and I bolted.

"My father was a healer in the royal court, and he along with my mother were murdered for their powers.

"Our family was cursed by the Witches of Endor, who we believe, want our powers.

"My mating with Henri wasn't complete, and I knew if I left it would keep us both safe.

"From what he said, he tried to look for me and when he couldn't find me, thought I was dead, so got on with his life the best he could, I guess.

"I stopped looking for a way to break the curse a long time ago and dedicated my life to the island and doing some good.

"I never felt the need for a relationship - with him or anyone else - to feel complete. I am happy as am.

"More importantly, I'm the last Beaumont so when I die, if I don't have children, the curse dies with me and no one else is hurt.

"Today when Henri showed up, my carefully constructed world came crashing in around me.

"Even if I wanted to - which I don't - we cannot complete the mating bond. If we do, I will be forced to endure watching him die, like my parents and every other member of my family for the last thousand years.

"I can't lose someone else to that damned curse."

They both remain silent while two and a half centuries worth of secrets come tumbling out. When I am finished, I can see a million questions in their eyes. I thought they would be angry with me for keeping my secrets, so I am surprised when they sit either side of me and hug me, tightly.

"I can't imagine what it must be like carrying that alone for so long," Mum says. "Will you leave again?" she asks sadly, clearly distressed by the idea. I shake my head.

"I *can't*," I say, remembering Henri's direct order, "I was going to, I ran home to pack a bag, but Henri caught me as I came back out. I don't want to leave anyway. This island is my home, and you are my family."

Mum isn't a spinner, so she doesn't pick up on the significance of what I said, but Ginny is. "When you say, 'you *can't*,' do you mean what I think you do?"

I attempt a smile, but I know it doesn't reach my eyes. Mum looks confused. "Yes, Gin, he ordered me not to run again." Ginny just nods accepting it. We are spinners and cannot defy a direct order from a member of the royal family - no matter how much it pisses me off, I have to obey.

Mum looks furious. "He did what?" she spits. I place my hand on her leg attempting to calm her. She is an empath, they are largely lone beings, choosing to live separate from others for everyone's sanity, so she doesn't fully understand the intricacies of spinner society.

"It's fine Mum, Henri just did what comes naturally."

"It is not fine; he can't just give out orders like that and expect you to what? Submit? You have never submitted to anyone in all the time I have known you, firefly." Ah there is the reference to my temper.

"I know it's not fine, but what would you have me do? All spinners are connected by our magic. I might not have much of that, but it means I physically cannot disobey him."

The truth is I am more than a little pissed off about it. I have lived a free life for so long, it doesn't feel good to be back under spinner rule. I refuse to let Mum know how much the prince's presence has affected me, though.

I know I will never get her to understand so I give up trying and say, "regardless, this is my home, and I am staying put.

"I know this is a lot to ask, but I need your help," I say after a few moments quiet. "Gin, I know this will be particularly hard for you, so feel free to opt out..." I take a breath before continuing. "I need to keep Henri at a distance. I need to convince him I don't want him and make him leave and forget about me."

The look on Ginny's face suggests she thinks I have taken leave of my senses. "Lex, I love you and everything. There isn't much I wouldn't do for you."

I sense a but... "But there is no way you will win this game. Ordinary spinners aren't known for letting go of their mates. Your mate is one of the most powerful spinners alive today, there is no way in heaven and earth he will leave this island without you."

"He is not my mate," I interject.

She isn't finished though. "And he has been forced to live without you for two and a half centuries. I can't imagine how that feels, but it can't be good. The only way you will be rid of Henri now is when you head off to the heavens."

Now she has finished, and she looks fairly pleased with herself. I scowl, looking to Mum for her answer.

"Firefly, I would do anything for you. You know I would. Your dad and I thank our lucky stars you came into our lives, every day." I sense another but coming... "But we can't get in the way of a spinner and his mate, and you know it."

I do, of course I do.

Shame washes over me. It was selfish to put either of them in that position. I just feel so bloody trapped.

"I'm sorry Lex," Ginny starts.

I cut her off, "No, I'm sorry, it was selfish to even ask. I will just have to figure out how to deal with this on my own." The look on both of their faces tells me they think I am crazy.

What would they know? Mum has Dad and couldn't imagine living without him. Ginny has dreamt of meeting her mate, her entire life.

Their lives aren't burdened by a curse and the royal spinner court.

Gin and Mum stay with me for the rest of the night. We all know we are neglecting our duties staying here, but I don't feel like facing anyone again tonight – it's been a long and trying day.

Eventually Ginny goes into the house and hunts around for something we can eat.

"Alexis, I can feel your fear sweetheart, I wish there was some way for me to take it away," Mum says when she hears Gin routing around my cupboards. She has waited until we can't be overheard. Her motherly instinct trying to protect my best friend.

"I just don't know how to deal with this, Mum. When I was in Asgard, I knew couples who were twin flames. My birth parents were and look how well it turned out for them.

"I loved watching them together, but I didn't want it. Maybe I spent too much time with Gran. She wouldn't tell me much about her past. All I knew was that her own mate betrayed her, before my mother was even born and she moved to Asgard to raise her child alone.

"Twin flames might seem like a fairy tale, but what if your mate is not prince charming? What if he is a lying, cheating ass, who will break your heart?" Mum is about to answer, but I'm on a roll now.

"Shall I tell you what happens? You physically can't hate them. You forgive every wrongdoing, but you can never forget. You live the remainder, of your very long life, heartbroken and alone, begging the Goddess to send him back to you."

A sob escapes as I think about Gran's life. She devoted herself to my mother and I, but even as a child I could see she was broken beyond repair after what her mate did. Mum wraps me in her arms offering the comfort I so badly need.

"Alexis, have you stopped to think that maybe, your mate *is* prince charming?" I pull away and look at her incredulously, my eyebrow raised in question.

"I'm not saying he is perfect. I am saying he spent a long time looking for you. There are no certainties in life, but if you don't take a risk, you will never know. Do you really think your Gran would want you to sacrifice any chance you have at happiness to keep your heart safe?

"Imprisoning your heart will keep it from being broken, Alexis, but at what cost? Spending eternity alone, seems too high a price to pay. I can't tell you what to do, sweetheart, only you know your own path, just don't give up, before you have even begun. The Goddess has given you both a second chance, don't waste it on fear."

"The Goddess?" I scoff. "The Goddess has never done anything for me. She made me a powerless spinner with a mate I can never be with. I watched Gran pray to her for years to bring her mate back and don't think I haven't done the same to find a way to fix the mess I left behind. She never answers. She has forgotten us."

Mum is shocked by my outburst. She loves the Goddess and doesn't appreciate any kind of blasphemy. "Alexis," she yells, "take that back. Never speak the Goddess's name in vain. Have you stopped to think that sending Henri here to find you is her answering your prayers? I don't know what happened with your Gran and I am sorry for what happened to her, but it is not the same. Henri is here for you. He hasn't left and betrayed you. You left him." She isn't finished.

"And powerless? You are far from powerless, young lady. You push it down and hide it away but it's there, it's always been there you are just too stubborn and afraid to use it. I think you need to ask yourself what you are really afraid of, because I know you and it sure as hell is not the Witches of Endor."

"She's right, Lex," Ginny says emerging from the kitchen. Gin isn't angry with me like Mum, but the set of her jaw is daring me to argue.

Between their words and the tension of the day, I can no longer hold back the emotions. Everything I have held in for two centuries comes pouring out me and I sob into Mum's arms. The rain starts to fall, lightning flashes and thunder claps over ahead. We jump, up heading inside quickly. Once there, Ginny runs around closing doors and shutters. The more I cry the worse the storm becomes. My cabin is being battered by it. Mum starts to look alarmed as realisation hits. "Alexis, are you causing this storm?" she asks. All I can do is nod as a new wave of tears hits and the thunderclaps again, directly overhead.

"You aren't afraid of anyone else, are you Alexis? You are afraid of your own power," Mum says answering her own question. "Did you know you can control the elements like this?"

I shake my head. "I wouldn't exactly call this control, Mum."

"That is because you have kept everything supressed for so long. You don't allow yourself to feel anything so now you are, you're losing control. But it is in you to gain it."

"See the storm is already settling." She is right. Distracting me from the emotions I was feeling has stopped the storm.

"Not bad for a powerless spinner," Mum says, with a triumphant smile.

The next morning, I am up early, having not slept a wink. Mum and Ginny stayed until late, and I told them stories about growing up at court. We'd discussed my thoughts on the curse and how it might be broken, but we hadn't really got anywhere. I needed to find the witch who cast it and I had no idea where to start and – I still believed – little power to kill her and break it, even if I did find her.

Being shut off in Serenity means we don't have access to many texts or seers that might shed some light on my situation. I'd already known that it's the reason I gave up and decided to just let it die with me in the first place.

Deciding I need to clear my head, I dress quickly and head straight to the hospital. Spending the day buried in my work seems preferable to sitting at home stewing. I message Ginny on my way, letting her know I don't need a wakeup call today.

It feels good to sit in my office and read reports. I let the mundane task take over my brain and revel in the normalcy of it, loosing track of time and place.

A while later, Mum pops into my office with cups and what I imagine is boxes of food in her hand. I look up startled, having been completely lost in my work.

"I thought you could use some lunch," she says, waving the boxes at me and smiling. I'm about to say I'm fine, when my stomach rumbles, giving me away.

She pops the box of steaming hot food on my desk and I breathe in the heavenly smell. Spaghetti Bolognaise. I open the box and start shovelling it into my mouth. It tastes delicious, I hadn't realised how hungry I'd gotten - I skipped breakfast in favour of getting lost in work. How long had it been since I ate? I try to think back, unsure whether I'd managed anything amongst the chaos of yesterday.

Once she is satisfied, I have eaten Mum clears her throat. "He's been asking about you, Alexis," she says. I knew it wouldn't be long until I had to face him, but I was hoping to put it off longer than lunch time. "I told him to give you some space." I am grateful for her help, even if she can't keep him away indefinitely.

"Thank you," I say. "I will speak to him soon, I just, -"

"I know. It will all work out, cherry blossom, I just know it will." Ah the optimism of an empath. I sigh and get to my feet. "I have some patients to see on the ward this afternoon," I say, hoping to end the conversation.

"OK, darling," she responds. Shall I meet you downstairs around 4? We'll pick up Ginny and get ready for the party at your house."

I close my eyes, for a moment. With everything that has happened in the last 24 hours, I'd completely forgotten about the party.

"I'm not…"

"Going?" Mum finishes for me. "Like hell you aren't Alexis. I'll pick you up at 4."

Another battle I'm not going to win. I nod my head as she walks out of the door.

The party to welcome our guests is the last place I feel like going but backing down is not in my nature and I sure as hell don't want the arrogant prince to know how much he got under my skin.

Seriously, the Goddess must have been having a great laugh at my expense when she gave me that domineering ass as my twin flame. Following rules has never been my strong suit.

A few hours later I am wearing a long flowing emerald halter neck dress that swirls around my ankles. I have taken my red hair down and it falls in waves around my face and down my back. Minimal makeup highlights my eyes and I've used some gloss on my lips - I've never needed colour on them, they are red enough without it.

"At least I look a bit more presentable and not like I've spent the last two days in turmoil now," I say with a small laugh.

"Presentable?" says Ginny, "you look amazing!"

"Thanks," I respond blushing. "You look beautiful too." And she does. Her floral dress highlights her feminine curves, falling just above her knees, leaving her golden legs on show. She has swept her hair to one side, and it cascades over her shoulder, like liquid gold.

Mum comes in, having transformed her usual all business look into a sensual Latino goddess. A skin-tight black cocktail dress hugs elegantly to her generous curves and her usually straight, jet-black hair, falls in ringlets over her shoulders and down her back. "You both look wonderful," she gushes a huge proud smile emerging on her face. We raise our eyes, both feeling frumpy beside her beauty.

Satisfied with our work, we set off back towards town and *my mate*.

Night is starting to fall around us as we approach the square. The little lights hanging above our heads twinkle like stars, making our surroundings look even more magical than they did in the daylight.

I am again momentarily filled with pride, to be part of this community, before a tight ball forms in my stomach.

I sense Henri, before we even get to the square. Not in the way, I usually sense energy – I usually 'see' auras with my third sight, my solitary supernatural power.

No, I feel my marks pulse in recognition. I gasp and look at my hand, sure enough they are glowing again and feel a primal need to be close to him. *Just great!*

Taking a few deep breaths, I will the glow to fade. It does but the pulsing doesn't stop. I still can't see the prince, though I know he must be close by.

I am greeted by Eleanor, another member of the council and the school's head teacher. She is a werewolf and the one responsible for organising the decoration of the square.

There are lots of myths about werewolves - as there are every kind of creature - but most of them are not true. They can shift anytime they want, and their wolf form is no scarier than their human. Contrary to popular belief, the full moon does not turn them into blood thirsty monsters.

Eleanor is possibly the most gentle and loyal person I have ever met. "Eleanor, this looks... magical," I gush, looking in every direction. Her face lights up.

"Oh, it wasn't me, we have the kids to thank, they made all the plans and designs and coordinated everyone. Haven't they done us proud," she says, and she really means it.

I couldn't agree more. I am hit once again by how far we have come and what can be achieved when all beings, magical or otherwise come together.

Eleanor's mate, Hugh comes over and hands us both a rum cocktail.

For werewolves, mates are much like a spinners twin flame, although they are not one soul split in two, they are two souls *destined* to be together. Hugh looks at Eleanor with such admiration its almost too much to look at.

I am about to excuse myself when a voice – Henri's – sends a jolt of pleasure through my core. "Well, hello, my love" he says smoothly. "I wasn't expecting to see you this evening."

I turn to face him with a questioning look. "I am not *your love*," I say witheringly, internally berating myself for the warm feeling I get when he calls me that. "And why would I not be here?" I ask, diverting the conversation away from dangerous ground. "This is my island, my party, where else would I be this evening?"

I can feel the anger rising in me. How dare he question my actions; he doesn't know the first thing about me. I fight for control, remembering the storm I created with my emotions last night. I wouldn't forgive myself if my temper ruined Eleanor's efforts.

Henri seems to sense my mood and tries to calm me. "I am sorry, Alexis, I didn't mean to insinuate anything. What I meant to say was, I am happy to see you again." His response is disarming.

I assumed he would come back with sarcasm, and I realise I don't know anything about the man facing me either. "Can we start over?" he asks. Can we I wonder? I should say no, it's dangerous to let him get close, but before I can stop myself, I say "yes."

Henri's answering smile lights up his entire face and I can't help the one that creeps over mine, in response.

Henri raises a hand, stroking a finger down the length of my face, leaving it tingling in his wake. "You are magnificent," he says, breath catching in his throat. I blush at the comment, so unused the attention.

When I arrived on the island, I made it very clear I was not interested in any kind of relationship. My feelings have mostly been respected and very few men have ever tried to sway me.

Well actually, only one man ever bothered, and it was an awkward end to a great friendship. He is now off travelling the world to get away from me.

Samuel is a human, born on the island. Humans don't usually live anywhere near as long as we supernatural's, but we came to an agreement long ago that as long as humans remain on Serenity, they would stop ageing as we do. So, while Sam is almost as old as me, he still looks 25.

We were friends before Ginny even came to the island. He helped me to build and develop the hospital. To the outside world, we probably looked like partners, but I could never feel that way about Sam. He was my dear friend who I love unconditionally but never anything more.

I told him time and time again, but he lived in hope I would one day change my mind. The argument that ended our friendship and sent Sam away still haunts me. We had left the hospital together and walked into to town to grab a drink in Dad's bar. Four or five cocktails later and the conversation moved from gossip about Gin's latest suitor to Sam's feelings for me.

"Not this again, Sam. You know how I feel, my feelings haven't changed. I love you unconditionally, you are one of my favourite people in the world, but we will never be together that way. You are the brother I never had." My eyes closed as I tried to reign in my frustration with my friend.

"Why though, Alexis? Why are you so determined to be alone? Spinners live a very long time; do you want to spend your entire existence lonely?"

"I'm not lonely, Sam. I have you and Ginny, Mum, and Dad. I am happy with my life as it is. Please don't do this again."

"Do what, Lex? Tell you I love you. That I would do anything for you. Well, I do, and I would. You always say you are happy alone, but I don't believe you. You mean the world to me, please at least tell me why."

I never could make him understand. "Can we not do this tonight, Sam? We've both had too much to drink. It's not the time."

"Fuck, Lex! When is it ever? There is always some reason not to have this conversation. I cannot carry on like this. I love you and I have for as long as I can remember. If you don't feel the same just say and let me, go." He had yelled me.

"I love you Sam, you know I do. I am just not in love with you. Please see that you are my friend, but we will never be anything more."

"I don't think I can live with that anymore." Sam closed his eyes, defeated.

"Please don't do this, Sam. I can't lose you too."

"Too? Who else have you lost, Alexis?" I sealed my lips unwilling to reveal my secrets. "Ah, and you aren't going to tell me, are you?" My silence was all the answer he needed.

"I thought so." With one last look in my direction Sam walked away from me. I figured I would let him sober up and find him in the morning when we could smooth things over. I never got the opportunity though. The next day, Sam had left a note saying he would no longer live on the island without me. He was going to travel until he found somewhere else to call home, where he could grow old and die like other humans.

It broke my heart to be without out him and to think that he would rather die than be around me, but I respected his decision. If I had that choice, I would take it too. I just hoped he could find love and live out the rest of his life happy.

Coming back to the present, I notice Henri is holding his hand out to me. Giving me the option to refuse his offer to dance. I place mine atop his and feel a spark of recognition again as I do so.

He gently guides me, leading us into the centre of the square, where others are already dancing. "Shall we?" he asks. His smile seems shy and slightly lopsided, like he is worried I will refuse. I can't resist. He pulls me close and begins turning us on the spot. He is a wonderful dancer, leading me around the square. We stumble over my clumsy feet, and he catches me expertly.

We both laugh, looking into each other's eyes. My earlier worries and protests evaporating as his strong hands hold me. Henri leans in slightly then pulls back, silently asking permission to kiss me.

Well, this is a first, I think. I'd like to wager he doesn't usually ask permission for anything.

I pull away, chiding myself for allowing him to get to close. I close my eyes, breaking his pull on me, somewhat. "No, Henri. I can't." I say, it kills me to see his face fall but, if I give in now, two and a half centuries pain has been for nothing.

"I'm so sorry, Alexis, I got carried away." He says politely. I can feel his rejection and desperately want to comfort him, but that will only make matters worse.

We continue our waltz around the makeshift dance floor, finding a rhythm, even my parents would in awe of. Suddenly Henri dips me back and I hold his strong arms to stop myself from falling to the floor. Caught in the moment I lift my head to meet his and kiss him.

When our lips touch electricity sets my body alight. All the sensations I felt around him earlier, are nothing compared to what I feel now.

The kiss is gentle at first, but the feeling intensifies, as it deepens. Henri slides his hands from my waist up my sides and gasps when they reach the bare skin on my back. He doesn't stop and before long, his hands are in my hair.

When we part, we are both breathless, Henri is smiling. I take a step back, realising a line has been crossed.

We stand for a moment to catch our breath.

"Henri, you need to know, I am not the kind of woman who will be caught up in a whirl wind, fairy tale romance –" he tries to cut in but stops when he sees the look on my face.

"All I am saying, is this is complicated. I have spent a long time on my own looking after myself, I cannot... no will not return to Asgard and follow anyone's orders."

"I wouldn't expect that for a moment," he says, eyes laughing.

"Are you laughing at me, *prince*?" I say glaring at him.

"I wouldn't dare, *princess*" he responds, holding his hands up in surrender, the amusement still apparent in his eyes.

I narrow my eyes at him, bristling at his choice of name for me. I'm not like most women. I've never fantasised about being a princess and feel the burden of what it would mean to be Henri's fall heavily on my shoulders.

"I need to speak to some of the other guests," I say turning my back and walking away from him.

Henri doesn't appear to be very happy about it but doesn't complain. I have the feeling, he thinks I will try to escape again at the earliest opportunity, he isn't wrong.

I leave Henri talking to Dad and join the group of people around Mum. They are discussing the island's solar farm. This is Mum's passion, so I am not needed to interject much and get lost in thought.

I try to work out how my quiet life got so out of hand so quickly. In all the time I have been here, I've just got on with my life, with little fuss. Most people know my boundaries and don't try to cross them.

However, I have a feeling the crown prince sees my boundaries as a challenge. I need to find a way to take back control. I can feel Henri's eyes on me as I make my way around the other guests.

Even as I think this, I know my life has changed forever. I know Henri won't just walk away from me now, and I am beginning to think I don't want him to anyway.

No Alexis, get a grip. No one is going to die for you. Especially not him - he is the future king, for Goddess's sake!

I shake the feeling aside and wander around the square stopping to talk to people here and there.

Eventually I find Ginny, who is looking at me with concern etched across her face. "How are you holding up," she asks. I shrug, not really knowing how to put it into words.

"I'm... Oh I don't know. This is such a mess, less than 2 days ago, my life was normal and now..." I'm not sure what life is now, a mess?

"I saw you kiss him, Lex. I don't think either of you will be able to walk away, even if you wanted to."

"I won't bow to him or anyone else in Asgard, Gin. Mate or not, I choose my own life." I sigh.

"You should tell him," She replies simply. I get the feeling she isn't talking about my comment. She means I should tell him, the real reason I ran away.

I briefly consider it. "No. He would want to try and break the curse, like my father did. He died trying, and I will not allow Henri to do the same. No one else is going to die for that curse... or for me," I add.

"I don't think that is your choice anymore."

Logically I know Ginny is right, but I am too stubborn to admit it.

The panic starts to build in me. It is my choice and if I have any chance of saving him, I need to get away - *now*.

Just as I am starting to form a plan, Ginny glances behind me and I feel Henri stalking towards us. She dips into a courtesy and greets him formally, "your highness," she says. I turn to him and see that he looks embarrassed by Ginny's formal address. "Henri, please," he says.

Ginny smiles and steps away, leaving me alone with Henri.

"Thinking of going somewhere, my love?"

Chapter 4

Alexis

S hit! How does he know that? What are his powers again? I can't remember, but I'm sure mind reading isn't one of them.

Pushing the thought aside, I repeat my earlier complaint. "I am not *your love*." How many times will I have to say that to make him understand?

"Let's go together," he says with a tight smile, completely ignoring my comment. The words are gentle enough, but I can see the menace in his eyes.

I somehow don't think, I'd come out of it very well, if I tried to take off now. Whatever came over him yesterday, when I tried to push him away is still there, simmering just below the surface.

I nod not trusting my own voice and we head out towards the beach again.

Neither of us speak for some time. Eventually I break the silence, unable to stand the tension that is growing between us.

"Well, it's been quite a couple of days," I say. I glance over at Henri. His face looks incredulous for a second and then he smiles slightly.

"Yes, you could say that" comes his polite response.

As we reach the beach his face has relaxed a little and the fury in his eyes subsided. We sit on the still warm sand; Henri's arm is touching mine and his proximity leaves me tingling. From the look on his face, I know he feels it too.

"This island really is something," Henri says. I smile, happy to talk about a relatively safe topic.

"It is, we are lucky to have it."

"How did it come to be? The community I mean?" Henri enquires.

"Mum and Dad were the first outsiders to come here. The indigenous humans were very welcoming, and Mum soon realised that different beings could live side by side. There was a spell cast over the island a few centuries ago and anyone who remains here doesn't age. That means the humans can live as long as the rest of us. If they ever get to a point where they want to live a 'normal' human life, they can leave and start ageing again." I say trying to hide the pain, the statement brings. *Like Sam my best friend.* I don't say the last part aloud.

"I'm not sure how word spread, but soon, others who wanted a different way of life joined them. I heard about it after..." I can't quite finish the sentence, so I change course.

"Well, when I arrived there was already a thriving community and over the years people have come and gone bringing ideas for development with them. We are now completely self-sufficient.

"I am a healer of sorts – I founded the hospital with the help of Mum, Dad, and a friend, I sit on the leadership council as well. We try to have two representatives for each species on the council, this helps to ensure, we can live together in peace.

"No one has more say over the others. When I first came, I didn't think it would be possible, Mum soon proved me wrong."

Henri looks at me with an awed expression on his face. "So, you're a healer, like your father?" He asks.

"Not like my father, no. I just use herbal medicine, I have picked up bits and pieces from other cultures over the years. I didn't inherit his abilities." I close my mouth before I give anything else away.

Henri still looks stupefied. I know how he feels, the rest of the world doesn't operate this way. Each species live in their own communities, rarely mixing with others. Fear of the unknown keeps them apart.

Spinners, as the most powerful of all creatures, are considered gods by many. In fact, it is said we descend from the Goddess herself.

Unfortunately, many spinners believe this. However, my time in Serenity, has proven that when everyone is considered equal, we all thrive, and we can create something wonderful.

"Why has it been kept a secret for so long?" Henri asks. "Surely if it can be done here, the rest of the world can do the same."

I know that feeling, it is the one I had when I first arrived. But I also know, not everyone thinks the same way as us.

"It has never been a secret, but not everyone views things like we do, Henri. There are those who like power too much." *Like the witch who cursed my family*, I think. "Can you ever see The Elders accepting this?" I gesture around with my open arms.

His face darkens, but he stays quiet, nodding in apparent understanding.

"Can I ask you something?" I say after a few quiet minutes.

"Of course, anything," Henri replies. I take a deep breath and ask the question that has been on my mind since I first saw him yesterday morning.

"Why are you here?" He looks confused and hurt. I'm not sure why this bothers me but scramble to explain my question anyway. "You weren't meant to be coming. We had a list of the ambassadors' names. Yours was not on it." Henri laughs then.

"I am being punished." Now it's my turn to be confused.

"Punished?"

"My father wasn't happy with me," he says. He is avoiding the question.

"Because?" I try again, raising an eyebrow.

He sighs clearly thinking about how to answer my question. When he does it comes out in a rush as though he needs to get it over with.

"I was engaged to be married and I called it off."

I feel like I have been hit in the stomach. I know it shouldn't bother me. I was the one who ran away, who will run again at the first opportunity.

Despite myself though, it hurts that he would consider being with another woman. I spent all this time turning down other men. I lost Sam because I could never consider being with someone else, and yet here Henri is telling me he was planning to marry someone else.

He must see the hurt on my face because he puts his hand under my chin, pulling it around to look at him. "It wasn't like that, Alexis. It was my parents' idea. I can't take the throne until I'm married.

"I couldn't go through with it though. It felt like a betrayal to you even though I thought you were dead."

His words bring back all my earlier worries and panic starts to rise within me. "You should have gone through with it," I say, feeling the bile rise in my throat even as I say the words.

Henri looks furious and the anger I saw simmering below the surface earlier bubbles out as he jumps to his feet. "How can you say that?" he forces out between gritted teeth towering over me. "I'd rather be alone for eternity than with a woman who is not you, Alexis."

His words hit me with such force I can't breathe. I feel the same way, which I why I have secluded myself here for so long, I just don't want that for Henri.

"No."

This can't happen, he will die, and it will be my fault. I don't care if I die, I made the decision to sacrifice myself, a long time ago to save Henri, but his love for me will kill him.

And you don't want a mate, I remind myself.

"No?" Henri repeats. "Alexis, it's not up to you. It isn't up to me either." He runs his hand though his hair in frustration.

It is the sexiest thing I have ever seen and the grip I have on my self-control slips slightly.

"How can I keep you safe, if you won't listen," I say angrily. He looks into my eyes for the longest time, and I start to think he is frozen.

"You ran away and hid here for all this time, to keep me safe." he eventually says. It's not a question. I can see in his face that he has pieced together some puzzle in his mind.

He knows about the curse. I never thought he would find out, but maybe he found out from someone back in Asgard. Maybe the family secret wasn't as secret as we believed.

I can't bring myself to ask him. I'm not sure I can explain if I am wrong.

Chicken, my soul whispers. It takes me by surprise, she has been quiet for so long, I'd almost forgot she was there. She seems to have been woken from a long sleep by Henri's arrival - and she is pissed with me!

Henri steps towards me never letting his eyes leave mine, like they are holding me in place. He takes me into his arms and bends his head, so his lips graze my ear.

"We keep each other safe Alexis. Now will you please stop running and let me love you." His voice is husky, and he trails kisses down my neck leaving patches of tingling skin as he goes.

I close my eyes and surrender for a moment.

But as his mouth reaches my collar bone, I push him away.

Henri looks me over, lust clear in his eyes. He closes them and takes a deep breath. When they open again, he gives me a small lopsided smile and wraps a protective arm around my shoulder.

"You're exhausted, you should get some rest."

"What is with everyone telling me how tired I am lately?" I ask. I wonder how he knows how tired I am, but I don't have the energy to ask. We stand and Henri walks me back to my cabin.

"I think you bring out everyone's protective side," he says with a small chuckle.

I don't need protecting, not by him or anyone else for that matter. I am the one who protects others. Although, given his current proximity, I'd say, I'm not doing a good job of it right now. I pose more of a risk to Henri than any other creature in existence. But I can't help the feeling of desire that runs through me when I hear the meaning behind his words. Henri wants to protect me.

At the door, he kisses me on the top of my head. It is a sweet and gentle kiss. I watch him walk back up the beach and out of sight then crawl into bed and quickly fall into a dreamless sleep.

Henri

Oh, my mate is wonderful, I think as I walk back to the guest house, I am staying in.

So strong and full of fire, but caring and soft at the same time. And stubborn, I can see that in the defiance behind her eyes, she will never bend to me.

Usually, I wouldn't put up with that. But oh, does it excite me from my mate. I can't wait to see how far I can push her. No one excuses themselves in the presence of royalty and yet Alexis didn't think twice about it.

She didn't even flinch when I caught her. There was no hint of remorse, and she would not beg forgiveness for her *insubordination*. She is my equal in every way. No, not equal, she is far superior to me. I should worship at her feet.

I have dreamt so many times of finding her. Seeing a smile light up the face, I'd last seen full of sorrow. The Alexis in my memory and dreams could never do justice to the real thing. When she smiles, she could illuminate the entire world.

My mind wanders thinking about what our life together might look like. Full of love and happiness, erasing the darkness within me.

For so long my purpose in life has been eradicating every creature that poses a threat. I have taken too many lives to count, and each one lays heavily upon me, pulling me further into the dark. But Alexis shines so bright and pure, I think maybe her light can counter the darkness in me.

She is clearly very attached to this island and its inhabitants, which might pose a problem for our future. I doubt Alexis would be happy to come back to court with me. Not that I plan on going anytime soon. But eventually...

No, don't dwell on that now, Henri. You need to focus on getting to know your mate. You are destined to be with her, everything else will fall into place.

I reach the guest house and see that, Ed; my best friend and regent is sat outside. Waiting for me, no doubt. I go over and sit beside him on the step.

"How'd it go? he asks. I filled him in on what happened when I returned from Alexis' house yesterday. I think Ed was more surprised to find Alexis alive than I was.

Ed has been with me through all of this. He shared the pain of losing Alexis the first time and the grief when the witch told me she had taken her own life. He kept me sane when I thought the rage would consume me whole.

"It's... complicated," I say.

He laughs, "I never expected it to be anything else, man. Did she say what kept her away?"

"She was protecting me. She thinks I don't know about the curse. But I am sure, she left so that it wouldn't take us too."

"I still can't believe she has been alive all this time and we never found out."

"I don't know her well *yet*, but I get the feeling that when Alexis sets her mind on something, she succeeds. She is the most stubborn and infuriating woman I have ever met." I speak.

"Oh, it's going to be fun watching her bring you to heel," Ed says, falling into a fit of laughter. I laugh too, already knowing that I would do anything for her.

"Seriously though, man, I can't tell you how happy I am for you. After everything you've been through, you deserve the happily ever after."

Ed's words sober me up. "I don't think it will be that simple," I say my face darkening. "Do I even deserve her after all the destruction I have caused? With the monster that lives inside me, always fighting to take over. It almost did. You warned me not to hurt her yesterday and it almost happened. When she defied me, it was urging me to use the dominance within me to make her submit to the bond." Ed looks aghast.

"I fought it and won, that time. If she keeps up this desire to sever our bond, I'm not sure I will be able to continue fighting it."

"Henri, I have known you longer than I care to admit. You are like a brother to me, and I know your burden lies heavily on you.

"You might think you have been lost to the dark for too long to come back now, but I know the light is still in there. You are a good man! You deserve all the happiness in the world. With Alexis by your side, you will never allow the darkness to consume you".

I smile at my friend and wish I could have the same faith in myself that Ed does. Maybe he is right, and this will all turn out well.

I might not have known it, but this amazing woman has spent 250 years protecting me. At the same time, she helped to build this community, becoming a leader worth following.

What a queen she will make.

Ed drifts off in thought for a minute and I can see a realisation in his eyes. "When you say she doesn't know you know about the curse, please say, you told her it is broken!"

I can't look at him and it is all the answer he needs. "Have you actually gone insane man? Why would you not tell her." I don't know how to explain but I try.

"I want her to be with me in spite of the curse, I couldn't bear to tell her the things I have done," I say. "I know I am a selfish creature and don't deserve her love, but man I want it more than anything." Ed looks uncharacteristically angry with me.

"She won't take kindly to you keeping this from her, Henri. You are not giving your mate the credit she deserves."

"She has kept plenty from me!" I retort, unable to contain my temper. It isn't really Alexis, or Ed I am angry at though. It's myself.

Will Alexis even want me when she finds out the things I've done? Will she run from me again when she learns of the lives I have taken? That I have lived a life filled with death and destruction. That the half of our soul living within me, shares a body with a monster so full of rage, it could end the world.

Maybe I should be the strong one and walk away this time. Leave her to live a happy and peaceful life on this island.

Even as I think it, I know I am too selfish to walk away from her now. I will never be able to leave her again.

Alexis

I wake early, feeling more rested than I have in years. Last night was the first night, I haven't been haunted by my parent's death since I arrived on the island. I stretch out and decide to do some yoga before Ginny gets here.

It's not until I sit up that I remember the events of the last few days. Henri, here on the island, me kissing him, dancing at the party last night.

I didn't realise until the feeling left me, but my soul had been in constant turmoil since the day I ran from Henri. Like she longed to reconnect with her other half.

My long forgotten and neglected power is also simmering just below the surface, like it's been tied down all these years and Henri's presence has somehow unbound it.

I am furious with myself for allowing this to happen. *Stop being so selfish, keeping him close will only get him killed.* You must send him away.

I resolve to put an end to this. TODAY.

As I'm sat thinking, there's a gentle tap on the door. "It's open, Gin," I shout. However, it isn't Ginny who opens the door. Instead, Henri stands looking at me. He is the picture of a Greek god, as he enters and closes the door behind himself.

I was so lost in my thoughts; I didn't sense him coming. This is not good. My senses have been all over the place since Henri arrived on the island.

A blush spreads across my face as I realise, I am sat in almost non-existent pyjamas and have messy bed hair.

I pull the sheet back over myself feeling self-conscious. "Sorry," I say, "I thought you were Ginny. She usually comes to get me moving in a morning." My heart rate kicks up a gear and I am sure Henri can hear it from across the room.

He is grinning like the Cheshire Cat. "That colour suits you," he says appreciably. I blush even more at his comment finally letting my eyes reach his.

The look on his face changes and he begins stalking towards me, never breaking eye contact. I feel like I am prey being hunted. The hungry look on his face suggests he would like nothing more than to devour me whole. I back away up my bed, but Henri isn't fazed and before long he pulls me towards him by one ankle, dumping the sheet on the floor. Suddenly he is over the top of me pinning my hands with his.

I want to tell him to get off. My head is screaming at me, telling me the reasons this man should not be in my bed. But my soul's desire to be close to her missing half is winning. She is revelling in his closeness, almost purring with delight. She is desperate to seal the bond and any slip of control on my part would have her doing just that.

Henri gently leans his lips towards mine and begins to move down my jaw to my neck. Never actually touching me, but his warm breath leaves goose bumps in its wake. I let out a gasp as he reaches the tender part where neck meets shoulder. I sense him smile, his head moving down further still as his sweet breath dances across my chest.

When he reaches my breast, my back involuntarily arches, urging him to touch me. I feel it in my very core, and I clench in anticipation. I am suddenly aware that the only force preventing me from pulling Henri towards me and sealing the bond are his hands pinning me to the bed. My soul is begging him to let go. She wants to be reunited with her missing half more than she has ever wanted anything in her life and will stop at nothing to get it.

No, Alexis, you cannot let this happen.

Regaining at least some control from my suddenly sex crazed soul, I half-heartedly try to push him off, but he doesn't budge. Just Henri's breath on me, is like nothing I have ever felt before. It's driving all rational thought out of my mind.

I sense how much he is enjoying driving me wild.

Henri stops abruptly. I can't help the disappointment I feel. When I open my eyes, he is grinning. "I knew you wanted me," he says.

Yep, arrogant ass!

I close my eyes again and try to regain control. I am breathless, panting even. Completely wanton. It's maddening how easily he could make me submit to him. To give over my body and soul, risking both our lives in the process.

Henri leans down and whispers in my ear. "You can't even imagine the things I could do to you Alexis. I could drive you insane over and over again, until you beg me to stop. But I won't touch you until you ask me to."

Henri lets me go and I manage to rearrange myself. His words are enough to snap me out of my daze. Finally, I push my soul back into her place and regain control of my body and mind.

I cannot believe he just did that and if he thinks I am going to ask him to touch me, he will be waiting a very long time.

As if on cue, there is another tap on the door. A moment later Ginny opens it, letting herself in. Her eyes widen as she sees Henri stood at the foot of my bed. "Oh... erm... sorry, I'll go," she stammers.

"No," Henri says, "I need to attend to something with my regent, I was just leaving." The lie flows so smoothly from his mouth, I almost believe him. Henri turns to face me. "Have dinner with me this evening." he says. It's not a question.

Say no, Alexis, my mind screams at me. "No," I say defiantly. He closes his eyes nodding and stalks from the room.

My soul retreats to her room pouting, slamming, and locking the door behind her. She has no sense of self-preservation at all. It's fortunate I have been in the driving seat for so long. We'd be dead if it was up to her.

Better dead than alone, she yells through the locked door. I choose to ignore her. She can sulk all she wants but the world won't lose its king for me, her, or anyone else. It's like sharing my mind with a teenager.

I hear what I think is a shoe being thrown at the door before she goes silent. No doubt plotting her next move.

ROCHELLE TATTERSALL

Chapter 5

Henri

As soon as I open my eyes, I feel the need to be close to her.
"Alexis!" I breathe.
I dress quickly, going straight down to her small cabin on the beach. Once there I hesitate, not wanting to wake her. I'm not even sure what to say. I just need to see her again. I need to prove to myself that it wasn't just an amazing dream, she is actually alive.

I hear movement from inside, so I knock on the door. "It's open, Gin," Alexis shouts. She thinks it's her friend. I shouldn't go in; I should shout and tell her it is me. I don't, the desire to see her unguarded is too great. I open the door and step straight inside.

The cabin is small, dominated by a large wooden four poster bed with white sheets covering the mattress and voile curtains hung from the posts swaying gently in the breeze. French style wooden doors with tiny square windows lead to a deck, and I notice the sea lapping at the shore beyond it. Yet more white curtains against the windows, wave in the wind.

This place is so inviting, fitting Alexis completely. Bright, warm, and peaceful. The scent of sea air mixes with her honey floral. It's both sweet and salty at the same time. I have never smelled anything more intoxicating in my life.

When my eyes meet hers, Alexis is blushing. She sits on her bed wearing a small pair of shorts and an almost transparent vest. I try to stay back, but the scent swirling round my head and seeing her sat there looking so radiant drive all restraint from my mind. I can't help myself; I need to feel her soft skin beneath my fingers, my lips, my...

I stalk towards her, even as she crawls backwards up the bed. I pull her back to me and position myself over her. I was only going to look, but her reaction as I hover over her spurs me on.

Her soft skin smells so good. I long to run my tongue over every inch of her. I don't. I hold back, in the hope of driving her wild.

When I reach her breast, she arches her back, asking me to take it into my mouth. I am overcome with pleasure - I won't rest until I have explored every glorious inch of this woman. I glance up and her chest is red from arousal.

I want to take her here and now; it takes every ounce of my self-control not to. However, I won't use the bond to force her into a corner. If we go much further, it will snap completely into place and I will never know if she is with me, just because the bond makes it impossible not to be.

I start to worry that I might have over stepped, using the bond to get her where I want her, but then she didn't exactly object.

I hear someone approaching and decide to back away to spare her the embarrassment. I don't care who sees, but I have a feeling my mate wouldn't be too happy about it.

I'm surprised I don't burst into flames from the look on Alexis' face when I pull away. She is murderous and a plan forms in my mind. She wants me, that much is clear. "I won't touch you, until you ask me to." I say with a slight smirk. The look on her face tells me I might be waiting a while, but the way her body responds to me says something completely different.

As Ginny knocks and walks in, I make my excuses to leave but not before doing something I have never done in my life... "Dinner this evening?" I ask.

I hope she says yes, but part of me knows she is holding back, I see the internal battle as she tries to figure out what to say.

"No," she says, with finality. I nod and leave. I knew it wouldn't be that easy, but I had to try.

Alexis

"Should I ask?" Ginny enquires, as the door closes behind Henri.

"No," I snap, before stalking off to the bathroom for a shower and slamming the door behind me. I am all too aware I am behaving like my irrational soul, but I am beyond caring.

I set the water running and step inside the shower, remembering the feeling I had the morning Henri arrived. Mercifully, the same doesn't happen this morning and I can try to process what just happened.

It's like I can't control myself when I'm around him. My rational mind takes a back seat, and my irrational soul takes over. I suppose that is because her other half lives in Henri and she wants to be close to him. She is still locked in her room inside my mind sulking. I make no attempt to draw her out, I need space to think and can't do that when she is pining to be close to her twin.

I sigh, turning off the water and stepping out of the shower. I look at myself in the mirror and notice how different I look today. My face is somehow brighter and the dark circles that have been a feature under my eyes for as long I can remember, have gone.

It's just because I got a good night's sleep, I tell myself. It has nothing to do with Henri.

I'm lying to myself. *"The only reason you slept was because he was here on the island."* My soul reminds me. "*I thought you weren't talking to me,*" I respond silently. No reply. Oh great, now I'm having conversations with myself.

I dress in my signature cami and shorts and head out to the deck where Ginny is sat at the small table, sipping tea. I take a seat and pick up the cup she has made for me. She looks pointedly at me but remains quiet, waiting for me to speak.

"Are you planning on telling me what's happened in the last 12 hours," she eventually asks when I fail to say anything. I know my friend too well to think she might let the subject go.

"Last night we talked on the beach. About the island and my life. I asked him what he was doing here. It turns out his father wanted to punish him." Ginny raises an eyebrow.

"How is sending him here a punishment, and come to think of it, what the hell is he being punished for?"

I choose to ignore her first question and simply answer the second. "Henri called off his engagement." Ginny's mouth drops open, and I can see a million questions in her eyes.

"He was engaged?" she asks, outraged. "What was he thinking? Is the man suicidal?" All spinners know tying yourself to someone other than your mate, is like a death sentence. It's why Sam and I would never have worked, even if I'd wanted us to.

"I'm not sure. He thought I was dead, so I guess in a way he was. Anyway, he told me he couldn't go through with tying himself to someone else, so he called it off."

"Wow."

"I told him calling it off was a mistake, he should have stayed in Asgard and married her. I thought it might be enough to push him away."

Ginny scoffs at the stupidity of my words. Even I know that plan had enough holes to be a tea strainer. "Given what I saw this morning, I'm guessing that didn't work."

"No, he got quite angry, said he wasn't going to just walk away. Then he kissed me – again."

"Did you..." Ginny starts but I cut her off.

"NO," I shout, knowing exactly what she is about to say. "He turned up early this morning. I thought he was you, so said to come in." I decide to leave out the finer details of Henri's visit. "We were just talking when you arrived."

"So, what are your plans now?" Ginny asks. "What are his, for that matter?"

"My plan is to go up to the hospital to check on a couple of patients," I say, ignoring the real meaning behind her words. Ginny narrows her eyes.

"That is not what I meant, and you know it," she says.

"I know what you meant, but it's complicated. It isn't safe for us to be around each other; I just wish he could see that. Whenever he is near me, I forget why we can't be together. It's the bond, though. I can't seem to be able to separate my real feelings from it.

"He can't stay here forever though, he has duties. If I can just keep him at arm's length until then..." I trail off, once again hearing the weakness of my own argument.

"OK, you keep telling yourself that," she scoffs. I flash a dirty look her way but drop the subject.

"Come on, I really do need to get up to the hospital," I say instead.

The day passes in a blur of meetings and patients. I am somehow able to get lost in my work and feel almost normal for a few hours. The rhythm of the day soothes the turmoil and I feel lighter as I leave the hospital.

Walking into town I am greeted by Dad, for our weekly date night. He hugs me close and kisses both cheeks. "How are you, firefly?" he asks, his Spanish accent so much thicker when he is worried about me.

"I'm fine, Dad," I say, trying to keep my voice steady. He sees through me and pulls me in for another hug. After a moment we walk towards his bar and find a seat in a quiet corner. Two drinks are placed before us and Dad glances up to thank the waiter.

I down my own drink in two gulps and Dad silently pushes his towards me. I take a sip, and sigh. "Better?" he asks.

"Better," I answer.

"You want to talk about it?" He asks.

"I'm sure there isn't anything Mum hasn't already told you," I say with a shrug.

"Mum told me the story Alexis, but that isn't what I want to know. I want to know how you are doing. I haven't really seen you since the prince arrived. I saw your reaction; you weren't exactly happy to see him – it's been a long time since you ran away to your hiding place. Now I know why, I can only imagine what you are going through. So no, Mum hasn't told me everything."

Mum is so intuitive and open; her questions never catch me off guard. Dad is usually so much more reserved, when he is this frank like this, it comes as a surprise.

"I'm terrified, Dad," I blurt, before I can stop myself. Tears I have been holding back since the storm incident finally begin to fall again and a protective arm wraps around my shoulder. I let it all out. The rain outside starts as suddenly as it did the night Henri arrived and I know it's me doing it. This time instead of the panic I felt before, it soothes me somewhat. The thunder never arrives.

"I know you are cherry blossom, I know," he sighs. He allows me time to wallow before pulling me back to the here and now. "I love you more than, I can put into words Alexis, and seeing you like this breaks my heart, but do you know what else breaks my heart? Seeing you spend your life alone.

"You put on a great show. Not many people see through your façade, but your Mum does and so do I. What happened back in Asgard was terrible but why does that one event get to define your entire life? Why does it mean you have to be alone forever? And when you are as close to immortal as it is possible to be, forever is a very long time.

"I'm not a spinner, so I don't know what the twin flame bond feels like. I only have my experience with Brighid to compare, but I do know I would rather have loved her and she I, for one day than endure a million years without her. If you close off your heart to even the possibility of love, they win. Do you understand? The witches who set out to ruin your family, they win Alexis."

"They won the day they took my parents, Dad," I snap in response. My anger elicits a bolt of lightning followed by a clap of thunder in the sky above us. Dad jumps at the sudden noise but doesn't back away from my anger. "And what would you have me do, give them another win?

"If life before I arrived on this island taught me anything at all, it is that there is evil out there, that will stop at nothing to win.

"Being away from Henri every day for the last 250 years has been like having half of my soul ripped out. No not like, it was exactly that, I left half of my soul on the other side of the planet. But what choice did I have? Allow my people, the world, to lose their prince and future king?

"I see the way you are with Mum; I know you love her and would do absolutely anything for her, but the twin flame bond is different. It goes far deeper than love. Henri and I are meant to be one. We each have half a soul, desperately searching for its missing half. It is agony to push him away. I wish there was another way, I spent a long time looking for one, but there isn't.

"I don't have the power to break the curse. If my parents couldn't do it with all theirs, what hope do I have? I did then, and continue to do now, the only thing within my power; keep my distance to keep the prince alive. If he dies, the world as we know it dies too." My voice has risen, and I take a deep breath to stop me from yelling. The storm outside is raging along with my emotions and the whole island doesn't need to know my secrets.

Dad is visibly fuming at my words. "Who are you trying to kid Alexis?" Dad asks more sternly than I have ever heard him. "You are unbelievably powerful. You have stuffed it down as far as you can. Hidden it even from yourself but it is still there alright. Fear is what keeps you from stepping into your true power.

"Your Mum and I have always known you were incredibly powerful. We didn't say anything because you never needed it here. But you need it now and I won't sit by and watch you waste your life because you are too afraid to step into it.

"It is time to own who you are firefly. No more hiding from us, yourself, Henri, or anyone else. If you don't have any power, how are you creating this storm. Just imagine what you could achieve if you stopped running from it.

"When you first came here, you wanted the world to know there was another way to live. I have always wanted the same thing, but who would listen to me? No one Alexis, no one. But you? You are mated to the future king and are more powerful than even he is. More powerful than even The Elders, I'd care to guess. You have it in you to change the world, if only you would stop running scared and own up to who you were born to be." By the end of his little rant, Dad's accent has become so thick I struggle to keep up.

I shrug my shoulders unable to respond. I am suddenly exhausted and long to be wrapped up in bed. Dad's tirade has run its course, and he goes quiet, giving me space to process what he has said. The storm is no longer raging, only light rain falls on the tin roof of the bar. I find the noise soothing.

We sit in silence finishing our drinks, as the usual early evening noises return with the slowing of the rain "I'm going home, Dad." I finally say as the tears run out and the rain stops completely. I say good night to Dad and to my surprise he allows me to leave without any fuss. He knows me well; his words have struck a chord and I need time to think. Slowly I make my way home in the twilight, rerunning the argument with Dad, in my head like it's on tape.

Did I hide my power, even from myself? I know I didn't have much when I lived in Asgard, but spinners don't usually come into their power until they reach adulthood. When mine never really matured I just assumed I didn't have any – I'd put it down to losing my parents so young. But maybe Dad is right, and it was there all along and I have suppressed it somehow. I never heard of a spinner who could control the weather, though. I know our power is second only to the Goddess, but even so, that seems excessive.

If I am honest with myself though, it has been stirring since the morning before Henri arrived – when my marks were glowing. Tonight is the second time I have caused a storm, what else might I be capable of. The thought both terrifies and excites me. My life has been serene and calm for so long, am I ready to face what this kind of power could bring?

Henri is sat on my deck when I get home. I'm not surprised to find him there. His face drops when he sees me. "You've been crying," he says. I nod, still unable to trust my voice. "I'm sorry, Alexis, I never wanted to make you sad."

I close my eyes and take a deep breath as I sit beside him. "You didn't make me sad, Henri…" I stutter not sure how to explain my feelings. "I'm confused. I have been telling myself, I did the right thing leaving and that I am happy with my life for so long I almost believed it.

"I met with Dad this evening and he has a way of seeing through things and then telling me what he sees." I don't go on; afraid I will say too much. Henri nods, appearing to understand and I begin to worry I already have.

"Alexis, I know why you ran all those years ago. Finding me at your parent's graveside must have been, *difficult*. I thought you might return when you had come to terms with their death, but I can see that you still haven't. I understand, we are supposed to live for hundreds, even thousands of years, to lose your parents so young…" he pauses and sighs, looking for the right words. "I can't even begin to imagine that kind of pain.

"No actually, I can. I lost you before I even had you and have carried that for a very long time."

I am stunned and hang my head in shame. I feel the weight of the world fall on me as I begin to see how much pain and suffering, I have put this man through. Fresh tears start to fall, and the rain soon follows. How can I ever be forgiven for hurting him like this?

Henri moves closer shielding me from the down pour I have manifested. I selfishly allow him to pull me in close. I don't deserve his comfort or compassion, but I will take it. I don't have the energy to push him away any longer.

We remain like this until darkness engulfs us and the tears run their course yet again – since when did I turn into this blubbering mess? I seem to have done nothing but cry for days. My eyes are so swollen and painful, I can hardly see. Henri stands, taking me with him and leads me into the house. He places me gently in bed, pulling the sheets over me. He plants a soft kiss on my forehead and whispers, "I love you Alexis, I always have and always will." I can't find a response so say nothing. Henri heads to the door but turns to face me as he gets there. "Alexis?" he asks.

"Mm" I mumble in response.

"Would you do me the honour of having dinner with me, tomorrow evening?" This time he is asking politely, like the prince he was raised to be. He is still giving me the opportunity to refuse again.

"OK," I reply, hesitantly. His smile is dazzling as he turns to leave.

Henri

As I head back towards the town, Ed's voice suddenly appears in my mind. *"Henri, you need to get your sorry ass back here, QUICKLY!"* I hear him say. I can feel his panic even through our telepathic mind link and set out at a run, back towards the guest house. *Be there in five,* I reply in my mind.

When I get there, Ed is in the dining room, pacing. He must be lost in his thoughts because he startles as I enter. "What is it?" I ask, not knowing if I really want to know the answer.

"She's left Asgard," he states, and my blood runs cold. By she, Ed is referring to my ex-*fiancé*, Lilith, who did not take too kindly to my calling off the wedding. It didn't matter to Lilith that we weren't mates. She just wanted the title and crown.

Lilith and Ed never saw eye to eye. He could see what she was doing from the start, and he was all too happy when I called the wedding off two days before the 'big day.'

Closing my eyes for a second, I take a deep breath and ask the only question that matters right now. "Where is she going?" I know the answer before Ed says it - he wouldn't be in such a state otherwise.

"Here," he says, confirming what I already know.

"Why?" I ask.

"For you of course," he replies. "It seems your father told her where you went, and she thought she should come and fight for her man."

"I am not and never will be *'her man'*," I seethe. Anger rips through me. Since my encounter with Alexis this morning, the rage had subsided, like her presence was soothing my soul. The very thought of Lilith being anywhere near Alexis, sets me on edge and I can't figure out why.

Maybe it is because Lilith has seen my rage, and I don't want Alexis to find out. Maybe it is because the only person I ever told about Alexis was Ed. Maybe it is because Alexis - ever keen on sending me away - might use this development to talk herself out of being with me.

Yes, maybe that's why!

Ed breaks through my thoughts. "She will be here in five days," he says.

Right! Five days to make Alexis realise she loves me and stop pushing me away. Nothing to worry about.

I am up early the next morning to meet with Brighid and her partner Matias, who I spoke to at length, the night of the party. Mostly about Alexis. I had to find out everything I could about her. I knew she wouldn't open up to me easily.

He told me, she arrived on the island around a month after her parents' funeral. She was in a bad way. Brighid, an empath, helped her to heal and in time convinced her to care for others on the island.

I see that both Matias and Brighid think very highly of Alexis. They took on the role of parents, essentially adopting my mate. I will need their help to win her over.

This morning Matias greets me with a friendly hello, although Brighid seems a little cold. Today I am to have a tour of the island, starting with

70

the school and ending with the building I am most interested in - the hospital.

I trail round, with a smile plastered to my face, counting down the minutes until we finally arrive at the hospital. I try to engage Brighid in friendly conversation, but she remains formal and distant.

Matias takes me aside to tell me she is just trying to protect Alexis, but not to worry she will warm to me.

This island really is amazing. In the school I spot more species of children than I ever knew existed. All learning together, fully accepting their differences without judgment or prejudice. I wonder again why the rest of the world can't be like this.

As children, spinners are taught about other species. However, what we are taught is that others pose a threat to civilised society and it is our job to maintain balance. I never really bought it, and it will be one of the first things I change when I am king - especially now I have seen it working, with my own eyes.

Here on this island, I have proof that when everyone is given the opportunity, amazing things can happen.

Many back in Asgard sneer at the mention of this island. I think that must be why it has been left alone for so long. It is thought of as 'backward.'

After the school we visit the food growers, Brighid's beloved solar farm, and many of the island's shops and artisans. Eventually we have toured around the entire island; the only place left is the hospital.

I can feel Alexis, even before I step inside.

Alexis

By 3pm, I have seen all my patients, done some teaching with the interns and almost completed my paperwork.

The normality of my day has helped to subdue the anxiety that has been growing since last night, somewhat.

As I sit in my office, attempting to write a lesson, I feel Henri enter the building. This is the first time; I've actually sensed him coming and I briefly wonder why that is.

I'm not sure I am ready to face him, but after neglecting my duties so far during this visit I know I must go to greet our guests. I grab a drink of water, wishing it was something stronger to steady my nerves and head down to the main foyer to greet the visitor.

Henri's face lights up when he feels me approach, but he remains quiet in the middle of the group.

He looks every bit the modern prince, in perfectly tailored blue slacks and a loose white cotton shirt, with the sleeves rolled up to the elbows. He fits in perfectly, but I have a sudden longing for his long-braided hair and beard, his muscular arms rippling below a rugged tunic. Looking at him like this from a distance, I notice how striking his marks are for the first time. They look tribal, but I can't be sure, given the majority are covered by clothing.

I see him lick his lips, and blush at the thought of what that mouth could do to me.

Get a grip, Alexis, I scold myself. Now is not the time.

Plastering on my most convincing smile, I warmly greet the group. "Welcome to Serenity Hospital," I say, avoiding eye contact with the prince.

We start the tour and I lead the way, explaining everything that we do. Unlike the healing centres back in Asgard, we treat all kinds of beings here, so many of the treatments are alien to our visitors.

"Each species has its own healing methods or medicine," I say as we near the research centre. "At first that meant we struggled to treat everyone on the island.

"However, we have now developed techniques that include numerous different methods, benefitting everyone." I beam thinking about how we have grown to understand each other and work together.

"This is especially helpful for those among us who have a mixed heritage," Mum cuts in.

I hear a few of the ambassadors' gasp at Mum's comment. They are clearly part of the traditionalist leagues, true followers of The Elders, who don't approve of our way of life.

"Are there many..." one member of the group speaks up, clearly trying to choose his words carefully. "Um, mixed heritage, beings on this island?" he asks.

I don't like his line of questioning or tone, so beat Mum to the answer. "No, not many," I say vaguely, looking at Mum silently begging her to stay quiet. Fortunately, she is an empath and has picked up on the feeling behind the man's words.

Another much younger looking man speaks up, obviously uncomfortable with the reaction of the old guard among their number. "This is truly remarkable," he says with a grin. "The rest of the world could learn so much from you. Couldn't they?" The question is directed at

Henri who looks at me smiling widely as he answers. "They could," he says, and I can even hear the smile in his voice.

I hear mumbles about nature and order among the other members of the group, but they are silenced by a deadly look from their prince. "Please continue, Ms Beaumont," Henri says with a twinkle in his eye. I notice the younger man who spoke earlier smirk at the prince.

"Beaumont?" another older spinner asks raising is eyebrows so far, they almost disappear into his hair line. "Are you related to the late Selene Beau..."

"I doubt it, my family are all here on the island," I cut him off before he can finish his question and glare daggers at Henri. He looks at me with an apology in his eyes.

I continue the tour, the group stopping to talk to a few of the doctors, nurses, and patients along the way.

When we finally arrive back in the foyer, I say my farewells to the group and turn to go back to my office. I need some space to gather my thoughts after that near miss.

Henri, grabs my wrist, holding me back, his demeanour less confident than usual. "I am truly sorry for that slip, Alexis," he says so earnestly, I believe him. "I will pick you up at seven," he says to me. I groan inwardly, I'd forgotten all about the 'date' I agreed to last night.

"Henri, I'm not sure..." I begin to say, but he cuts me off.

"No funny business, I just want to talk, that's all. I promise," he says, drawing a cross on his chest. I sigh but nod my agreement.

"OK," I say, feeling like I am agreeing to both of our deaths.

Chapter 6

Alexis

Ginny is waiting for me as I set off home. We walk past the square and along the dusty dirt track that leads to the beach and my cabin. Ginny is unusually quiet and seems to be having some kind of internal battle with herself. I realise I haven't seen her since my argument with Dad. I wonder if he has said something to her.

Eventually, I can't stand watching her any longer and blurt, "come on, out with it." She looks at me innocently with wide eyes, but I can see straight through her.

"What? What do you mean? I'm fine." I narrow my eyes, refusing to back down.

"Try again, Gin. I know you too well. If you have something to say, I want to hear it."

"I found my mate," she eventually says. I freeze in shock as I try to process what she is saying. I selfishly thought her ruminating was about me. When did I become this person, who believes everything revolves around my life.

"What? Who? How? When? Where?" I ask, unable to form a coherent sentence. I know it must be one of the group of ambassadors, we have known everyone who lives on the island too long for it to be a resident and there are no other visitors here at the moment.

It takes her a while to answer, but when she does the words rush out, like she is trying to get it over with as quickly as possible.

"I saw him when they arrived but never made eye contact, you know with everything that happened. Yesterday we bumped into each other in town. It was like I had been hit by a bolt of lightning when our eyes met. We both knew straight away.

"Oh, he is amazing, Lex. We walked and talked for hours; it was like we had known each other all our lives.

74

"He is the prince's best friend – his regent. He is called Edward, but prefers Ed. I am meeting him tonight." Her words tumble out and she is flushed with excitement.

I can't help but be happy for my friend. She is overjoyed, but the fact that she worried about telling me makes me frown. "What is it?" Ginny asks.

"I was just wondering, why you were worried about telling me? I couldn't be happier for you, Gin." She looks away and I can see the worry there again.

"It's just... well... I mean... with what you are going through, it just doesn't seem right." I am aghast at her compassion and my eyes fill with tears. I gain control quickly, not wanting to be caught in the middle of another deluge.

"Hey!" I say. "I know how much you have dreamed of meeting your mate. I am truly happy for you." I put as much emotion into the words as can muster. I need her to see that I mean every word.

"I never wanted a mate, and I didn't need the happily ever after. I am, and for a long time, have been at peace with that.

"That does not mean I would be bitter, that my best friend in the world has found hers."

I hug her tightly, letting her know how happy I am for her. When we part, both our eyes are filled with tears.

We don't need to say out loud that our simple lives have been forever changed by the arrival of the Spinners Court to our tiny corner of the world.

There will be trying times ahead, but for now we will act like teenagers gossiping about the first throws of love. I listen on as my best friend gushes about her mate and lays out her hopes for their future together.

A future, I know, I can never have with mine.

Henri

I am more than shocked, when Ed tells me the girl who walked in on Alexis and me the other morning - Ginny - is his mate. But I am made up for the guy.

He has been with me through thick and thin, man he deserves to find his soul mate.

However, as I wait outside Alexis' cabin looking out at the sea, I can't help the jealousy I feel. Ed's union with Ginny will be so much easier than ours. It's how it is meant to be with our twin flames.

Nothing in my paring with Alexis will be easy. My anger rises to the surface again with this dark thought.

I feel Alexis step onto her porch and her presence soothes me instantly, anger all but gone.

I turn to face her and what I see takes my breath away. Alexis is wearing a tightly fitted knee length, sleeveless dress, that highlights her beautiful rainbow-coloured markings perfectly. They wind up her leg, out of view under the dress, only to emerge again at her breast and wind elegantly down her arm.

She blushes at my appraising look. "You are breath-taking," I manage to force out. Again, I am filled with the urge to grab her and make her mine. "Thank you," she replies, almost shyly, looking down.

Alexis is not used to compliments. *Well, she better get used to them,* I think to myself.

She walks towards me, appearing to recover herself. "Shall we?" she asks repeating my own words from the other night back to me. She gestures toward the path back into the town.

"I thought we could take a walk first," I say, reaching for her hand and moving to walk along the beach.

We aren't eating in the town's restaurant this evening. I need to talk to her away from prying ears. Matias and I have organised our meal to be delivered to the small dock, where I have set up a private table for just the two of us.

I am surprised when Alexis easily agrees to the walk. I'm even more surprised when she lets me take her hand. The feeling of her soft skin against mine sends a jolt of pleasure through me - this is where I belong, tethered to this amazing woman.

As we walk, I ask her more questions about her life here and her work. I have noticed she is happy to discuss these subjects and I want to put her at ease.

She opens up about her friends and what it meant to be welcomed here without question. As I thought, Brighid and Matias took her in, becoming her adoptive parents when she was alone in the world.

She tells me how she had lived with them for a time and how they never forced her to talk about what happened to her birth parents.

They had hoped she would find love - not knowing of my existence. Even attempting to pair her up with someone. I feel a pang of unbridled jealousy as she imparts this information, but hide it well, *I hope*. She tells me her adoptive parents had long since given up hope for her on that front. *Good I won't have to kill anyone,* I think.

Eventually the subject of Ginny comes up and we both express our happiness at her mating with Ed.

Alexis becomes very animated talking about her friend. It seems that even though she was happy on the island before Ginny arrived, she longed to have another spinner around, she could relate to.

It was with Ginny's help that Brighid eventually convinced Alexis to use her healing knowledge again. Ginny - like Ed for me - has been always there for Alexis.

I was particularly awed by the fact that it didn't matter to her that Alexis wouldn't disclose the secrets of her past, she was still there for her on the darkest of days.

Alexis

When I walk out of my cabin, Henri turns to look at me and the look on his face brings yet another blush to my cheeks.

He looks amazing, wearing a smart pair of shorts and short sleeved shirt, giving me a proper look at his markings for the first time. I was right in thinking they looked tribal. It is clear they distinguish him as a warrior.

It takes a great deal of control not to run my hands across them. You need to be more disciplined than that, Alexis, my mind screeched.

No, you don't my soul countered. She has been blissfully quiet all day while I worked. Henri's presence has to roused her, though.

As we walk along the beach, he asks me a thousand questions about my life here in Serenity. I am happy to answer them, rather than discussing our ill-fated relationship.

We are approaching the dock, when I notice a table and two chairs arranged under a small canopy. *That's unusual*, I think. Then turn to see the small smile on Henri's face and realise it is his doing.

"I thought we could dine in private," he says. I frown slightly, feeling this may not end well. I was counting on being around other people, to prevent anything like the other morning happening again.

My soul on the other hand is doing her victory dance again.

When I look at Henri, his face full of hope and longing, I can't refuse. "OK," I say. His face breaks out into the most magnificent smile, and I can't help but do the same.

He pulls out a seat for me before taking his own.

One of the young waiters from Dad's bar, approaches us with drinks held on a tray. "Your favourite, Lex," he says as he places a rum cocktail in front of me. I smile up at him as he places Henri's drink down. "Thank you, Tom," I say.

I sip my cocktail and look out at the sea. We should have a restaurant here, I think. It's the perfect spot. "The people here really do love you, don't they," Henri says breaking through my thoughts.

"We are a small community," I say. "I love them too."

"Why are you not the leader," he asks not mincing his words. This is a subject I'm *not* keen to discuss.

"We don't have a leader per say. If we did, it would be Mum, she is the council chair." I answer, hoping this will be enough. It isn't.

"I can feel your power, Alexis. You are a born leader." I sigh unsure how to explain why I wouldn't want to be this role. Mum has asked me more than once to take over her seat. Why does everyone feel my so-called power, other than me?

"Power brings out the worst in people. Those who have it often want more. Those who desire it, will stop at nothing to get it.

"Mum is perfect for the chair, empaths by nature are not interested in having power over others.

"My family's power was its downfall. I didn't inherit it, I can barely see auras, never mind do anything with it, but I wouldn't want more anyway." I feel the blood drain from my face as I realise what I just said. *Shit!*

Henri stares at me with a knowing look. "Your parents were killed for their power, so you hide yours in the hope of not following them," he says, understanding the meaning behind my words.

"You claim to be powerless and the other beings here on the island, haven't uncovered your secret, but I am the prince and your mate, I could feel it the second I stepped foot off the boat, before actually. The force field is your doing too." It's not a question.

I don't answer. How do I explain that I am not the heir the Beaumont's hoped for. Fortunately, I am saved from having to, as our food arrives. I suddenly realise, we haven't actually ordered any food. Henri must see my confusion.

"I had help," he says simply. I narrow my eyes at him.

"Who?"

"Matias." Hmm, figures. He is determined to meddle.

I smell the food before it gets to us. It is my favourite, Paella. Dad's too, from the smell of it. He has a traditional Spanish recipe that has been passed down through generations of his family.

I look up to thank Tom, but find someone else entirely, looking back at me. *Fuck, fuck, fuck!*

Henri

I am just starting to feel like Alexis will open up to me, when we are interrupted by another waiter bringing food. I instantly take a dislike to him. The way he looks at Alexis, leads me to believe he wants what is mine.

One look at Alexis' face and my thoughts are confirmed. There is history there.

"Samuel," she says trying to smile, but I can see his presence is unsettling her. "I thought you were still travelling. Africa, wasn't it?" she asks, politely. Her address appears to be formal, but it is far from it. I can hear an undercurrent of sadness in her voice.

"I was back in Australia actually," he replies. "I couldn't keep away, though." I can see from the look in his eyes he means he couldn't keep away from her. The rage comes bubbling back up and I feel the need to put this *rat* in his place.

It looks like I might have to kill someone tonight after all.

I clear my throat and his attention turns to me, as if he hadn't seen me before. "What's this Lex?" he asks.

"None of your damn business," I say before Alexis can answer.

"Oh yeah? Says who?" he retorts. I almost fly out of my seat at the insolence. Before I know it, I have my hands around his throat. He is up against a wall, feet dangling inches above the ground. "Mind. Your. Manners." I grate out. I know he can feel my power and the anger coming off me in waves.

I can almost hear Alexis roll her eyes and it is enough to snap me out of it. She places a soothing hand on my arm, calming me fully. Samuel notices the gesture and grimaces.

"Henri, put the boy down," she says. Her voice is steady, but I can feel her fury under the surface. I wonder momentarily who it is aimed at. Me or *him*.

My answer comes quickly.

Alexis

The minute I see Sam, I know this isn't going to be pretty. We were so close before he went off travelling. I know he had always hoped there would be more, but I could never reciprocate his love. I really did think he was gone for good. Why would he choose now to return.

I'd said it wasn't him, that I loved him but would never be *in love* with him. I would never be with any man in that way. The argument we'd had the day he left comes back to the front of my mind and my heart shatters all over again. There is so much I didn't get to tell him. Sam is my family, I never wanted to break his heart and I can only imagine how much he is aching right now.

I see the emotions going through his mind as he takes in the scene in front of him. We look like a happy couple on a date.

The emotion he settles for is anger. *Quadruple fuck.*

Sam can be so sweet and kind but his hot temper lands him in trouble often.

He is hurt, I can see that in his face. I told him I would never be with anyone that way and then accept a date from a stranger when he is gone.

Henri is much stronger than Sam and won't take kindly to another man trying to stake a claim on me. Before I can formulate a plan, the two men exchange heated words and Henri has Sam up against a wall.

I am suddenly furious. Who the hell do these men think they are fighting over me as though I am some sort of prize to be claimed. *I think not.*

Instinctively I know how to calm Henri. I say the words he needs to hear to put Sam down and place my hand on his arm. He turns to me, smiling. Clearly thinking he is out of the woods.

Boy is he wrong.

I set off once again at a run towards my cabin, kicking off my sandals as I go.

Henri catches me easily, his own anger matching mine. "I said don't run from me," he actually growls.

I spin around out of his grasp, anger fuelling me on, power ripples just beneath the surface of my skin. It's unsettling. Something, I have never felt before. *Where is this coming from?* I feel heat pricking at my fingertips and I think they are seconds away from catching fire. He tries to pull me back to him. I can see his need to touch me, which pushes the flames threatening to burst out over my skin back, but I still back away.

The sky goes dark as menacing thunder clouds roll in. Sure, enough moments later the thunder and lightning begin. At least I am angry and not sad, or we'd both be soaked to the skin in no time.

"I am not your property, Henri" I shout. "You do not own me and you sure as hell, are not going to have everyone, you think is a threat to your manhood up against a wall. I can take care of myself. I don't need a knight to rescue me."

"A threat to my manhood?" he asks, sounding almost amused.

His amusement only serves to fuel my growing anger and the flames come dangerously close to the surface again. I push it back but do nothing to quell the raging storm above us. "Yes, your fucking manhood, Henri. You go storming in there acting like some Alpha wolf, when another man dares to touch his Luna. Well, the she wolves might find it sexy, but I am no she wolf.

"I don't need a Neanderthal to hit a predator over the head for me." I scream as actual fire shoots from my fingers. I pull my hands behind me to protect my arrogant ass of a mate from them.

Henri's eyes widen but he doesn't comment. At least my words seem to have succeeded at wiping the smile off his face.

"You think I want to be like this, Alexis?" he says as calmly as he can, I can still feel his fury matching my own. I look at his hands to see if he is also shooting fire from them. He isn't - I guess that's just me then! "I have spent so long without you, the need to possess you and keep you safe is all encompassing "

"I am safe, or I was until you turned up. Your presence here is the only danger I face. Can't you see that? I never wanted you to save me. I wanted you to leave me alone. I am not your princess, Henri." I somehow get the words I have been trying to say since he arrived, out of my mouth. I need to make him see we can't ride off into the sunset together.

Although I can see my words cut into him like a knife, he doesn't back down. The rage has shifted, another emotion now swimming in his eyes, but before I can figure out what it is, he speaks.

"For more than two centuries, I have been a shadow of a man, forced to walk the earth with only half a soul. First, slaying every single creature who sought to do you harm. Then when I was told you were dead, I killed even more. This rage has been my constant companion Alexis, and you are the only antidote.

"I will no longer live in a world where you are not by my side. You can try and deny our bond and use harsh words to send me away, but know this, my place is by your side and come what may, we will face the future together."

His words take me off guard. What does he mean, he has been out there killing other beings? Why would he do that?

"I don't want you Henri." The sudden pain in my chest feels like it will kill me as I say the words and tears spring into my eyes, but I need to send him away. I won't allow myself to be hurt like Gran and certainly I won't leave my people without an heir. Rain now starts to fall in time with the tears streaming down my cheeks.

Henri looks thoughtful as though he can see into my mind.

"Go ahead Alexis, hate me. But I think you are running out of steam on the whole keeping me safe bullshit. Maybe you can hold onto the fear of betrayal thing long enough to spend the rest of your life alone.

"You never struck me as a coward, so what are you really afraid of, Alexis? The hardest thing is loving someone and having the courage to let them love you back."

I'm stunned into silence. How does he know so much? I look again at him, as our eyes meet, I can almost hear his thoughts. He says them out loud anyway.

"I know about the curse, Alexis."

Chapter 7

Alexis

My mind is reeling. He knows about the curse, and he isn't running for the hills. The anger that overtook us moments ago is gone and the sky clears. Henri looks up, understanding dawning on his face. He doesn't comment though.

"How?" I ask. "How do you know?"

"I was frantic when you left, and I was unable to find you. I searched all Asgard for you and when you weren't there, I went to a seer."

Ah, yes that would do it.

"She told me of the curse. With the ties that bind, the clock begins, to drain these spinners for their sins, as they fall, we hear their cries and witches of the world will rise." He repeats the words, I have only ever heard once out loud, but which have been etched onto my brain forever since.

"I understood at once why you left. It didn't matter to me. I searched for you anyway." My heart breaks at the thought of him scouring the earth for me.

"You said, you thought I was dead," I say. "Why?" He closes his eyes as if trying to shut out a painful memory.

"I went to the Witches of Endor in Budapest. I found the one who created the curse. She told me, you had taken your own life in fear. That you were too weak to fight for me.

"That is when the rage took over. I killed her and the rest of the clan, it broke the curse, but what good was it me when you were already gone. I kept hunting down *witches*, I needed to put an end to them, so they could no longer inflict pain on others."

I hang my head in shame. The witch was right. I ran away in fear. I am weak. Henri was out there making a difference, fighting our battles alone. And where was I? Sitting pretty, safe and sound, on my paradise island.

Henri gently lifts my chin so that he can look deep into my eyes. "You are many things, my love, but weak is not one of them."

I quickly close the distance between us and his arms snake around me holding me close. Henri leans his head down to kiss me and for the first time, I don't try to pull back. The kiss starts off slow and gentle, but soon lust takes over intensifying it. My hands find his arms and move up into his hair pulling him even closer.

He groans in satisfaction at the close contact, and I feel a smile tugging at his lips. I am lost in the kiss, falling into an abyss as the world tilts slightly and I know the bond has snapped fully into place.

Henri accepted me the moment we locked eyes 250 years ago and now the Goddess acknowledges that I have accepted Henri as my mate. I can almost feel her presence, the joy she feels as our soul reconnects.

When we finally part, gasping for breath everything seems different, yet the same. There is an awareness deep within me that no matter what happens I will love this man unequivocally for the rest of my days. I feel my power fully waking as if from a long sleep. I suddenly understand it was always there, my fear had closed it off. I groan, knowing I will have to admit that Dad was right.

Henri looks at me, as though I am the most precious thing ever to have walked the earth, and I know that he too will love me for the rest of time.

We silently walk hand in hand back towards my small house. Henri sits on the sand leaning back against a post and I sit with my back against his chest as we watch the sun set over the crystal blue sea.

Neither of us speak for a long time. Henri absently runs his fingers across my bare arms, leaving goosebumps in his wake.

"Alexis," he whispers in my ear.

"Hmm," I say. Relishing the feeling of his fingers on my skin.

"The storm, that was you, wasn't it? Not just tonight, the others as well." I don't trust my own voice, so I nod my head. My growing power still terrifies me. Everyone believed any child of my mother and father would be incredibly powerful, but only the Goddess herself should have the ability to manipulate the elements.

Henri doesn't question me further and I drift off into my thoughts.

I can't believe what I have been missing out on all these years, without Henri by my side. The feeling of completeness is indescribable. My thoughts turn dark as I think again about the pain I have inflicted on my mate. How can he ever forgive me for my selfish actions? He is so strong, he deserves better. All this time I was running from Asgard and my responsibility, wanting to be free. How did I not see, I was trapped in a prison of my own making? I closed off my power, part of my soul, denied my lineage and what good did it do?

None. *Selfish, selfish, selfish!*

I am about to speak when Henri stops me. "I know what you are going to say, and I won't have any of that," he says quietly into my ear. His warm breath sends shivers down my body. I suddenly realise he knows what I am thinking.

I turn to look at him, quirking an eyebrow up. "You can hear my thoughts?" He laughs out loud at the incredulous look on my face.

"Yes, my love, I can," he replies simply. My brow furrows as I try and fail to hear his. "It will come, give it time. The mind link develops over time, much like an infant learning language. You need time to settle into the reconnection. It's a lot for the body, mind and soul to deal with."

I am amazed by how much he knows about this and how little I do. Henri chuckles softly. "I've had a lot of time to learn," he says.

"OK, do you think you could try to stay out of my head?" I ask. This could get very annoying and embarrassing for me. A laugh rumbles through his chest as his arms wrap tightly around me. "Not a chance," he says, and I can hear the mischief in his voice.

I could get lost forever in the sound of his laugh. I would happily suffer the annoyance and embarrassment to hear that sound even just for a moment.

I say my next words as the thought forms. This way he can't cut me off. "Henri, I am truly sorry for the pain I caused you. I will spend the rest of my life trying to make up for it."

Henri presses his face into the back of my head. I hear him inhale deeply taking in my scent. He is quiet for a few moments, clearly choosing his words carefully.

"Alexis, there is nothing to make up for. This moment right now, is more than I ever imagined it would be. We are together now and that is all I need." My heart swells listening to his kind words. I don't deserve this man, but I vow to spend the rest of my life trying to.

I don't say this out loud, but Henri's arms tighten around me again, in response to the thought. "And I you," he says.

I close my eyes and lean my head back on Henri's chest, the rhythmic sound of his heartbeat, lulling me to sleep.

Henri

We are both quiet for some time. I realise Alexis has fallen asleep when her thoughts go quiet. I remain still watching her sleep peacefully in my arms, where she belongs.

I still can't quite believe this amazing powerful woman is mine. I know the power in her veins scares her. How could it not, when she has watched everyone, she loved, suffer for theirs? She doesn't scare me though. Although witnessing the storms she has been producing, is certainly something. She could give the whole of Asgard a run for its money, The Elders included. A spinner who can manipulate the elements – I would never have thought it possible if I hadn't seen it with my own eyes.

Even with my arms wrapped around her, Alexis' body temperature starts to fall as her sleep deepens. Though I am reluctant to move, afraid to end this perfect evening, I sigh and easily lift her, carrying her into the house and her bed.

I plan to leave and return early before Alexis wakes. However, as I place her on the bed, she reaches out for me. I lay and wrap a protective arm around her, marvelling at how well we fit together, with her back pressed into my front.

Ed has been trying to mind link with me for a while and I have kept him shut out. Eventually I open the link to find out what he wants. Before he realises, I am there, I hear him grumbling but can't quite catch what he is saying.

"Something wrong?" I ask in my head.

"Hen! What the fuck, I've been trying to reach you for hours." There aren't many people who would get away with speaking to me like that, Ed is one of the few.

"Sorry, it's been an interesting night." I link back. *"What's wrong?"* I ask again.

"Oh nothing," He replies. Even through the link I can hear his sarcastic tone, which has my hackles up immediately. Ed only uses sarcasm when he is really stressed. Something is definitely wrong. *"Nothing, other than your 'betrothed' arriving on this island in less than 12 hours."*

"Shit! You said five days. And. She. Is. Not. My. Betrothed."

"I know that, but it seems Lilith doesn't. Apparently, she thinks you didn't mean it and she is coming here to 'work things out.'"

"Oh no, no, no this is bad, very bad." I start to panic. I have just found Alexis, our bond is still tenuous, not yet complete. The presence of Lilith could bring it all crumbling down.

Alexis

I slowly start to stir, smiling as I realise, I have slept through the night for the second night in a row. I open my eyes and find Henri propped up on one arm, watching me from the other side of the bed, eyes twinkling.

"Good morning," I say stretching out my stiff limbs. His answering smile is breath-taking.

"Good morning, my love. Sleep well?" he asks.

"Yes actually, very well," I answer with a smile of my own. Two days ago, I'd have chided him for calling me that but this morning, it fills me with joy. Henri slowly bends down to place a kiss on my lips. I respond instinctively, parting them slightly as his tongue runs along them. My body flushes with heat, and I groan, letting the feeling take over.

Henri moves, his body now hovering over me. I use my hands to pull him back down against me. My nipples pebbling as arousal blossoms between my legs. He pushes his crotch into mine and I feel the growing bulge as his own arousal takes over.

I groan in pleasure again as Henri's lips move from my mouth to my neck. Slowly he trails kisses down my chest to my tummy.

He sits, pulling me up with him and lifts my dress (I am still wearing the dress from last night) over my head, leaving me naked other than my panties. Henri stares down at me, a rapt expression on his face, but makes no move to touch me. I begin to squirm under his scrutiny as a wicked look appears on his face and he quirks up an eyebrow.

"Do you want something, Alexis?" he asks. I nod, but Henri continues to watch me. "You have to ask." I close my eyes in frustration.

"Please touch me, Henri." I gasp throwing an arm over my face in humiliation.

Henri pushes me back again resuming his trail of kisses. When he reaches my panty line, He begins to plant kisses across it. My back arches in response and I feel him smile against me.

Oh, so slowly his kisses move down to my core I gasp at the sensation. Henri looks up at me again and I buck my hips in frustration. The sudden lack of contact leaving me wanting.

It is all the motivation Henri needs as he pulls down my panties and drops them to the floor. I suddenly feel self-conscious and try to cover my body, but Henri smiles shaking his head. "You are so beautiful," he says, voice full of lust.

Without a moment's hesitation Henri swoops back down, tongue easily finding my centre. I gasp again, pushing my hips up to meet his mouth. Henri groans as he slowly circles his tongue around my clit and down my seam.

The feeling is unlike anything I've ever known before. My own fingers could never match the sensations of Henri's touch.

I quickly feel myself getting closer to the edge. Henri seems to sense how close I am as he leisurely moves further down lapping my arousal.

His tongue finds its way to my entrance. I cry out in pleasure as he pushes it inside, tasting all of me.

He licks all the way back up to my clit, almost tipping me over the edge as my legs tighten around him. Laughing lightly, he uses his hands to hold them open.

Henri refocuses his attentions on my sensitive bud, sucking and licking rhythmically pushing me all the way over the edge. I come spectacularly, bucking my hips, and screaming out his name. Henri continues to lap up my orgasm as the spasms wrack through my body.

I lay trying to catch my breath as Henri comes lay beside me. He plants a chaste kiss on my lips. I taste myself on him, which quickly reignites my arousal and I begin to trail my fingers down his arm.

Henri suddenly stiffens a look of fury coming over his face.

Henri

Alexis looks so sexy when she wakes. I can't help but lean in and kiss her. Like yesterday, I don't mean for it to go any further than that. But the way her body responds to my touch urges me on.

Pleasuring Alexis is better than I even imagined it would be. The scent and taste of her arousal, better than the finest food imaginable.

The way she calls my name as she reaches her release, almost drives me over the edge.

I know she isn't ready to 'mate' and seal the bond - that was clear last night when I could hear her thoughts, but she couldn't hear mine.

That doesn't mean I can't show her what she's been missing all this time.

As she lays back down, I kiss her, and her eyes widen as she tastes her arousal on my lips.

"Times up, Hen. She's here," Ed mind links me and fury boils through me. He feels it through the link. *"Henri, get control, you are still with Alexis,"* he reminds me.

I close my eyes and take a deep breath willing them to remain my normal colour, not allowing the blackness to take over. When I open them, Alexis is looking at me curiously. I lean my forehead on hers breathing in her sweet scent.

I'm not sure where to begin explaining but after a moment's hesitation I opt for telling her enough to understand the situation. It will be the truth just not in too much detail.

88

"I need to tell you something," I start, "but I need you to keep an open mind and not do anything... reckless." Her eyes widen and a small smile appears on her face. *"Oh Goddess, what now,"* she thinks.

I can feel her inner turmoil at my words, she can't hide it from me, but she puts on a great calm facade. She simply nods, silently telling me to go on.

"I mentioned the other day that I had been engaged, before I left," I start, trying desperately not to listen to her thoughts. She tenses, but nods, encouraging me to continue. "Well, Lilith, the woman I was engaged to, decided to follow me here, hoping to rekindle our 'relationship'."

She is stunned into silence, not even forming thoughts. I wait, counting to 34 before she speaks. "Well, we will just have to make it clear that you are mine!" she says, voice calm and steady, eyes full of defiance.

My heart surges hearing her words. She said I am hers. I've waited so long to hear those words from this woman's mouth. I pull her into my arms, as my lips find hers, my earlier arousal returning in earnest.

I groan hearing a small knock on the door, it opens without waiting for an answer and Ginny pokes her head around the corner. "Sorry to bother you, love birds," she says with a hand over her eyes. "We have an unexpected guest on the island. You should probably both come."

"We'll be right there," Alexis says, making me sigh with frustration. I don't want to share her with anyone, I only just got her back.

Alexis doesn't need to hear my thoughts. She can read the look on my face. "We have all the time in the world," she whispers into my ear before standing and going into the bathroom.

"You can uncover your eyes now," I say to Ginny, who is still in the doorway. She enters and heads straight to the small kitchen area, where she bussies herself making tea. From the precision of her moves, it's clear she's done this a million times before.

Ginny returns, handing me a cup. She looks me straight in the eye - not something a lot of people do. "Ed told me who this 'visitor' is," she begins. "If you hurt my friend, I will hurt you so badly, you will wish, you had never been born." The fierceness in her voice, leads me to believe she means that. It's actually very sweet that Ginny thinks Alexis needs protecting from anyone. The love of my life is a force of nature.

"I have searched for Alexis for a very long time, Ginny. I would protect her with my dying breath. I loved her every single day of the last 250 years and more, I will never hurt her. I can promise you that."

"Can you?" she asks. "Mates or not, you know so little about her. She enjoys her quiet life here, she never told me what brought her to this island, but I do know she was broken when she arrived. It has taken a long time for her to become the woman she is today.

"We all know that being mated to *you* will force her to leave. Are you ready for the consequences of her return to Asgard? Are you prepared for her grief?" She keeps her voice low, clearly worried her best friend will overhear her concern. "She didn't grieve the loss of her parents before, she was too busy trying to keep herself and you" – she jabs a finger in my direction – "alive. Asgard will open up wounds that have barely begun to heal. You know she is the one who's been causing the storms, don't you?"

I think she is trying to shock me, but it won't work. I figured that out last night. My hope is that when we do finally return to Asgard, we can find a teacher to help her gain control of her powers, rather than allowing them to burst out whenever she is feeling strong emotions.

"I do and I know it won't be easy, we will face her – no, our – demons together when the time comes. I wish we could remain here forever but as I was born to be king, Alexis was born to be queen and we will deal with that together now." Ginny shakes her head and I know what her response will be. I hold up a hand, silencing her protest.

"Alexis might not have been born royal like me, but she is the other half of me, so yes, she was born to be queen. If the Goddess hadn't intended for that, she would not have made her my twin flame. She is destined to rule beside me, 250 years of hiding can't change that.

"You love fiercely Ginny, that is clear, I am truly grateful, Alexis has had you as her friend during her time here and I am so happy you are Ed's mate. You are exactly what he needs, just as Alexis is who I need, and I her."

I can see she won't be won easily. I give up on words and hope that in time I can show her, how much her friend means to me. Ginny nods, she isn't happy with my response, but the discussion is over for now.

A few seconds later, Alexis emerges from the bathroom looking absolutely breath-taking, wearing another cami top tucked into high waisted shorts. Her dazzling red hair falling loosely down her back – exactly how I like it.

Alexis smiles at Ginny, taking the cup she holds out for her. They exchange a meaningful glance before Alexis turns to me.

"Shall we?" she says gesturing to the door. *That is rapidly becoming our catchphrase*, I think with a smile.

ROCHELLE TATTERSALL

Chapter 8

Alexis

The woman Henri had been engaged to when he thought I was dead, is here in Serenity hoping to get him back.

I'm speechless. Even my thoughts go blank. My soul who had been in the middle of her happy dance was momentarily stunned into silence, before she began cheerfully plotting this woman's death. I am grateful Henri's conscious mind can't hear her. She is truly insane. If anyone ever wondered what happens to a soul denied its other half, the answer is more disturbing than you would think.

She is thrilled when I say "Well, we will just have to make it clear that you are mine!" Hopefully that will appease her for a while.

Henri told me they meant nothing to each other. Clearly that wasn't true, at least on her part, he meant something to her. Why else would she follow him halfway around the world. Whether that something is love, power, or *lust* I'm not sure.

I spend longer than usual in the bathroom, attempting to compose myself. I'm grateful when I hear Ginny quizzing Henri. Although I can't quite here what she is asking, it will, at least, keep him out of my head for a few minutes.

When I emerge, Henri's look almost makes me blush. I plaster on my game face - something I have mastered over the years to prevent others seeing my true feelings - and gesture for us to leave. I know it won't work on Henri; he knows exactly how I'm feeling but hopefully I can keep my true emotions from the others.

Emerging from my cabin into the bright morning sunshine, Henri reaches for my hand. I gladly allow him to take it. It feels like the most natural thing in the world to be touching him.

The three of us head towards town in silence. I peek up at Henri, trying to work out what he is thinking. He smiles at me and squeezes my hand, reassuringly. I roll my eyes knowing he is reading my thoughts but has no intention of sharing his.

We arrive in town, and I can see a group of people gathered outside the guest house where Henri, Ed and some of the ambassadors are staying. I spot Ed facing off with a tall blond-haired woman in designer clothing.

Henri stiffens looking at the two of them and I know this is her. "Lilith," Henri says, nodding confirming my thought. I keep looking straight ahead.

Lilith is beautiful, there is no doubting that. Her aura on the other hand is anything but. She is trying hard to conceal something, I just can't figure out what. Yet. Henri's demeanour changes as he feels what I am sensing through the bond.

"I sense aura's," I tell him silently. *"Usually, I have to concentrate to see them, but my third sight just shot open. She feels wrong."* Henri looks again at Lilith, eyes narrowing. I wish I could hear his thoughts so I could know what he is thinking.

As we reach the group, Ginny goes straight to Ed and their hands join. Lilith looks at them and scoffs. She still hasn't realised; Henri and I are behind the group.

"Where. Is. He." she spits out. Ed laughs, enraging her further. He inclines his head slightly, acknowledging Henri and I. Lilith spins around, glowering as she sees Henri's hand in mine.

It doesn't take her long to gain control of her emotions and plaster a fake smile on her face. "H," she breaths. "I've been looking for you, for an hour. *He* wouldn't tell me where you were." she whines. *Pathetic,* I think. Henri smirks hearing my thought.

"Lilith," he replies ignoring her statement. I can feel the fury coming off him in waves and I rub circles on the back of his hand with my thumb, trying to sooth him. Lilith finally turns her attention to me, narrowing her eyes.

"And who might you be, holding the hand of my fiancé?" she asks. Before I can speak, Henri has angled his body to put me slightly behind him. I sigh, how long will it take him to realised, I do not need to be protected from her or anyone else.

"Alexis, this is Lilith, the woman I told you about." he spits. He then turns his attention back to Lilith. "What are you doing here?" he asks. "I thought I'd made it very clear before I left Asgard, that I will not be marrying you." I can feel how hard Henri, is working to keep control and I squeeze his hand in the hope it will help.

My own power is again simmering below the surface, and I check to ensure I haven't set Henri's hand on fire. Henri, chuckles following my line of thought. "I'm fine my love, no flames," he says. Lilith flinches hearing his words but chooses to ignore them.

Her voice turns sickly sweet as she reaches for Henri. "Oh, come on H, I know you were getting cold feet. I forgive you for that and for whatever this is," she says, nodding her head in my direction. "I gave you space and can overlook one last *indiscretion*, but it's time to come home now, darling, we have a wedding to rearrange."

Her words have taken on a strange flow, spell like, almost. I shake my head trying to dislodge the feeling that comes over me. Henri does the same, but no one else seems to notice anything.

My blood boils at her words and this time I know my fingers are sparking. I quickly pull my hand out of Henri's so not to harm him. She is a spinner; how can she not feel our mating bond. My anger propels me forward. Clouds form above us once again and I fight for control. I can't cause a storm every time I lose my temper. "This," I spit, "is Henri's true mate, his twin flame." She looks appalled and for a moment I think she is planning to attack me. "That's, that's not possible," Lilith says so quietly, no one else hears.

"Liar!" She shouts. This time everyone hears and an audible gasp ripples around the people gathered. "You've tricked him." Lilith is starting to lose control. I don't need to do anything. She is showing herself for what she is.

I laugh and move back to Henri's side, taking his hand back in mine, finally able to get control of the flames in my blood. The clouds dissipate.

"As you can see, Lilith you had a wasted trip. I am sorry I let things get as far as I did, but I could never tie myself to someone who is not my mate. Alexis is my mate. No tricks, no lies. She is my twin flame," Henri states. "I suggest you leave. Now." He adds coldly.

I know she can't just leave now. There won't be another boat off the island for days, even if we could arrange an earlier trip, it would take more than a day. I'm not sure we will all survive that long.

It is Mum who breaks the unnerving silence that settles over the group following Henri's declaration. "Unfortunately, there isn't a boat back to the mainland, for three more days," she says. I hadn't even realised she had arrived. "Ms. Jones, we have another guest house on the edge of town, you can stay there until then."

"I think I will be more comfortable here," Lilith replies smugly. Mum simply smiles back at her, revealing none of the emotion I know she is feeling.

"I am sorry, but that is not possible this one is full."

"No matter, I can share H's room," she says triumphantly.

Oh no, not going to happen, I think. Henri's rage begins to ebb as he hears the plan forming in my head. "That's fine, Mum. Lilith can stay here. There is more than enough room for Henri at my house." I say, mischievously. Lilith is seething, I feel it coming off her in waves. Henri moves to put his arms around me, pulling me back to rest on his chest.

"That's sorted then," he says grinning. Ed nods at us and tells one of the other men to gather up, Henri's things and have them moved over to my house.

I hadn't planned on having Henri move in with me. I was hoping to have a bit of space to get my head around things. But I sure as hell wasn't going to put him back into the arms of that *creature*.

I still can't put my finger on why she seems so 'off.' Maybe it's just because she is trying to place a claim on my mate. This is all so new to me; it's throwing my intuition off.

I still can't hear Henri's thoughts, but his emotions are getting stronger, and I know he is trying to figure out what my own feelings mean.

Lilith looks at me in utter disgust, and I realise I may have won this battle, but the war is far from over. Someone like her is not going to give up the opportunity to rule easily.

Bring it bitch, I think, and Henri actually snorts before kissing me deeply. "You are magnificent," he says, making me blush so hard, I think my skin may be the same colour as my hair.

I was supposed to be spending the day at the hospital. However, the arrival of our latest 'guest' changed my plans. Instead, I have the restaurant make up a picnic and take Henri to my secret cove.

Hidden away from the rest of the island, the cove is my special place. It is the place I came to the day Henri arrived. My place of solitude

The cove is where I go when everything is too much for me. I have kept my past so deeply hidden; most people never really knew my pain. Occasionally when it became too unbearable, I needed to let it out. The cove always manages to soothe me. I can cry, scream, and shout knowing I won't be discovered.

At first, I thought it was a place to communicate with the Goddess. It's the place I felt most connected to her, I thought she might hear my prayers and guide me. While I know it is her cove. She never answers me.

It is magical though. And not just because the shallow waters always warm and calm. The white sand is as soft as silk on my skin. It's such a contrast to the burning turmoil within my soul. There is actual magic here. I have always felt it.

"Wow," Henri says as we climb down the rocks surrounding the cove. "Here I was thinking this island couldn't get any better. How did you find this place?"

"I was out walking alone one day and suddenly had the urge to change direction. I'd never been this way before, I just stumbled across it.

"There is some sort of magic here, it seems to repel others. I sometimes think the Goddess knew I needed somewhere to be completely alone, when I felt like the pain would consume me. I have always been alone here though. She has never answered my prayers. Today is the first time, someone has been here to share it with."

A shadow crosses Henri's face as I talk about my pain. I am aware that my thoughts are sharing more than my words intended, but I don't stop them. I need him to know how hard it has been to stay away for so long. That he wasn't the only one suffering.

"No more pain now, my love. Just joy," he says earnestly. I raise my eyebrows at him. Surely, he isn't naïve enough to think our fight is over. "I'm not," he answers my thought again. "But, as long as you are in my arms, I will feel joy, no matter what is thrown at us." My heart fills as I hear his words, knowing he means every one of them.

I chastise myself again for ever leaving him. He deserves so much better. Henri's eyes darken listening to my unspoken words. "No more of that," he says sharply.

We sit in the sand looking out at the sea for a few minutes before tucking into our wonderful picnic. The food is delicious as always and the company couldn't be better. I know we still have so much to work out, but in this moment, it is difficult to feel anything other than peace.

I'm not sure how long we lay in the sand talking after we finish our picnic. It feels like minutes but the sun's movement across the sky suggests it is more like hours.

Henri tells me all about his travels around the world, his family who are desperate for him to find happiness - his words almost make me forgive them for wanting him to marry Lilith.

He tells me about Ed, who is more like a brother than a friend. Ed has been there for Henri every day. He is fiercely loyal and there are no secrets between the two.

It fills me with such joy that Ed is Ginny's mate. It seems I couldn't wish for a better man for my best friend.

Henri even opens up about his anger. I am surprised that he wants to share this side of himself with me but remind myself that he knows I would find out sooner or later, thanks to the bond.

"You would," he says answering my thoughts again, "but that isn't why I am telling you, Alexis. I want you to know all of me, good and bad. I have done terrible things. Some I am sorry to say, I am not proud of.

"When the anger takes over me and I lose control I am no longer my own person. When that happens, you need to stay away from me. I would never forgive myself for hurting you."

I look at him, in awe. "IF that happens, you won't hurt me," I say with conviction. "We have both done things we are not proud of, but you have accepted all of me - light and dark - and I accept all of you. I don't know everything that you have done, but I do know you didn't do anything lightly, and will have had a damn good reason for it."

I don't add that I would never forgive myself if the fire in my veins harms him, when I lose control and with his ex so close by, that might be sooner rather than later.

We stay quiet for so long; I have to check Henri hasn't fallen asleep. He is looking up at the sky a small smile playing on his lips. "What?" I ask. He suddenly sits up and comes to hover above me. "I was just wondering how I got so lucky," he answers.

I roll my eyes. *Lucky, yeah sure. If you call finding your mate at her parents' funeral and her running to the other side of the world lucky. I'm not sure lucky is the right word.*

Henri laughs, hearing my thoughts. "Well, when you put it like that..." he says. I pretend to be offended and hit is chest. His face turns to mine, and I see a playful glint in his eyes. "Did you just hit me, my love?" he asks. I gulp and nod giving him a shy smile.

"And you have rolled your eyes at me twice today." Henri leans down to kiss me slowly. "You know, anyone else who did that would be punished," he says against my mouth. His words send a thrill through my body. "Hmmm what am I going to do with you?"

1. He moves so fast; I don't even register that he is pinning me with both hands above my head. Henri is physically much stronger than me and I know I wouldn't be able to get away - without using my power - even if I wanted to. His mouth is so close to my ear, his breath tickles the sensitive skin.

Henri slowly moves his mouth down to my jaw, never actually allowing his lips to touch me. The proximity is enough to drive me crazy and I'm almost begging for him to put his lips on me again.

This playful side is new, and I love it. "I'm going to let go of your hands, keep them there," he says huskily. I nod, telling him I will. He continues to move across my body, never allowing us to touch. I arch my back in frustration, desperate to feel his soft lips on me.

Henri laughs softly. "Is it nice to hit me?" he asks.

"No," I breathe.

"Is it nice to roll your eyes at me?"

"No."

"Will you do it again?"

"No."

"Good girl. If you do Alexis, I will drive you wild. I could keep this up all evening." His words send a thrill of excitement straight to my core and I can feel the arousal pooling between my legs. There is a dark warning there, but to my surprise it doesn't scare me.

Henri presses his body against mine and I groan as I feel his hard bulge against me before he captures my mouth with his. As I feel him relax, I quickly flip so he is laid on his back and I am straddling him.

Henri's eyes widen as he registers our new position. I lean down and begin trailing my own kisses across his jaw. He has had more than one opportunity to explore my body, I want to discover his. He is wearing a button-down shirt; I slowly open each one kissing down his torso as I go.

When I reach his shorts, I feel his length twitch against me, straining to be set free. I happily oblige, pulling the zip of his shorts down. Having never done anything like this before, I expected to have some trepidation, but my body just reacts and takes on a mind of its own, knowing exactly how to please my mate.

There are no other words, he is magnificent. I just stare for a moment, before licking my lips in anticipation. Henri looks down at me, silently telling me I don't have to. "I want to," I tell him, before lowering my head to taste him.

Henri shudders at the contact and I take that as a sign to keep going. I start by licking up and down the length, then circling the tip. He growls, grabbing my shoulders.

I love the reaction and take the end into my mouth. I hear a gasp escape his lips as I push further taking as much as I can, until he hits the back of my throat. He easily fills my mouth and I swallow hard, then relax allowing more of him into my throat, earning another groan of pleasure.

I move slowly at first, gradually picking up the pace. I sense he is getting close, and he half-heartedly tries to pull me away. "You don't have to," he says, but I don't move. He tasted my orgasm; I want to taste his.

Before long he begins to buck and warm fluid fills my mouth. It tastes slightly salty, but not bad. I swallow every drop and lick him clean.

When I look up Henri is still breathing hard, but a smile is playing at the corner of his lips. "That was..." he doesn't finish, but I take it as a job well done.

I lay back down beside him, and he takes my hand in his. We stay for a few more minutes before I say we better get going. It is difficult to get back in the dark; there is no artificial light on this part of the island, and we are expected at the council building for dinner with the ambassadors.

I don't want to leave. I'm not ready to share Henri with anyone else. I feel like we have so much lost time to make up for. But my loyalty to the island spurs me on. It is my duty to be there, and I've already neglected the rest of them today.

We arrive back at my cabin to change. I marvel at how we move around each other getting ready in the tiny space. It's like a perfectly choreographed dance. The way I remember my parents moving together.

Someone – I suspect Mum – has delivered a stunning cobalt, satin evening dress for me to wear. Wide straps sit perfectly, just off my shoulders, plunging to a V between my breasts, the dress sinches in at my waist before flaring out to my knees at the front and the floor at the back. I pull the top of my hair back and pin it in place, leaving the rest to fall down my back in its natural waves. I leave my face free of makeup other than a quick brush of mascara and some lip balm.

Henri's eyes widen again as I walk out of the bathroom. "Just when I start to think I am used to your beauty, you walk into the room and take my breath away again," he says.

I blush at his remark, so unused to compliments but smile when I look at him in a crisp white dress shirt and dark blue slacks. I know what he means. He looks more like a Greek god every time I look at him. I still pine for his more rugged Asgardian look though.

His lips find mine and my arms automatically circle his neck. We are breathless when we part. "Maybe we should stay here," I say, looking up at him through my lashes. Given Lilith will be there tonight, this feels like a really good idea to me.

Henri raises an eyebrow at me. "As much as I would love nothing more than to stay here and peel you out of that dress, we both know, we have to go."

I take in a deep breath to steady my nerves. Ed mind linked Henri as we walked home, telling him Lilith will be at dinner this evening. "Ready?" I ask.

"Not even remotely," he answers with a smile. Again, I know what he means. I would love to just remain here alone with him, but we both have responsibilities and if I am going to be with him for the rest of time, I should get used to this.

The dining room is full of people when we arrive. I spot Ed and Ginny talking to Mum and Dad, so I walk over to them.

Dad wraps me in a tight hug, "You look beautiful, firefly," he says, thickly accented in Spanish. It has been a long time since Dad lived in Spain, and the accent is all but gone, apart from when he is feeling emotional. My Dad might be a cold-blooded vampire, but he is a big old romantic at heart. He is thrilled to see Henri and I together.

"I knew that dress would look good on you," Mum says, as I turn my attention to her.

"Thanks, Mum," I say, moving back to Henri's side.

I sense Henri ask Ed a silent question and Ed shakes his head slightly. Ginny notices too. "Care to share with the group?" she asks, sounding like a school marm.

Ed is about to answer when there is a flurry of activity at the entrance. I turn to see Lilith enter wearing a red, floor length gown with slits right up to her thighs. The colour suits her creamy skin and platinum hair perfectly and I'm hit with a pang of jealousy. I am frumpy and clumsy by comparison.

Henri doesn't like my train of thought. He pulls me round to face him. "You are the most beautiful women in this room. The most beautiful woman in every room on the planet," he says planting a soft kiss on my lips.

I glance up to see Lilith looking over with a scowl marring her beautiful face.

We take our seats, Mum, and Dad at the head of the table flanked on either side by Ginny, Ed, Henri, and I. Lilith is at the far end of the huge table, seemingly engrossed in conversation with one of the ambassadors. Every now and then she looks our way, but she is hiding her feelings well.

Dinner passes pleasantly enough, we talk and laugh, resolutely ignoring the elephant at the far end of the table. The food has been brought from the restaurant and it is delicious. It showcases the best of what our little island has to offer. I didn't get to eat my paella last night, so I am thrilled when huge pans of it arrive at the table.

The first mouthful is exquisite the earthy taste of the saffron giving way to tangy tomato, before you get the hit of lemon at the end. I finish my first bowl quickly and help myself to seconds. Henri watches astonished as I devour the two helpings. I stop myself going for a third, but he pushes another plate in front of me, nonetheless. I eat that too, finally feeling satisfied.

Before dessert arrives, I excuse myself and go to the bathroom. I am pleasantly full and just a little tipsy from the wine. I wash my hands marvelling at the bright eyes and flushed cheeks in my reflection. I don't remember the last time I felt so alive. I am actually starting to believe Henri and I can have a future together.

When I leave the bathroom, Lilith is standing against the wall opposite with a grim look on her face. I try to walk past not wanting her to put a dampener on my good spirits. Tonight, will be the first time Henri and I spend a night together in our cabin. I have always loved my little house, built by Dad just for me, but with Henri there it finally feels like home.

Still Lilith is able to block my path.

"What have you done to him?" she asks.

"Excuse me?"

"His mate died a long time ago. You don't get more than one. I know you have done something to him, to make him believe you're his mate," she practically snarls.

Anger flares within me and I feel flames licking up my arms. I don't need to look down to know I am dangerously close to setting my dress on fire. From here, I can't see outside to know whether the storm clouds have come rolling in, I am sure they will make an appearance soon, though.

How does she know about me? He said the only person who knew was Ed. Maybe there was more to their relationship than he told me.

"You might want to check your facts, Lilith. I am not dead actually; I am here alive and well. You're a spinner, don't tell me you can't feel our bond. Stop pretending you can't." She cringes at my words, clearly uncomfortable.

"Henri is my prince, not yours," she spits.

"The thing is, Lilith, I don't care whether he is the crown prince, court jester or a penniless farm hand. It wouldn't make a difference to me if all he had were the clothes on his back. He is my mate, and you will never change that."

Suck on that, bitch! My soul is yelling furiously at the woman who is threatening to take her other half away. Yes, definitely unhinged. I never realised how many swear words she knew.

"*He. Is. Not. Your. Mate.*" Lilith seethes, stating each word clearly as though she is speaking to someone who doesn't speak English. I can see she is fighting hard to keep her fury controlled. That just makes me smirk. I know I am winning.

Her face changes and I see she has rained herself in. "He tells me everything. He told me how his mate left him lonely and in pain. She was such a selfish creature she only thought about herself. I made him feel better, helped him forget her. Oh, the nights we shared together. Well, you know how good he is in bed."

No actually I don't, we have never slept together. Lilith sees the answer on my face. Hers contorts into one of false sympathy. *"Oh darling, see you are just a distraction for him. Something to play with before he comes back to the palace and takes me as his queen and wife. You would never be enough for him, sooner or later he would come back to me. He will betray you."*

A strange feeling comes over me. It is hard to describe, but I am suddenly filled with doubt as my worst fear plays out inside my head. The picture is as clear as if it was happening right before my eyes. Henri's body writhing against Lilith's, his beautiful blue eyes looking deep into hers.

"Lilith, I love you," the Henri in my head says. Bile rises in my throat, and I start to regret the third bowl of paella. How could he do this to me? He doesn't love me; he is just playing with me. Like Gran's mate. How could I be so stupid.

I don't say another word, just turn and walk away from her, out of the building into the fresh air. Sure enough the storm clouds are overhead, rain is pounding down on the ground and thunder claps loudly through the silent night.

I take off at a run, unsure where I am going. I can't go home there is too much of Henri there.

ROCHELLE TATTERSALL

Chapter 9

Henri

The day with Alexis was perfect. I can't wait to get out of this event and back home with her. Home, I have come to understand is not a place, but anywhere my mate is.

She excuses herself to go to the bathroom and Ed comes to sit by me. We are in the middle of a conversation when I sense her pain then hear the thunder. That can't be good.

I realise Alexis hasn't come back from the bathroom. And worse, looking around I see Lilith isn't in the room either. Panic runs through me. If Lilith has hurt a hair on my mate's head, I will kill her with my bare hands.

Ed senses the change in me and stiffens.

I stalk out of the room and find Lilith waiting for me in the hall. "Where is Alexis?" I ask, trying to contain my fury. Lilith shrugs her shoulders.

"Never mind your little toy, you need a real woman to help you burn off that anger, darling."

"What. Did. You. Do?" I grate out. She comes to place her hands on my chest, and I step back out of her reach. "Answer me Lilith or so help me, I will tear your throat out."

"I just told your little plaything some home truths. Like how she can't be your mate because she already died, you told me so. And that you need a real woman, like me. Not some hippy who spends her days taking care of all these disgusting creatures."

My fury burns so hot, my mind shuts off as I reach my hands around her neck. I know my eyes are seconds from becoming completely black but with Alexis in pain, I have lost all control. Even without the storm outside, I could still feel her anguish.

"Henri," Ed yells, pulling me back. My grasp loosens and Lilith stumbles backwards out of reach.

"She isn't hurt, physically at least," he continues as my vision returns. "Ginny saw her running off towards the west side of the island. She says it's where Alexis goes when she needs to be alone. She will come back, but no one knows exactly where it is she goes, so there is no point trying to follow her." Like the day I arrived.

Only now, I know where she has gone, and I know how to get there. We were there only a few hours ago.

I just pray the Goddess will allow me to find it again.

Alexis

I'm surprised when I reach the cove. I hadn't even realised my feet were bringing me here. Although the place is now tainted by Henri, there is a cave at the back I didn't show him. I set off towards it, my soaking dress and hair clinging to me in the down pour. If I don't get a grip on this power, I will spend the rest of my life wringing out my perpetually frizzy hair.

Walking into the cave is like entering another world. Small, coloured gemstones embedded in the walls and ceiling glitter like stars. It's like the entire universe condensed into this tiny space.

I fall to the ground and let the grief I have been holding at bay wash over me. Outside the rain intensifies, huge drops hitting the sand like rocks. I curl in on myself and sob.

How could I have been so stupid? Of course, he was just messing with me. I'm the silly little girl who ran away from him. He was probably going to lead me along, have some fun then run back to his perfect life at the palace when he got bored.

I opened the box containing my heart, hell, I gave him the key and now as everything burns around me, my heart is cowering in a dark corner. My heart break turns to anger as I look around the goddess's temple.

"Is this your idea of a joke?" I yell. "I was doing just fine and then you send him here. Was my heart not broken enough? You thought it would be a good idea to twist the knife a little more!" I don't know why I'm talking to her; she never answers. "Nothing to say for yourself, as usual. That's it, you come up with some grand plan, leave us here to do the actual work and don't bother to show up when we need you. Well thanks for nothing.

I hate you; I hope you know that. I. HATE. YOU. You allowed everything to be taken away from me. EVERYTHING. I build my life back up without any help from you and you allow it to be torn down again. What sort of Goddess does that?" The last words come out as a sob as my anger fades and grief takes over, once more.

A noise just outside silences my cries. I'm just starting to think, I imagined it when, I hear his voice. "I know you are here my love; I can hear your thoughts." He sounds a little worried but mostly furious. I take comfort in knowing the rain is currently battering him while he searches for me. Hopefully the Goddess is done breaking me for one night and he won't find me, "Do you really believe that I was just leading you on?" There is menace in his voice. I can't tell if he is mad with me for running or Lilith for making me run.

Why has he bothered to follow me here anyway? It's clear he wants her really.

Henri growls. "You are everything I could ever want or need, Alexis, my love. You have to believe that. I have spent too long searching for you, to give up now."

He is punishing me for the mistakes of my past. My heart shatters into a thousand pieces at the thought.

I remain silent, knowing he hasn't pinpointed my exact position yet. I try to close off my mind, so I don't give him any clues. I begin reciting the kings of England in reverse chronological order, to drive any other thoughts from my mind.

He sighs when he figures out what I am doing. "OK, if that's how you want to play it. I haven't got anywhere else to be, Alexis." I hear him sit down in the sand and my heart skips a beat.

My entire being is yearning for him. I need to touch him. My soul, who stormed off in a huff when I ran from Lilith, is yelling at him in the hope that he will find us.

Closing my eyes, I lean my head down on my knees and try to hold the tears in. Eventually, completely wrung out, I relax and doze off for a moment. That is all Henri needs and he finds where I am, from my errant thoughts.

I jolt awake as he wraps strong arms around me, carrying me back out to the beach. The rain has stopped, and the night air is warm on my cold skin. It is lighter out here than inside the cave. The almost full moon shining brightly on Henri's handsome face.

Once he has placed me back down on the sand, his eyes find mine. The fury is still there in his eyes. I can feel how much he is fighting for control.

"Good!" I think and he chuckles lightly.

I know he can see the anger in my eyes and feel it in my thoughts. I am still too angry to speak, so I go over the conversation with Lilith in my head.

When I am finished, he looks down. It is all the confirmation I need. "You lied to me," I force out as another sob escapes.

"I'm sorry," he says hanging his head in shame.

"You're sorry?" I ask anger flaring again. "What are you sorry for Henri? Leading me on? Telling me that there was never anything between you? Clearly there was, seen as she knows you thought I was dead!"

His head snaps up. "I never told her that, Alexis. I swear."

My voice has risen to a yell by the time I finish, and I realise I'm beginning to sound hysterical again. "You slept with her, for Goddess' sake." If I'm being honest, its vein but the last part is what hurts the most. "How could you do that and then lie to me about it?"

"I am so sorry my love, but you have to believe, I never told her about you!"

"Then how does she know Henri? How?"

"I… I don't know." We are quiet for a moment. I begin to think he isn't going to answer my other questions.

"I am sorry for not telling you the whole truth my love. I promise, my feelings for her were never more than a convenient arrangement that would allow my father to retire.

"The moment I saw you, there was never going to be another woman for me. Only you, always.

"But I'm ashamed to say, I gave into her attempts to seduce me. I still don't know how it happened. I don't even remember it. I just woke up the following morning and she told me what had happened. I'd had… encounters before, but I'd never had anyone like that… in my bed."

"Not helping, Henri." I am aghast that he was able to sleep with someone else. I know I never could, I pushed Sam away time and time again even though I did love him. Then I knew Henri was alive, and he thought I was dead, so I guess it's different.

I am just starting to wonder what he means by encounters, when Henri closes the distance between us and lifts my chin to look straight into his eyes. "I am yours, always," he says with such conviction it almost knocks me over. "My love, you are everything to me. Please say you know that."

I sigh and take a deep breath. *I do, of course I do. I'm not sure what came over me. I don't usually doubt myself like that. How had I let her get under my skin so quickly.* The picture she painted was my worst fear brought to life. I've spent my entire existence afraid of being betrayed and hurt beyond redemption – like Gran – and Lilith effortlessly used that against me.

I know Henri has heard my thoughts, but he wants to hear the answer out loud. "I do," I say, nodding.

"I have loved you since we were children, Alexis and I will love you until my dying breath. I could never betray you. You are my world, if I lost you again, I don't know –" I place my finger over his lips, silencing him.

"I love you too, Henri, with every fibre of my being. Goddess knows I have tried not to, but damn it, I do." His eyes shine with happiness. It is the first time I have acknowledged my true feelings for him. Henri lifts me into a hug and my legs automatically wrap around his waist.

He kisses me deeply but makes no move to go any further than that. He can sense that wouldn't be a good move right now. Lilith planted a seed of doubt in my broken mind and I'm not sure I can fully trust myself yet.

This is the problem with a twin flame. Unconditional love sounds romantic and wonderful. Forgiveness comes automatically, but that doesn't mean we can forget as easily.

It dawns on me; this is the reason Henri doesn't hate me for the unending pain I have caused him. He physically can't because of the mate bond.

"Bond or not, Alexis, I have always loved you. From the moment I saw you as a child, playing in the castle grounds with the other children. You were so unlike the others. Never bowing down to anyone. Determined to live on your own terms - a free spirit my mother called you.

"Yes, the bond strengthens that feeling. But I loved you before our souls recognised each other as one. Even without the bond I would never hate you for the decisions you made. Decisions that cost you so much - you left your home and everything you had ever known - to keep me safe," he tells me.

"You're wrong, I am not strong, I am weak and that is why I ran away. I didn't want to continue my parents' fight. Maybe Lilith was right. I am not enough for you," I reply.

"You are so strong, kind, and loving, never letting your pain or fear turn you into something you are not. The darkness never won." The look on his face is daring me to contradict him, but I remain quiet, trying to process the route our conversation has taken.

I don't remember Henri being there when we were children. The first memory I have of him is at the funeral. He never came to play, always too busy learning what he must, to become the next king, I thought.

"I was drawn to you even then," he says. "I always watched you from a distance. Even when we got older, and the other boys would try to court you and you would brush each of them off. Every time I would pray that you would turn them down, and you did," he says with a smile.

"I was never interested in them," I say simply. "Never interested in anyone in that way. Even though I saw what my parents had, I didn't want it. Gran's mate betrayed her. He broke her heart and left her alone with a child to raise. She didn't know it, but her sorrow taught me to be cautious with my heart.

"Then when my mother and father died, and I was told there was a curse, it just cemented my belief that I was better off alone. Of course, when I learned what you were to me, I knew I had to leave. You are the crown prince. Destined to be king. If I was selfish and stayed our people would lose you."

The curse might be broken, but I don't think for one second the witches will allow us to sail off into the sunset.

"Alexis Beaumont, mark my words, neither our people nor you are going to lose me. We will fight every enemy together and we will win, that is a promise."

Henri's words leave no room for argument. Unlike me, he is a warrior and has never backed down from a fight.

For the first time in 250 years, I see a break in the clouds; I have hope.

Henri

I almost lost her again last night, is my first thought as I open my eyes. Anger threatens to overtake me, but the feeling of Alexis sleeping in my arms, is the antidote to my rage. I hold her closer, and she stirs, I try to shush her back to sleep but it is too late.

Alexis looks up and kisses my lips lightly by way of good morning. I respond moving my mouth against hers. She moans softly and I am tempted to take things further, but I stop myself. I want her to trust me, and the bond before we do anything more - again. When the lust takes over it skews everything else.

I pull away and see the dejection in her eyes, which almost makes me cave. Instead, I hold her tighter, letting her know that I still want her.

"Soon," I say. Hearing the confusion in her thoughts I go on. "A lot has happened in the last few days, my love. When we make love for the first time, I want it to be special. We have waited more than two centuries; we can wait a little longer."

She frowns but nods in agreement.

"I have some things to take care of with Ed today," I say. I don't want to be away from her at all, but I need to get to the bottom of how Lilith knew where I was and what she said about Alexis being dead.

The more I thought about it last night, the more it bothered me. Alexis said Lilith felt 'wrong.' I trust her intuition and need to know exactly who, or more accurately *what,* I'm dealing with. I don't like to be taken for a fool and I have a sinking feeling, Lilith was taking me and the rest of my family for just that.

"OK," Alexis says. "I should probably go to the hospital and check on some patients anyway."

"I will meet you there when I am done," I say.

Alexis smiles, "I would like that."

We walk into town together and say goodbye as we approach the square. Alexis turns to head towards the hospital. I force myself not to call her back. Instead, I go to find Ed.

I hunt him down helping Ginny unpack boxes in her shop. They look the picture of domestic bliss and I wonder if my relationship with Alexis will ever be that easy.

"Sorry to interrupt," I say to Ginny. "Could you spare him for a few hours?"

"Yes, please take him," Ginny says laughing. "He is messing up my system." She is more relaxed than I have ever seen her. But I note the frosty glance she gives me. I am clearly not forgiven for breaking my promise, to not hurt her best friend, so soon.

I wish I could explain that it wasn't my doing, but deep down, I know, it is my fault Lilith is here, so really it is entirely on me.

Ed pokes her in the side mumbling, "I was only trying to help." The childish hurt look on his face makes me snort.

Ginny softens, "I know, I'm only joking, baby," she says sweetly. Ed smiles clearly smitten and kisses her. Maybe he can help smooth over my rocky relationship with her. She means a great deal to Alexis, and I don't want to come between them.

"Laters," Ed says, winking. I roll my eyes.

Walking out into the sun, Ed can't wipe the stupid grin off his face. I am so happy for him. He has been alone with me for so long, it's good to see him this way - carefree and boyish, a far cry from his life, ensuring I don't destroy the world.

"I really am sorry to pull you away," I say.

"Don't worry about it, I still have a job to do," he responds. "So, what exactly happened last night?" I rub my eyes, trying to figure it out and let him into my thoughts to see for himself. "What does Alexis mean by Lilith feels 'wrong'?"

"I'm not sure, Alexis' power – the one she is willing to admit to – I believe is linked to the healing abilities passed from her father. She sees auras with her third sight – that's how healers cure people; they balance the energy.

"Lilith's doesn't feel right to her, but she can't figure out why. I think Lilith is blocking her somehow. Also, Lilith said she knew Alexis was dead. It's not something I ever shared with her - you are the only one I ever told, so I want to know how she knows." Ed looks worried.

"I swear I never told a soul, Hen."

"I know, I trust you completely, but someone found out she was my mate, then went on to share that information and I want to know who!"

"I didn't say anything before, but I'm not sure Lilith is who she says she is," Ed says after a moment's thought. "I checked out her story back in Asgard and no one was able to corroborate."

"You never said," I say with a frown.

"Well, I wanted to be sure before I came to you with anything. I was still trying to gather evidence when you called it off, so I decided to let it go, thinking it no longer mattered."

"It matters now, what have you found out so far, Ed?"

Alexis

I can't focus on anything today. I have a stack of documents on my desk that need reading and a few patient notes requiring my attention. By lunch time, I have read the same page countless times and still have no idea what it says.

The last few days have been a rollercoaster, and I am still trying to come to terms with everything. The strong feelings that I have for Henri are almost unfathomable. He annoys, scares, intrigues, and excites me all at the same time.

I brushed off every man who ever made a play for me - even before my parents' death. I was never interested in a relationship, too busy protecting my fragile heart.

But this twin flame bond - now that I have accepted it - has me feeling things I never wanted to feel and have no idea how to handle.

111

Lilith bothers me more than I want to admit. Yes her 'relationship' with Henri makes me murderously jealous. Yes, the way she got under my skin and had me doubting everything with so few words annoys the hell out of me.

But the thing that bothers me more than any of that is the way she feels. She feels so wrong. I can read all auras - no matter what the creature - but hers is so murky, she is hiding something.

My own, like my mothers and Gran's, is mixed with every colour of the rainbow and more I don't have names for. I have never worked out what it means, why we have so many, when others only have three or four at most.

Spinners usually have white, gold, and silver auras with other colours thrown in, depending on their power.

Lilith's looks like it's true form is concealed. The right colours are there but they seem to be overlaying something else. It puts me on edge.

"Agh," I scream in frustration, throwing the page across my desk.

"Penny for your thoughts?" Mum says coming into my office. I smile at her as she takes a seat on one of the comfy sofas at the far end of the room.

"It's nothing," I say.

"It certainly isn't nothing. I can't get any work done because your frustration is so strong."

"Oh, sorry," I reply weakly, before explaining my issue to her. She nods along thoughtfully, taking in every word.

"Let's try something," she says gesturing for me to join her on the sofas. I do as asked and she faces me, taking my hands in hers.

"Close your eyes and focus on your breathing," she instructs. I follow her instructions, gently closing them. Then breathe in and out slowly, feeling the air as it enters my nose, making its way up then down, all the way to my tummy and back out again. "Let everything else fall away. Don't hold onto any thoughts. Let them simply come and go." Mum says in a soothing, melodic voice.

We remain like this for a few minutes until my mind clears and I begin to relax. We have done this countless times over the years. Mum uses her subtle power to drive my anxiety down, it helps to calm my mind and allows me to gain perspective.

"What is it about Lilith that bothers you most?" She asks in her meditative voice.

"Her aura is odd. I feel like she is trying hard to conceal something," I say thinking back to yesterday. "I didn't have to focus on it like I usually do. My third sight just opened, and it was there."

"Anything else," Mum asks. I concentrate trying to remember exactly why I knew she was hiding something.

"It seemed to be overlying something else. The colours were so much less vivid than usual."

"Open your eyes," Mum says.

When I open them, we are stood in the square. We watch on as a group of people argue. I gasp realising we are watching the events of yesterday morning, play out again. This has never happened before. I wonder if it is an extension of my powers or Mum's.

"Focus Alexis," Mum says as the vision begins to fade, and my office comes back into view. I refocus on my breath. Closing my eyes once more and connecting with my long-forgotten intuition. I open them and we are once again in the square.

"What are we doing here?" I ask.

"What do you see?" Mum asks, ignoring my question. I describe the scene in front of me and confusion clouds my words as I take in Lilith's strange aura again. It is the same as it was yesterday, almost smudged, like someone has drawn it on.

"Stop forcing it, Alexis. Breathe and see what is really there. I do as asked, closing my eyes once more, forgetting the scene I just saw. I almost stumble back when I open my eyes.

Lilith's aura is no longer murky. It is as vivid as all the others I see. Only, now there is no hint of white or gold, or any other colour I would expect to see on a spinner. It is devoid of all light, pure black – a symbol of evil.

Gran taught me how to recognise the signs of evil when I was young. Their power has a distinct smell, like something decaying, left out to rot on a warm day. The scent of death. There are many other signs that most people can spot if they look hard enough.

One sign, that can only be seen by certain spinners, is their aura. I can now see that not only does Lilith's aura mark her out as inherently evil, but it shows me what kind of creature she is.

I close my eyes on the scene before me and take another deep breath. When I open them again, Mum and I are back in my office. Panic surges in my chest. "Lilith is a witch and not just any witch. She is a Witch of Endor. Her clan killed my birth parents."

Chapter 10

Alexis

There are many magical creatures in this world. From fae's and trolls to empaths and werewolves, dragons, and giants – Dad even claims he once saw a unicorn, I'm not sure I actually believe that.

We all have different types of magic. Fae's have power over the natural world. They help the plants to grow and seasons to change, Werewolves have their strength and undying pack loyalty, empaths have dominion over emotions.

Spinners, literally spin the fabric of the world, we can see the threads that bind it together. Threads maybe isn't quite the right word, it's more like ribbons of light energy. That's all there is really, billions of connected ribbons of light energy. Spinners can use these ribbons to create new spells, protect those who need it and do the Goddess's work here on earth.

Spinners use the ribbons that shine brightest to them and that creates their power. I see them all the same – I always thought that was because I had so little power, none shone bright enough for me to use. I have never told anyone. Never wanting to admit how little power I thought I had. Recent events have made me re-evaluate that theory though. I clearly have plenty of power. I just can't seem to use the threads like other spinners.

I've never been in danger here in Serenity but figured I would let people believe I was like other spinners – call it an insurance policy. I believed it might just be enough to prevent someone from attacking me – should the need ever arise.

My Gran warned me, power like hers is feared and coveted in equal measure. There are those who want to use it for evil. Then there are others, who are afraid of so much power in one being.

Most creatures are neutral - nether 'good' nor 'evil' - spinners fall into this category. We are capable of light and dark, good, and bad. It's how the Goddess intended it - free will, so to speak.

Some say that witches descend from the original spinners, the ones placed on earth to maintain the balance. Not all witches are evil, far from it and their powers can be similar to ours. I don't know whether this is true, but I do know the Endor clan is inherently evil. They went down a path far removed from that of your average spinner or witch.

Endor magic is limited because they only use it to gain power over others. They fail to see the way every creature helps to spin our world. Spinners have been at war with the clan for millennia.

My intuition tells me Lilith was hoping to marry into the royal family to gain more power for her clan. Any child she and the prince bore would inherit half its DNA, and as such power, from Henri.

Everything clicks into place. Lilith was using her magic to block her aura. The doubt that crept into my mind when she was talking to me last night was her magic. She is clearly a very powerful witch - I shudder to think just how powerful a child shared with the future king of spinners would be.

That and their claim to the spinner throne might have been enough to give the clan leverage to win the war. No wonder Lilith is so angry. Henri and I have spectacularly ruined a plan that has no doubt been centuries in the making.

Lilith is not as powerful as spinners though. Even with the limited control I have on my power I was easily able to see through her disguising spell and quickly shake off the doubt she spun around me.

She might have fooled the entire royal court, but she couldn't fool me for long.

The urge to get this woman off my island is stronger than ever. She must be arrested and taken back to Asgard to stand trial. I know it will mean her death and that of her entire clan, but I can't bring myself to care. They killed generations of my family. If that wasn't enough, tried to take over the throne and dupe my mate.

She deserves to die for the latter reason alone in my book - my soul nods in agreement as she sits sharpening her sword – where did she even find that?

Mum looks at me as though I have lost my mind. "Are you sure, Alexis?" She asks. I nod, unsure I can speak without showing the fear that has come to sit on my chest.

She smiles warmly at me. "Empath remember." Of course, she knows how afraid I am, no matter how calm I appear on the outside. "What is it, firefly?" she asks. I frown at the use of my old nickname. I really hope Henri doesn't learn of it.

I sigh shaking the thoughts of Henri off to answer mum's question. Just the thought of my mate is enough to distract me.

"Lilith's kind, killed my parents. It was one of them who cursed us. It can't be a coincidence that she wove her way into Henri's life."

"No, I wouldn't have thought so," says Mum. "What are you going to do?"

"I'm not sure. I need to tell Henri, but we need to be smart about this. I doubt Lilith is working alone and it won't be easy to take them down."

I should have known; you can't outrun your problems forever. They always find a way to catch up with you in the end.

I approach the square and see Henri and Ed who are occupying a table off to the side, their heads bowed together. Lilith comes up behind me before I get to them. I spin to face her as she spits my name.

I narrow my eyes but remain silent. I have no intention of confronting her before I have told Henri what I know. Neither will I give her the pleasure of seeing my fear. She feeds off it.

We face off for a moment before she eventually speaks. She was clearly expecting me to say something. "I see you still haven't given up; you fool." The venom in her voice enrages me.

"What do you want, Lilith?" I ask. I don't want to look at her, no less talk to her.

"I just thought I should let you know, where Henri went when he left your bed this morning. Can you guess?" She waits for a response but continues when I don't offer one. "He came running straight back to me. He said you can't give him what he needs, and he will be coming with me when I leave." An image of them writhing in bed appears in my mind.

This time I can hear the spell in her voice. I didn't notice it last night. Maybe because I didn't know what she was then. I do now though, and I easily push away the mirage. Her words have no effect on me.

Lilith can make others believe anything she says. It's a rare power, that can have devastating effects - I briefly wonder who she stole it from. It isn't working on me though. I laugh at her ridiculous words, and she is instantly enraged.

"Something wrong?" I ask, innocently. Henri is suddenly here; I didn't even see him approach. He angles his body, so he is stood just in front of me, blocking Lilith. It is a protective gesture, a warning.

I place a soothing hand on his arm, letting him know that I don't need protecting from her and that I won't bolt again.

"H, I was just congratulating your *mate*," she almost purrs. Henri looks to me and I nod. I want her to think she has the upper hand - for now.

"You are both *so* lucky, to have found each other." There is an undercurrent to her voice that I don't like. I try not to dwell on it knowing that Henri will pick it up and start asking questions.

I wish I knew what Henri was thinking. He still hasn't relaxed his protective stance. I see a slight smile at the corner of his mouth, no doubt my frustration is amusing.

Henri

Ed tells me that he hasn't found out much about Lilith. No one seems to know where she came from. He has reached out to every spinner town known to man.

She claimed her family were English aristocracy, but Lord Frederick, the highest-ranking spinner there, has never heard of Lilith or her family.

Ed didn't think much of it at first, just thought she was a social climber looking for some royal action. Now he isn't so sure.

Neither am I. Something isn't right.

We're in the middle of discussing our next steps when I sense Alexis close by. Her thoughts are a jumble and when I look up, I see her talking to Lilith again.

Rage rushes to the surface. The last time Lilith spoke to my mate, Alexis took off. There is no way, I will allow that to happen again.

I jump up, running straight towards them. Placing myself firmly between my mate and Lilith, I am ready to rip the latter's head straight off, if she makes one wrong move.

Alexis places a hand on my arm, I can see from her thoughts she is trying to reassure me, she can handle Lilith and she won't be running anywhere.

My heart fills with pride and admiration for the wonderful woman stood beside me. She is stronger than anyone I know.

"Shall we, firefly?" I ask. I feel her embarrassment but can't help the laugh that escapes. Matias told me this was the nickname he and Brighid gave my mate when she first came to live with them. It's so endearing I just had to use it.

Alexis' embarrassment quickly fades, turning to wonder as I laugh.

Alexis is quiet as we walk back towards home, hand in hand. Outwardly she seems content just to walk in silence, but inside I can feel her unease. She is trying hard to cover it, thinking about the wonderful times we have spent together. I can tell she is trying to hide her worries from me.

I remain quiet, deciding not to ask her what she is worried about until we get home.

I sit on the deck looking out at the sea, while Alexis grabs us drinks from the kitchen. "Thank you," she says as she sits beside me. I look at her puzzled, unsure what I am being thanked for. "For not questioning me while we walked back." I smile, knowing it must be so difficult to have me inside her head all the time.

"Are you ready to tell me?" I ask. I am trying my best to stay out of her thoughts. Alexis swallows hard, before launching into her story.

"I couldn't focus on anything today. I kept going over what happened last night. The way Lilith got under my skin and how wrong she felt." I listen patiently, making myself focus on her words rather than her thoughts.

"My emotions were getting on Mum's nerves, so she came up to see me. She used her power to help me focus..." She doesn't finish the sentence out loud, allowing me to see the rest in her thoughts.

I am looking in on the scene from yesterday where Alexis met Lilith for the first time, only I am on the edge looking in. I can see the aura around Lilith. What I see in Alexis's thoughts confuses me. I know she is trying to tell me something, but I don't know what.

"*Look at the colours surrounding everyone,*" Alexis's mind-links me. Ah, now I understand. The other spinners in the scene have bright auras, Lilith's is dark and forbidding. "*Lilith isn't a spinner*" Alexis thinks.

I pull back out of Alexis's head and give her a questioning look. She takes a deep breath, before answering my unasked question. "Lilith is a witch... and not just any witch. She belongs to the Endor clan."

Alexis

Henri doesn't speak for quite some time, while trying to process what I have told him. His thoughts aren't as clear to me, as mine are to him, but I am starting to pick up more on his emotions.

"Alexis, my love, that isn't possible," he finally says. "I rid the world that clan, long ago." I think he is trying to convince himself.

"You must have missed some." I say in response. I feel his rage erupt in my own head and have to fight to stay calm. "They are powerful beings,

Henri. Lilith appears to be even more powerful than most. It wouldn't have been hard for her to slip away and lay low for a while."

I feel his rage subside to be replaced with shame and regret. Henri closes his eyes for a moment and the pain I see there when he reopens them makes me gasp.

"I am so, so, sorry, my love. It is my job to keep you safe and I have failed so spectacularly time and time again. You kept us both safe for two centuries and I brought that creature right to your doorstep. Can you ever forgive me?"

Tears blur my vision as I hear my mate's words. I place my hands on either side of his face, forcing him to meet my eyes. "We have been keeping each other safe. That *witch* took advantage of you and the entire court. She played on your vulnerability and the courts need for a new queen. There is nothing to forgive.

"I love you, Henri, my prince, my mate, my twin flame. Now it is time we fight our enemies together and show them just who they are messing with." I say with as much force as I can muster. Henri's answering smile is breath taking.

"I love you too, firefly. Now and forever," he says, leaning in to give me a chaste kiss. It isn't enough and I move to straddle his knees, bending my head down to reclaim his mouth. It parts slightly and I playfully bite his bottom lip, sucking it into my own mouth.

That is all the encouragement my mate needs. Henri moves his hands under my butt and easily lifts me, taking me into the house. He throws me onto the bed and stands looking at me with lust in his eyes.

I start to squirm, feeling uncomfortable under his scrutiny. Henri smiles then slowly covers my body with his. "Stay still, firefly I was enjoying the view." There is menace in his voice, but I can hear a playful note there too. I swallow hard and do as I am told. "Good girl," he whispers in my ear before standing once again, bringing me with him.

I grow wet at his words. I am a strong and independent woman, being called a 'good girl' definitely shouldn't turn me on, but oh it really does. Henri smirks, listening to my confused thoughts.

He stands behind me, pressing his hard member against my back. I lean into Henri's muscled chest as he plants wet kisses on the sensitive place between my neck and shoulder.

I let out a soft moan. "I love that sound," Henri murmurs against my skin, before pulling away and spinning me to face him. "You are wearing too many clothes, my love. Fix it."

Shit, he wants me to strip, I think, suddenly feeling very self-conscious. Henri grins hearing my thoughts. "Yes, I do, Alexis. I want to see all of you." I hesitate for a moment; unsure I can do it.

Henri notices my hesitation and comes back towards me, sighing. "Why do you continue to defy me?" He says, commanding as ever. I am not used to submitting to anyone. I like to have the control but damn me if I want to submit to this man. Give control to someone else for once.

Henri grasps my chin tilting it up so he can kiss me deeply on the lips. I am breathless when he pulls away. "You are the most beautiful creature; I have ever laid eyes on. I want to see all of you, now take off your clothes."

He is so controlling, and I love it - in the bedroom at least. Still, I hesitate.

"Alexis, I am not a patient man, I told you to take off your clothes. If I have to do it for you, there will be consequences."

"Consequences?" I ask in a whisper.

"Yes, my love consequences," Henri responds. I am torn, I want nothing more than to make love to him and seal our bond, right now, I want him more than I have ever wanted anything. But... the thought of Henri's consequences shoots desire straight to my core.

Henri is clearly out of patience. Reaching down, he pulls my vest top up and off, before kneeling to pull my shorts down. Dutifully I step out of them. He throws them across the room, then trails his hand up the inside of my leg. My panties are the next to go, and I try to cover myself, feeling very exposed with his head inches from my core.

Henri isn't having any of that, he pushes my legs apart and admires the view. I start to squirm again. "Still," Henri demands. I stand as still as I can and gasp when he slaps my inner thigh. It stings a little but sends another jolt of pleasure to my core. I didn't think it was possible to be any wetter, but I feel another gush and my arousal drips onto Henri's hand.

Henri leans his head in and laps it off my leg. My knees feel weak, and I grab hold of his hair to steady myself. Henri stops before he reaches my core and I groan in frustration.

He stands and lifts me onto the bed. "Now, if you'd been a good girl, you would be moaning in pleasure right now, but you weren't, were you?" he asks. I look deep into his eyes before answering. Why is this turning me on so much, I wonder?

"No," I answer, quietly.

"What was that, Alexis? You will have to speak up. Have you been a good girl?" Embarrassment floods my body, but rather than wanting to escape it, it makes me want to please him.

"No," I repeat, louder this time. Completely humiliated by my sudden need to submit. I always knew Henri was domineering, but this is more than that.

"No, you weren't, so now I have to punish you." My eyes go as wide as saucers at his words, and I start to panic. "I won't push you too far – this time – firefly, trust me," Henri says softly. I can feel his need to dominate me. He wants us to be equals in life but needs control somewhere. I am more than happy to let him have it here.

"OK," I say, knowing he won't, and if I'm honest, the thought of Henri punishing me is thrilling. Henri sits on the edge of the bed, immediately pulling me across his lap, face down, giving him full access to my up turned backside.

I am alarmed, realising what he is about to do, but he runs his fingertips over my back and bottom, raising goosebumps as he goes. I relax into the feeling, letting out an involuntary moan when the sensation stops.

Henri brings the flat of his palm down hard on my ass cheek and I scream out a mix of pleasure and pain. He gently rubs circles over the spot where he slapped me before bringing his hand down on the other cheek. He repeats the rhythm a couple more times and I think I might explode from this alone.

He dips his hand down between my legs and lets out a soft chuckle feeling how wet I am. I groan as one digit enters me slowly and begins pumping. I am desperate for release, but just as I feel my climax building, he withdraws the finger.

As my breathing begins to calm, Henri reaches further round and finds my clit. He rubs small circles around the little nub, and I feel myself building again. Again, he stops before I find my release.

"Henri, please," I almost beg.

"Please, what, Alexis? What do you need?" he asks. I can hear the grin in his voice even though I can't see his face. I again flush with humiliation. He is going to make me beg for my orgasm.

"I was so close, I need to come, please," I say pleading in frustration.

"Is it frustrating baby?" he asks. I nod, keeping my face pressed into the bed, my feelings are too confusing to process right now. "Well now you know how I felt when you wouldn't show me your beautiful body," he says, pulling me up. "Now, lay back on the bed." I do as asked, still feeling self-conscious. I try to cover myself with my hands but stop seeing the look on Henri's face.

He raises an eyebrow. "I could keep this up all night, Alexis, if you deny me seeing your exquisite body, I will deny you the release you so desperately need." I remain still, hoping to show him, I can behave.

Henri leans down and spreads my legs wide apart giving him full view of every part of me. I squirm again under his scrutiny. "Keep them like this," he says before coming to kiss me again. He takes hold of my wrists and places my arms above my head, "and keep them here," he says again. "If you move them, I will tie you up like this and we can play this game all night." I nod to show I understand.

Henri stands again, taking in my entire body before slowly removing all of his own clothes. I drink in the sight. He really is magnificent. He is toned to perfection, and I long to run my tongue over every part of his body.

I know better than to move right now, though. I will get my turn. Henri sees me raking my eyes along his body and he smirks at me. "Like what you see?" he asks. *Arrogant ass,* I think. Then gulp remembering, he can hear my thoughts. His eyebrow quirks up at me and I can see the mischief in his eyes.

"Oh, arrogant, am I? I think you enjoy being punished, Alexis."

I shake my head, "No."

"Hmm, that's funny because your mind and body are telling me something different. I think you're enjoying me taking control of that beautiful body of yours." I close my eyes unable to answer.

I feel him join me on the bed. "Now how should I make you come," he says reaching down to pinch my nipple. "Like this," he asks squeezing it gently. "Like this," he asks again moving his hand down to my swollen clit, eliciting a moan of pleasure from me. "Like this," he asks moving his hand even further down sliding one finger into my soaking entrance, earning himself another moan.

Henri withdraws his finger and moves to press his naked body against the length of mine. I feel his cock press against my entrance. "Or like this," he whispers into my ear.

I want him inside me right now. Nothing else matters. I buck my hips silently begging him. "Oh no Alexis, you have to tell me what you want," he says.

"You, I want you," I say in breathless frustration. "All of you, inside me, *now*." I grit as he teases me with the end of his cock. It is oddly freeing to give into him, to let him take control of my body and pleasure.

He doesn't need any more encouragement and he eases himself inside me right up to the hilt. I moan in pleasure and pain. He is big and this is my first time - if you don't count my own hand. Which feeling Henri inside me, I definitely do not.

Henri stills giving me chance to adjust to him inside me. The pain subsides quickly, and I rock my hips telling him to move. He starts gently.

Slowly easing back almost completely out and all the way in again. The pleasure grows and I know it won't take me long to reach my climax. Henri lifts his head to look into my eyes, he kisses me deeply and it is enough to push us over the edge. We look into each other's eyes as we simultaneously find our release.

I feel my soul fully reconnect with his, a bond that can never be broken. We are joined together as one, his pain and pleasure are mine, and mine his.

The feeling is euphoric, bliss. Everything that came before no longer matters. Nothing and no one can ever come between us.

I cry tears of joy and Henri holds me in his arms for minutes or hours, it might even be days. I'm not sure.

All I know is I am home.

Chapter 11

Alexis

Every Saturday night for the past 100 years, Ginny, Eleanor, Mum, and I have a girl's night, with some of the other women on the island. Even finding our mates, isn't enough to stop us. Mum and Eleanor would never allow it. We get ready at Mum's house. Laughing, drinking wine, and helping each other with hair and make-up. I protested at first, not wanting to be away from Henri, but I needed the normalcy of tonight.

Ginny has pulled my hair into an artfully messy high pony and found me a dress that she insists I wear, even though the back dips to just above my ass and the front shows more than a small amount of cleavage. The skirt (if it can even be called that – belt might be a more appropriate a word) clings tightly to the top of my thighs. The silver material is soft against my skin, even though it looks metallic.

When I first saw the dress, I worried what Henri would think, but after my third glass of wine, the girls convinced me I look sexy as hell and shouldn't care what Henri thinks. It's my night and my body... plus this is girls' night, no men allowed.

So, here I am in Dad's bar, more than a little intoxicated. We finished several bottles of wine before we left the house and I've lost count of the number of cocktails I had since we got here. The alcohol has reduced any inhibitions I had about the dress, and I am giving it my all on the dancefloor with the girls. Lights flash in time with sultry music, and I move in circles, against Gin, who is pressed up against me, hands on my hips, laughing. The song ends and I tell the girls I am going for more drinks.

I lean over and wave at the bar tender, who approaches me, eyeing my generous cleavage. I raise my eyes and he snaps his head up to meet them.

"We'll have another round of..." I don't get to finish my order. Strong hands grasp my hips and I hear a low, menacing growl.

"The next word out of your mouth had better be water, Alexis. You've had enough to drink already." I can hear the threat in his voice, but I'm too drunk to even care. I don't even acknowledge my mate's presence.

"Cocktails, please, Tom." I finish my order as though Henri wasn't even there. He growls at me again and spins me to face him. I wobble and he catches me expertly. Tom has scuttled away, I glance over my shoulder and am relieved to see him preparing cocktails, not water.

"Something I can help you with, Henri? This is girls, night. That means no boys." I say, accusingly, slurring slightly, attempting to ignore his furious stare.

"You're drunk Alexis." It's not a question, so I figure it doesn't need an answer. I shrug my shoulders, keeping my lips firmly pressed together, holding back the smart remark that sits behind them. His arms come to rest on the bar either side of me, caging me where I stand. The look of fury is still on his face. I know I shouldn't antagonise him, but he shouldn't have interrupted girls' night. He and Ed, who I see timidly approaching Gin, with an apology on his face, had strict instructions to stay away. Ed isn't to blame. I already know Henri is the reason they have gate-crashed. The look on Ginny's face says she doesn't care either way.

Henri lowers his head towards my ear, so no one else can hear our conversation. "Alexis, you have already had too much to drink, no more." Unfortunately, I am too stubborn to back down and right now, will not be told what I can and can't do.

"If I want more, Henri, I will have more." I turn to take the tray of drinks Tom has placed on the bar behind me. To my complete surprise, Henri allows me to take it and head back to my friends. We each take a cocktail from the tray, and I down mine in one, feeling Henri's eyes still on my back. Pulling Gin away from Ed, we head back onto the dance floor and begin dancing again. Henri watches for a while but doesn't approach.

Maybe he will be content to watch from the bar, at least if he stays, he will know I am safe and I can still enjoy the night with my friends.

Unfortunately, the arrival of another group of people puts an end to that idea. I am lost in the music again when someone approaches me from behind. I can still feel Henri watching from the bar, so I know it's not him. Hands grasp my hips and pull me back.

I spin to see Sam. I smile and hug my friend, but there is no warmth in his eyes as he looks over my shoulder. I don't need to turn to know Henri is stalking towards us. "I'm sorry," I mouth to Sam before turning to face my furious mate.

"We're leaving, NOW, Alexis." His words leave no room for argument, but I am not one to back down.

"You can go, Henri but I am staying." I say with finality of my own. Henri takes a deep breath, in an attempt to stay in control.

"We can do this the easy way or the hard way, my love, but either way we are leaving," he says softly.

"No," I say, refusing to bend to him. Suddenly I am swept off my feet and the wind is blown from my lungs as Henri lifts me onto his shoulder face down. I squeal and attempt to cover my backside which is dangerously close to being on show in this dress. Henri's hand comes down hard on my thigh. "Ow," I scream.

"Enough," Henri growls. The girls look on, amusement playing around their mouths. They think we are playing. I know different, Henri is beyond livid, and I am in a world of trouble.

Once out in the cool evening air, Henri lowers me until my feet hit the floor. The area outside the bar is deserted. I am alone with a very angry mate.

I look at the floor, unable to meet his eyes. "Look at me Alexis," his voice is commanding, and I have to obey. When I look at him, I can see his fury, but there is something else too. Is it lust? I wonder.

I don't have to wonder long. Henri pushes me back against the wall and claims my mouth. I want to protest but his demanding kiss leaves no room. I relent and kiss him back with the same passion. We are both breathless when we part, and Henri leans his head down on mine.

"What the fuck are you wearing, Alexis?" I am suddenly self-conscious and try to get away. Do I look that bad? He holds me firm, hearing my thoughts. "Alexis, that dress is… wow, I mean wow. You look amazing. But as you know I am a possessive and jealous man, and I don't ever want ANYONE else to see that much of you."

"Oh," I say softly. I knew this is how he'd feel about the damn dress. I try to stay angry with my mate for his behaviour, but the change in his eyes melts my core. He wants me. No, he needs me. He needs to possess me, in a very primal way, and I can no longer remember why I was so furious with him.

"Oh," he repeats. "Now what am I going to do with you?" His words light a fire in my core.

"Anything you want," I say.

"It was a rhetorical question, my love. You have been a very, very naughty girl tonight." He comes back towards me and roughly pushes my legs apart. He actually tears my lace pants off and pockets them. His hand comes back and finds my centre. He lets out a soft moan when he feels the wetness already there, before a wicked gleam appears in his eyes.

"Do you enjoy me taking control, Alexis?" I nod, unable to look at him. "I asked a question," he says.

"Yes," I say, colour heating my cheeks.

"I think you enjoy more than that. I think you like to be humbled."

"No," I begin to deny it, but a look from Henri stops me. I look at the floor, shame washing over me.

"Why would you be ashamed by that, Alexis? I love it. In fact. I think we should go home and see just how much you enjoy it…"

By the time we have walked back to the cabin, I am wound so tight I could explode from just the friction of my dress against my clit and Henri knows it. How is he so in control and I am here ready to explode.

He says nothing as he beckons me to him. I walk forwards and he pulls me into his arms. "If you want me to stop, promise me you will tell me, Alexis." I nod not trusting my voice. What is he planning if he has to tell me this? "Words, Alexis." The command is back in his voice.

"I promise," I breathe.

"Good girl" he says, as he pushes the straps of my dress off my shoulders and soft material slides down my body leaving me naked. Henri takes a step back to survey me, then bends to help me step out of the dress completely.

Henri and I remain at home in our small cabin - occasionally venturing out onto the beach - for almost a month. We talk, make love, feed each other our favourite foods, and fall in love, in the human sense.

I can now hear his thoughts as well as he hears mine. We show each other things we can't find the words for. I show him the pain I felt running away from him. He shows me the grief of believing I was dead. There will never be any secrets between us, the bond has seen to that.

On the second day Ed mind-linked Henri informing him that Lilith had gone. No one was sure how she managed to disappear - Serenity is protected against apparition - but after a very thorough search of the island it was clear she had done just that.

Ed being Henri's second in command, contacted the palace and organised a man (or woman) hunt for her. Henri was adamant that we do not go after her straight away. "She will lay low for a while now, let's leave it up to palace security to find what they can," he had said to both Ed and me.

I didn't want to argue with him so grudgingly agreed. We needed time alone to adjust to being together and Ed needed time with Ginny.

Alone in my cabin with Henri, it is easy to forget what awaits us, out in the world. At some point we will have to leave Serenity, the place I have called home, for most of my life.

Henri and I are destined to rule though, and as much as I don't relish the thought of leaving, my home is with my mate. Henri is home.

We have so far avoided talking about this, but I know the time is fast approaching, when we will need to. The royal ambassadors are set to leave the island in a week.

It's almost lunchtime when we make it out of bed. I shower and Henri makes tea for us both. I find him looking out at the sea. He is so peaceful I almost don't say what I have been thinking, not wanting to burst our bubble.

My hesitation is all Henri needs and I feel him in my thoughts. Pulling out what I don't want to say.

I come to sit beside him and wait for a response. "We will stay," he says so passionately, I want to agree.

"We can't stay Henri, and you know it," I reply.

"This island is your home, Alexis. I drove you out of your first home. I will not take you from another."

I slowly shake my head and turn his, forcing him to look at me. "You are wrong," I say. "You are my home, my life, my love. As long as I am with you, I am home."

"What about your friends, your family? Brighid and Matias?" I have been trying hard not to dwell on them. Leaving them feels like losing my parents all over again.

"Mum and Dad will understand. Their love has never been easy, but they would be nothing without each other. They know what it means for me to have found you.

"I will miss them, of course. But the Goddess has a plan, and we have to follow it. We will leave in a week - together - and that is final." My mind is made up and I know the longer we put it off, the harder it will be. I am still not on speaking terms with said Goddess, she has a lot to answer for, but I can't deny she planned for me to rule alongside Henri, even if she has abandoned me – Henri and I won't do the same to our people.

I have things I need to put into place. Someone will need to take over the running of the hospital and my seat on the council will need to be filled. I'm not sure if a week will be long enough, but the others will help.

Henri is stunned into silence for a moment. So unused to being spoken to like this. He is usually the one calling the shots. I can hear his thoughts as he tries to make sense of being told what to do.

Eventually a breath-taking smile spreads across his face. Henri pulls me up to stand in front of him and dips before me on one knee.

"What are you doing?" I ask nervously.

"Alexis, my love, my firefly, my queen. You are the most amazing, beautiful, strong, and infuriating woman I have ever met. I love you with every fibre of my being. Will you do me the honour of marrying me, in front of everyone you hold dear?" Henri asks.

Now it is my turn to be stunned into silence. I can hear Henri starting to panic when I don't say anything. Eventually, when I can speak, I give him my answer. "Yes," I say, eyes filling with tears again.

Henri stands lifting me easily into his arms and kissing me. I deepen the kiss, wanting to show him just how much I love him. We are breathless when we part.

He slowly lowers me back to the floor, but I am not done yet. I pull his t-shirt up over his head and bend to remove his shorts. I quickly pull mine off too and take his hand, heading in the direction of the sea.

We step into the warm water and walk until it reaches our waists. I turn to Henri, hungrily reclaiming his lips. He lifts me again and walks further until our bodies are hidden by the crystal ocean.

I am ready for him, and he easily slides inside me. I gasp at the feeling, my body weight ensuring he is deeper than ever before. Henri's strong arms lift me slightly before he lets me drop back down hard, the fullness is exquisite, and I want to stay like this forever.

Henri moves me slowly at first, letting me enjoy every inch of him inside me. His moans of pleasure soon have me veering towards the edge. Sensing my climax approaching, Henri whispers in my ear, "Come for me my love." His words send me right over the edge. I feel his climax, as my walls continue contracting around him.

We stand in the ocean, my head leaning down on his, while we catch our breath. Neither of us make a move to separate and he stays buried deep inside me, as he carries me back to the cabin.

Henri sits on the edge of the bed, holding me tight against his chest, both of us dripping water onto the wooden floor.

"I love you with every fibre of my body and soul, Alexis Beaumont. I cannot wait to show the world that you are mine and I yours," Henri says.

"You are my life, my soul and my home Henri and I cannot wait to spend the rest of my life by your side," I answer.

"I guess we have a wedding to plan then," Henri says with a smirk.

The thought of getting married would have filled me with dread just a few short weeks ago and while I'm still not thrilled by the idea, I do want to give my friends and family in Serenity something to remember. I know there will be another formal wedding when we are back at court, but for me this is the one that really matters.

The next few days pass in a blur. I barely see Henri as he makes the arrangements for us to leave and I spend time with Mum and Ginny, making plans for our wedding.

Mum graciously offered to find my replacement at the hospital and on the council so I can enjoy the last few days I have on the island.

The thought of leaving Serenity and my friends behind breaks my heart, but I belong with Henri and can run away from my destiny and responsibilities no more.

Ginny is coming with us. She would follow Ed to the ends of the earth, and I am so happy to share my new life with my closest friend.

The wedding is two days away and the square has once again been transformed for the event. Millions of twinkling fairy lights hang above my head, as I admire the handy work of Serenity's children.

Tears fill my eyes and my chest swells with pride looking around me.

Strong hands wind their way around my waist, and I smile when Henri rests his chin on my shoulder. "Don't be sad, my love," he says.

"I'm not sad," I say turning to look at him. "I'm the happiest spinner to ever live." A wide smile erupts across my face in response to his.

"Shall we go home?" I ask.

"Already there," Henri says, taking my hand in his, as we set out towards the beach.

"How was your day?"

A frown crosses his face, but he straightens it out before I am even sure what he is thinking. "Long without you by my side," he responds.

"You're trying to hide something from me, my prince," I say with a frown of my own.

"It's nothing, *princess*, just exhausting trying to explain everything to the palace." I panic immediately, thinking they won't accept me as Henri's mate, the future queen.

Who am I, after all? Some lowly spinner who has spent the last 200 plus years hiding out on an island, living amongst other species. My very way of life will be frowned upon at the least.

Not for the first time, I wonder if my bond with the crown prince, will destroy everything we have worked so hard to achieve on Serenity. Will the palace see this way of life as a threat, when they learn the full extent of how we live?

Henri stops, pulling me into his warm embrace. "Stop with your doubts, Alexis. I love you; Ed thinks you're amazing, my parents and everyone else will too.

"What you and the other inhabitants of this island have created is nothing short of a miracle and it might just change the future of the Earth." His eyes twinkle with pride and I can feel his love for me through our connection.

"You were born to be my queen. No one will be able to question that when we return." With his words I understand what the frown was about.

"Who is questioning our bond, Henri?" I ask. Henri rolls his eyes at me - something I would be punished for if the roles were reversed. "Sometimes you are too intuitive for your own good, my love." He is trying to deflect me again. I stand my ground, stubborn as ever.

Henri heaves in a huge sigh. "My mother was caught up in Lilith's spell. She doesn't believe Lilith was trying to fool us. Everything will be fine once she meets you, Alexis."

I know he is trying to protect me, but I don't need protecting. "You aren't telling me the whole story, Henri. I can feel it." I seethe. "Stop trying to protect me and tell me the damn truth, NOW." Sparks fly from my fingers and lightning flashes across the sky as I lose my grip on my temper.

"Firefly, please let me deal with it." Henri says as calmly as he can, though I can feel his frustration rising along with my own. Henri is showing as much restraint as he can, right now. I should let it go, but never one to back down, of course I don't.

"No," I say, stubbornly digging my heals in, while trying to reign in the fire.

"No?" Henri asks, "are you defying me again, Alexis? How do you think that will end for you?" The fire I see behind his eyes lights a spark in my core which spreads between my legs in a completely different way to the one in my fingers.

I know he's had a trying day, and I shouldn't push him, but I can't help myself, it's not in my nature to submit. I need to know what I am facing when I return to court.

Henri looks at me, silently telling me to stand down. I set my jaw and stare deep into his eyes, stubbornly refusing.

Before I know what's happening, Henri comes forward, sweeping me off my feet, to carry me over his shoulder - fireman style. I screech, clenching my fists and pummelling his back. "Henri. put. me. down." I say pausing to hit his back between each word. *This could not be any more embarrassing or demeaning if he tried.*

Henri slaps me hard on the bottom, eliciting another scream from me. "Stop now, Alexis. You are already in a world of trouble. If you carry, on you will get your punishment right here," here he growls.

OK, so it could get more embarrassing and demeaning.

I can hear the lust in his voice and another jolt of fear mixed with pleasure shoots to my core. His words are enough to silence me though. I don't think I could bear the humiliation of anyone else seeing whatever my mate has in store.

Henri's rage is never far from the surface. He controls it well, most of the time, but his need to keep me safe is the thing that most threatens his control.

However, I am not a China doll, and do not need his protection from real or perceived threats. I know I have lost the battle today, but this is a war I won't be backing down from.

I am strong enough to fight by his side.

At the present moment though, I am looking forward to whatever punishment my dark prince has in store.

We arrive back at our cabin and Henri roughly throws me on to the bed. I back up as far as I can. He smirks when I hit the headboard. "Nowhere to run now, firefly," Henri says stalking towards me.

He reaches for my ankle pulling me down the bed. "Stand," he commands. I do as asked and stand in front of him, looking up through my eyelashes hoping to look as sweet as possible.

"It will take more than that to save you now," Henri purrs. I swallow hard, making him laugh. "Are you worried, my love?" I decide not to answer. My mouth isn't likely to be any help.

"Take off your clothes." I do as I am told, slowly easing my shorts down and stepping out of them. My top follows leaving me in nothing more than my bra and panties.

Henri eyes me appreciatively, slowly walking around me. "Continue," he says with a smile, coming back to stand in front of me.

Once I am totally naked, Henri lets out a slow breath. "You are the most beautiful and infuriating woman I have ever met, Alexis Beaumont.

What am I going to do with you?" I can almost see the cogs turning in his head as he ponders his own question.

"Don't move," he says, before heading into the bathroom. Henri returns quickly carrying the belt from my bath robe. Panic sets in as I realise what he is planning to do with it.

Henri senses the change in me and strides forward wrapping his strong arms around me.

"Do you trust me?" he asks.

"With every fibre of my being," I answer.

Henri steps back and takes my hands in his. He uses my belt to tie them together in front of me. I have never been as turned on in my life. I am always so in control of everything, it is liberating to hand the control to Henri.

Henri guides me back on to the bed and raises my arms above my head, securely fastening my bound hands to the headboard. Once he is satisfied, I can't escape, he uses my legs to pull me back down the bed, so my arms are straight.

Placing one knee between my legs he roughly pushes them apart. "Keep them like this," he whispers into my ear. "If you move them, I will tie them to the bed as well. Do you understand?"

"Yes," I answer, voice quivering.

"Good girl." Henri stands at the foot of the bed, openly ogling me. I feel so vulnerable. He can see EVERYTHING, and he is still fully clothed.

I begin to squirm, feeling uncomfortable under Henri's penetrating gaze. He quirks up an eyebrow, silently daring me to close my legs. I immediately still, knowing he will follow through on his threat.

Henri walks into the kitchen, leaving me in my vulnerable state. *Goddess, I hope no one decides to call in on us.* I hear a small chuckle as he moves around the kitchen. He returns less than a minute later.

Henri carries something behind his back, obscuring it from my view. He bends and places the mystery object on the floor.

Starting at my foot Henri, plants cold kisses all the way up my leg. I realise now, he went to the kitchen for ice. Each spot Henri kisses freezes, then instantly burns.

Reaching the apex between my legs, he stops, returning to my feet and kissing his way up my other leg. I moan in frustration and feel him smirk against my leg.

"We've been over this my love. If you would just learn not to defy me, you would be having an orgasm right about now." Henri continues his cold exploration of my body, moving onto my stomach once he has finished with my legs.

My body is already dying for its release, but I can sense Henri is nowhere near done with me. He loves exploring every inch of me with his wicked lips.

Picking up another piece of ice, Henri comes to kiss my lips. I take the ice into my mouth, then offer it back to him. He takes it between his long fingers rubbing it over my breasts. My nipples already hard as bullets, harden further at his touch and my back arches involuntarily.

Henri trails the ice down my stomach, and it comes to rest in my naval. "Stay still, Alexis," he says quietly. "We wouldn't want to make a mess on the bed now, would we?" I can't answer, my body is so tightly wound. I watch him move down again, popping another bit of ice in his mouth. He stops right between my legs.

As soon as the ice touches my swollen clit, I let out a moan of pure pleasure. The feeling is so intense, hot, and cold at the same time. I instantly know, there is no way I can stay still.

I feel the ice move along the slit, exploring every inch of my aching core. Using his tongue, Henri slides the ice inside me. "Hold that there," he says. I can feel it melting inside me but do my best to hold onto it.

He lowers his head back to my clit and lightly flicks his tongue over the tiny bud, sending jolts of electricity through my entire body. I try to stay still but it's impossible. Henri's hand slaps my inner thigh, in warning. It stings slightly but mixed with all the other feelings almost sends me flying over the edge into oblivion.

"Henri, please," I beg, I know I won't be able to hold back for long.

"Please what, Alexis? What do you want my love?" He says, while continuing his assault on my core.

"I need to come," I answer breathlessly. Henri slowly slides one then two digits inside me, rubbing what is left of the ice against my walls.

It is enough to push me over. I come harder than ever before, my walls contracting hard against his fingers. I feel the gush of my orgasm between my legs and Henri lets out his own moan.

"Oh, I love how your body responds to me," he says, but doesn't stop his assault. I writhe under him, trying to pull away, the pleasure is almost too much to bear.

"Stop, Henri, please. It's too much." My pleading falls on deaf ears. His fingers continue their relentless circling inside me as he sucks my clit into his mouth. Before long, my orgasm is building again, and I see stars as I come again and again and again.

I have never felt so conflicted, I never want him to stop but it's getting too much, too intense. As I come again, I scream his name and finally, he stops the movement, but leaves his fingers inside me, feeling my muscles contract around them.

I still, trying to calm my erratic breathing. Henri removes his fingers and brings them to his mouth. "You taste so good," he says, and I blush. He unbuttons his shorts, allowing his huge member to burst free.

Without warning, Henri flips me over landing a hard slap on my backside. I gasp at the pain; I haven't recovered before another one lands on the opposite cheek. "Hmm, that colour looks good on those cheeks too," he says, pulling me up onto my knees.

I barely have time to register, my new position when he slams into me, hard. I scream out as he starts to move inside me, hard and fast. The feeling is so exquisite. He is usually so gentle with me. *Clearly, he has been holding back,* I think.

"You haven't seen anything yet, firefly," I hear him think. I am about to come again when Henri abruptly pulls out. He stands and I watch over my shoulder as he takes all his clothes off.

Coming back onto the bed, Henri unties my hands and brings me to straddle his lap. He stares deep into my eyes as he expertly slides back inside me. He starts to rock us back and forth, eyes never leaving mine.

I am building quickly, and I can feel Henri won't last much longer either, as much as he wants it to last. Pulling me down so my lips cover his, he kisses me deeply. The sensation pushes us both over the edge and Henri calls out my name as he finds his release.

Once our breathing returns to normal, Henri adjusts our position, so we are laid looking at each other, never breaking contact.

He is still buried deep inside me. In this moment it is impossible to know where Henri ends, and I begin.

Chapter 12

Henri

I sit on the steps of the council building, watching my mate instruct a group of children, who are setting up tables for our wedding. I have never met a more competent woman. She is calm and confident. She isn't easily thrown.

Right now, I know she can hear me thinking about her, but she never lets on, though I can feel her squirm internally. I chuckle and turn my attention back to Ed, who is going over the arrangements for getting us back to Asgard - again.

"Ed, you worry too much," I say with a sigh. "No one tried to attack us, on our way here, returning will be no different." Ed raises his eyes at me.

"If you think that, you are a fool, Hen!" Ed replies, frustration rising. The truth is I don't think that, but I am trying to hide my feelings from Alexis. Dwelling on all the possible threats, we might face now I have found her, won't do me or her any good the night before our wedding.

Hearing my unspoken thoughts, Ed backs off. "I'm sorry, Hen. You're right. We will be fine." I nod, my attention already back on my mate.

Ed follows my gaze, and his attention is caught by his own mate. "How's Lex, feeling about leaving?" he asks. "Gin is excited and terrified in equal measure. She lived in the north before finding her way here, she's never been to Asgard."

"*Alexis* is much the same." I say, emphasising my mate's full name. She will always be Alexis to me, and it irritates me a little that he uses the shortened version – though most people call her Lex.

My best friend and mate have become close in the short time they have known each other. I am relieved they get on, but I don't like any male near her, that includes Ed.

"She knows what to expect, she grew up at court. She's just worried about how she will be received, having been away for so long. Returning as the future queen is a lot to deal with."

There is no doubt in my mind that my mate was born to be my queen, she is everything I am not. Calm, kind, open, selfless. Our people will be in good hands. I just wish Alexis would see that.

A small smile lights up her face, as she hears my thoughts. *"And you are everything I am not, my prince. The protector of our people, the love of my life,"* she mind links me.

I stand clearing my throat. "Excuse me," I mumble in Ed's direction. Closing the distance between us in a few short strides. I gather her up in my arms and kiss her hard.

Alexis

My head is spinning when Henri puts me down. The whole square has stopped to watch us. I hear a few wolf whistles amongst the crowd and my cheeks burn as bright as my hair.

Movement at the opposite side of the square suddenly catches my attention. I see Sam's face drop as he walks around the corner. I feel like I have been kicked in the stomach at the look of betrayal on his face.

Henri's gaze follows mine and he stiffens, pulling me closer when he sees Sam watching us. *"Henri, he is hurt, I need to speak to him."* I mind link. *"Before anything else Sam has been a good friend to me, I owe him an explanation, at the least."* Henri stubbornly refuses to back down. I haven't seen Sam at all since the night in Dad's bar when Henri carried me out over his shoulder. I still haven't had the chance to explain.

"Please Henri, be reasonable. I broke his heart, forcing him to leave his home and when he returned, I was there with you. I just need a few minutes to talk to him. He is – was – one of my best friends and has been here with me for the last two hundred years." I don't want to make Henri feel bad, after all none of this is his fault, but Sam deserves an explanation at the very least.

Henri's response is lightning quick in my head, *"No."* It's final, I know there is no point in arguing further and I don't want to fight with him, hours before our wedding. I hang my head not wanting him to see the pain in my eyes. I have made my choice, and nothing would change that, Henri is my world. I let it go for now, hoping to have another opportunity to speak to Sam before I leave.

Henri narrows his eyes at me and growls at my thoughts. *Not if I can help it.* He thinks.

"Time's up, love birds," I hear Dad say as he approaches us breaking the tension. I roll my eyes. Henri smirks - thinking about what he would do to me if I rolled my eyes at him. I squirm at his errant thoughts.

Ordinary spinners don't always bother with a wedding. Nothing is more binding than the twin flame bond, in the Goddess's eyes we are already bound to each other. But given the circumstances, we decided to hold a ceremony here on the island, to celebrate our union with my friends and family.

There will be a big formal affair in Asgard, unlike the rest of us, the royals always host a kind of wedding. It allows everyone to celebrate.

Dad and Mum have made it clear that if we are having a wedding, it should be done right. I will be staying at their house tonight and won't see Henri again until the ceremony tomorrow.

Ginny has planned a 'girls' night for us, and I have been informed the island's male inhabitants have planned *a night to remember* for Henri.

I am slightly worried for the wellbeing of my prince. Serenity's men know how to party. "Don't drink too much and stay out of my head," I tell Henri as sternly as I can. "It's bad luck to see the bride before the wedding," I add with a wink. Neither of us believe in these silly human customs, but we are going along with it to make the others happy.

"Alexis," Henri looks at me sternly, "remember what happened the last time you went out… don't make me punish you again – this time I might not be able to wait until we are home." He is teasing me, but I can see the hope in his eyes. He loves to punish me.

I don't need the warning though. We are getting married tomorrow; I don't want anything to spoil that.

The girls brought me down to the dock, which has been transformed into a bar, complete with music, cocktails, and games. I am trying hard to stay out of Henri's head, but I occasionally feel him trying to push into mine.

I am dancing with my arms wrapped around Ginny, slightly unsteady thanks to the cocktails – I am nowhere near as intoxicated as the last time I was out with my friends, though. We are laughing and singing at the top of our lungs as we spin in circles.

The song ends and we come to a wobbly stop. "Water," I say giggling and heading to the bar. I down the glass in one, immediately feeling better.

Ginny heads back to the dance floor and I sit watching my friends enjoying themselves. *Goddess, I will miss them.* I think before pushing the thought away. Everyone has made it very clear this is a night for celebration, no tears allowed.

I gulp down more water and head back to my friends on the dance floor, who hum 'Here comes the bride' as I approach. We all fall into fits of giggles.

Once I have regained my composure, I notice a figure watching us. I immediately realise it's Sam. This is my chance, it's now or never. Henri has stopped trying to get into my thoughts, I will deal with the consequences later. I need to explain things to my once friend.

Henri

Being away from Alexis is so hard, especially when the little minx is keeping me out of her thoughts. Every fibre in my being wants to run to her, just to see she is OK. I won't though. She won't admit it, but it means a lot to her, doing this right, for her adopted family.

Her birth parents didn't live long enough to see what an amazing creature she has grown into. The least I can do is give her this time with her adopted ones. I can't even begin to imagine how hard it is for Alexis to leave them.

I have spent the last two hours listening to stories about Alexis and her exploits on this tiny patch of paradise. It is clear she is loved. It's not difficult to see why. Whatever she thinks, my firefly was born to lead, to be queen.

"Henri," Matias's voice pulls me out of my thoughts. I smile at the man who helped to bring my queen back from the brink. "Matias," I greet him as he sits beside me.

"I was hoping to have a private moment with you," he says.

"Of course, is everything ok?" I ask.

"More than OK if you ask me, son." I smile at his choice of name for me, so ready to accept me into his family. "Alexis may not be ours by birth, but her Mum and I love her as such, all the same. I couldn't be happier that she found her mate in you. I know you will love and care for her always.

"She isn't the easiest creature to live with and she *loves* to break rules," I smile having learned that for myself, not that I would admit that to her dad. "Just know that she always has a good reason for her actions, so don't be too hard on her.

"I have never seen my daughter as happy as she is with you by her side. Cherish each other always."

"I intend to spend every day of the rest of my life, proving my worth to your daughter sir," I respond, attempting to swallow the lump that has formed in my throat.

However, the overwhelming joy I feel speaking to my mate's dad is suddenly replaced with sheer panic. "Alexis," I say, my voice full of desperation.

"Henri, what is it?" Ed has noticed my sudden change in mood.

"Alexis is in trouble," I say, doubling over, as pain shoots through my stomach.

Alexis

Checking that no one else has noticed, I skirt my way to the edge of the dock and follow Sam to the beach. He is a way in front of me and I have to run to keep up.

"Sam stop, please," I shout as soon as I think we are out of earshot of the party. He turns to look at me, his expression unreadable.

"I'm surprised your *prince* has let you off the leash long enough to speak to me," he grits out. I am shocked by his coldness.

"It's not like that, Sam. Please try to understand."

"Oh, I understand well enough, *princess*. No man was ever good enough for you, God knows I tried to be. I could have made you happy if only you'd given me the opportunity. But no, we were all beneath you. Then Prince Charming comes along, and you fall head over heels for him. I don't know who you are any more, Alexis. You make me sick."

I am reeling at his words. I can see that he means every one of them. He really does hate me now. I try again to explain. "Sam, I swear it's not like that. You've heard the spinner's tale. He is my soul mate, my twin flame. Nothing could stop that."

He isn't a spinner; my words aren't likely to help him understand the twin flame connection. Until you have experienced it for yourself, it is impossible to truly understand. I have to try though.

"I met him before I came here when I lived in Asgard. My parents worked for the royal family. When they died, the king and queen attended the funeral. Henri was there. It was the first time we had been close enough to make eye contact. I'd only ever caught glimpses of him, from a distance before.

"I knew instantly what he was to me, but I ran away. My parents were killed by a witch, I knew she would kill us too if we accepted the bond.

"When Henri arrived here, he recognised me straight away. I tried to fight it Sam, to push him away, but I love him, and nothing can change that now. Please believe me when I tell you, my intention was never to hurt you." I don't know why I am telling Sam all of this. I just can't stand the thought of him hating me.

"We have been friends for so long, please understand, I don't want to lose you. Henri is jealous and possessive. That is on me, I made him live without me for so long. He will come round though. He knows you are very important to me." My words trail off and I give up trying to explain.

I look at him, but his face hasn't changed. All I see is a mask of hatred. I lower my gaze, defeated. I knew the bond Henri and I share, would earn me a few enemies, I just didn't expect someone so close to be one of them.

"You're lying," Sam finally says. "It's a nice story, Lex, real fairy tale stuff, but I know better. You are nothing more than a gold-digging bitch, well I am sorry I was not enough for you."

His words are like a knife. There is nothing I can say, to change his mind. Henri was right, I should have stayed away. I turn to walk back to the party, but Sam jumps forward, grabbing my wrist, pulling me back to him. I try to push him off but can't. I instantly regret that last cocktail. The alcohol is slowing my reactions.

I start struggling, until I feel something cold and sharp dig into my side. "Hush now," Sam says in a mock soothing tone which makes me shudder with disgust. "You and I are going to have a little party of our own, whore."

I am really panicking now. All rational thought has gone, and I curse myself for being so stupid. This isn't my friend; I don't know what has happened to him, but I can't see the Sam I know and love anywhere in him now. It's like he has been possessed.

Sam pulls me into the tree line, I can tell there isn't anyone around. I am about to scream when his hand comes to cover my mouth. "Tut tut, I thought you knew how to behave," he says.

Reaching into his pocket, Sam pulls out a scrap of material, which he uses to try and gag me. I bite down hard on his hand, earning myself a swift punch to the stomach, as he roars with anger.

I almost double over at the pain but refuse to bow to him. No matter how afraid I am, I will not give this monster the satisfaction of showing it. Where have my powers gone? Have I spent so long supressing them, that I no longer have any control over my magic. The fire that has been so close to the surface for weeks, has disappeared. I feel like a weak human, unable to defend myself.

I open my eyes and glare at him. I wonder what happened to him. Sam was always so sweet and understanding.

He comes back and leans the length of his body against me, and I shudder in disgust, feeling his bulge hard against my stomach. Pulling back, Sam uses the knife to slit straight up the front of my dress. "Not so confident now, are we, *witch*? Nothing but a little whore.

"Do you know what I'm going to do to you bitch? I am going to have my way with you and then kill you. If I can't have you, that jumped up *prince* won't either."

"He'll kill you, you know," I say, playing for time and reaching out my mind to Henri. "If you let me go now, I might be able to convince him otherwise, but if you hurt me, I won't be able to stop him."

"You're going nowhere slut, keep that mouth shut, or I will make you," he roars, slicing his knife along my jaw. I wince at the sudden sharp pain, feeling the blood fall onto my bare chest, soaking into the fabric of my bra.

"What happened to you, Sam? Where has this hate come from? I can understand you being angry with me, but the man I know would never go to these lengths to get his way. The man who had more compassion than anyone I ever knew, who helped me to build a hospital, who ran it by myside for so long. Sam, please don't do this. I love you; you are my family."

"You don't love me Lex, you never did!" He roars. "If you did, you'd be with me and not *him*."

"Sam, please," I beg, squeezing my eyes shut, unable to believe what is happening.

He grabs me roughly by the hair, forcing me down onto my knees, I use my hands to steady myself, then punch him hard in the crotch. He responds, using the blunt end of the knife to strike my face. I feel my cheek bone crack, but don't give into the pain blurring my vision.

He is far enough away now that I can get to my feet. I take off at a run without a backwards glance. I just start to think I've gotten away when I hear footsteps approaching. He grabs me around the waist and wrestles me to the ground, knocking the wind from my lungs and my remaining energy to fight.

Sam binds my hands together behind my back and trails his knife up the length of my body. Tears form in my eyes, and I squeeze them tight trying to shut out what's happening. He yanks my head back, pulling hard on my hair and a gasp escapes my lips feeling his knife slice the side of my face again. "Do you think your prince would want you now? Caked in dirt and blood, bound and ready for me like the whore we both know you are," Sam snarls in my ear.

I feel bile rise in my throat; I couldn't be more disgusted by the man I thought I knew if I tried. He wants me to fight him, he is taking pleasure in it, and it makes me sick to my stomach.

"Yes," I choke out, "I know he would want me no matter what. Henri loves me Sam, and no amount of pain inflicted on me by you will take that away."

"Will he still want you, when I've made you mine?" He lets go of my hair and I feel his weight lift from my back. I close my eyes again trying to shut him out. They fly open as I hear his zipper. I squeeze my legs shut tight; I refuse to let him take me. My body and soul belong to my mate, and this sorry excuse for a man can have neither.

I close my eyes again, thinking of my prince. What this will do to him. *"I'm so sorry Henri, I love you."* I think, hoping he can hear me. *"Don't you dare give in"* I imagine him responding fiercely. The thought of Henri's voice in my head is enough to stir me. I sit up, feeling the flames lick at the ends of my fingers.

Before I have chance to use them though, Sam pulls me to the ground, and I hit my head on a rock.

Chapter 13

Alexis

When I come to again, everything is dark. I can tell from the air; I am no longer in the forest. As my eyes adjust to the darkness, I realise I'm in a cave, but it's nothing like the Goddess's cave at my cove.

My hands and feet are bound, and a filthy rag is in my mouth. I start to struggle, attempting to free myself, but freeze as someone moves towards me. "Sam, please don't do this," I try to plead, although, it comes out more of a muffle due to the gag.

It's not Sam, who approaches me though. Lilith's victorious face comes into view.

"Not so clever now are we, little spinner," she sneers approaching me. I try to bring my power to the surface, to let the emotions she elicited from me before, spur me on. Nothing happens. "Oh no, there will be none of that," she smiles, while using her own power to lift me from the ground.

She leaves me dangling in the air, the earth beneath me just out of reach. I can feel now that she has done something to block my power. "I've been trying to get my hands on your considerable power for quite some time," Lilith says, with palpable excitement. "I am going to enjoy taking it from you."

Pain slices through my head and I try hard not to cry out as tears spring to my eyes. I will not give her the satisfaction of breaking me. I focus my energy on not letting her in. I might have ignored my power for a long time, but it is mine and this witch cannot have it.

Lilith sighs in frustration when she can't breach my mental barrier. "You will pay for that, *spinner*," she says, while using her magic to turn me away from her. I feel another pain down the length of my back, it feels as though I have been whipped. My skin has broken and blood pools on the floor beneath me.

I feel her attempting to breach my mind again. It's painful but not as bad as before. Using Mum's technique, I focus on getting air in and out of my lungs, letting my mind drift to a happier place.

I think about Mum and Dad, their unending love for me over the years. Ginny and her daily wake up calls. Finding Henri again. Thanks to my stubbornness and stupidity we haven't had long enough together, but the time we have had, has been the happiest of my life.

Lilith screaming, brings me back to the here and now. She is bent over with the exertion of pushing against my barrier, she soon recovers, and I feel another lash across my back. She turns me to face her again.

"Have it your way," she says coming towards me with a knife pointed at my chest. I can just make it out in the dim light. It's nothing like any knife I have ever seen before. It appears to be emitting a greenish light. The blade twisted like a corkscrew.

"Do you know what this is?" she asks. "It's a witch's blade. Once I plunge it into your heart, it will transfer your power to me and kill you in the process," she continues when I don't offer her a response. The knife is now pressed against my sternum with enough pressure for me to feel its sharpness but not enough to draw blood.

A movement in the darkness, just beyond my line of sight catches her attention. "NO," Sam yells and Lilith backs away from me slowly turning to face him. "She is mine, you promised," Sam says, coming into view. Lilith sighs.

"Fine, you have one hour to break her," Lilith replies. "If I can't get into her head after that, the kill is mine," she says before turning and walking from the cave. I crumple to the floor in a heap. The blissful oblivion of unconsciousness overtaking me, once more.

When I open my eyes again Lilith, the cave and Sam are no longer there. I am in a huge temple. Enormous white marble pillars are holding up a ceiling I can't see. It reminds me of the palace in Asgard but, there is something different about it. White mist swirls around my feet and I see the same mist outside the windows. I am alone. "Hello," I shout into the cavernous space. "Hello" my own voice echo's back.

I start to panic. I need to get back to Serenity, to Henri. Where am I? "Alexis" a sweet melodic voice calls from behind me. It's both familiar and strange. Slowly turning around, I come face to face with the most beautiful woman I have ever seen. She has almost pure white hair which flows behind her all the way to the floor. The only thing whiter than her hair is the dress she is wearing. Realisation suddenly dawns on me.

"You're…"

"I am," she responds with a smile.

"So, am I… dead?" I ask, shakily. I have only just found Henri again. I can't die now, I can't.

"No, daughter, you are not dead," the Goddess responds.

"Then where am I?"

"Neither here nor there," she answers cryptically. I close my eyes and take a deep breath, hoping that the Goddess who has ignored me for 200 years can't sense my frustration.

"I can," she says with a small chuckle, "you have been around mortals for too long, daughter your emotions are easy to read."

"Why am I here," I ask, no longer attempting to hide my frustration. "Why now, when you have ignored my pleas for so long?"

"The earth is not yet finished with you child; I need you to return and restore the balance. But you cannot do that without stepping fully into your power.

"If you do not accept it, when you awaken, you will be killed and your power, my power will be transferred to a witch. You are more important to the earth than any creature who ever lived."

"Oh really, and how exactly do you expect me to do that?" I ask, completely out of patience with her riddles. "For a Goddess you are exceptionally selfish, do you know that?" I ask. I am far beyond caring about her wrath. She abandoned me and allowed everything to be taken from me. I will not allow her to use me for her own ends.

She simply smiles at me indulgently, like a parent waiting out a child's tantrum.

"I am sorry your life has been so hard child. If there was another way, I would have done it." I am beginning to think we are having two different conversations. "You will come to understand more in time, but for now you need to fully accept your power and who you are. Do you think you can do that, Alexis?"

"I, I don't know how," I say panic again returning, replacing my anger and frustration.

"Yes, you do. Look inside, do you know why the threads all shine the same for you? You are the embodiment of power, Alexis. Call out to them, what happens?"

I don't reply, but the room around me is suddenly illuminated by millions of threads all colours of the rainbow and some I've I don't know the name of. I call out and they all respond, ready to do my bidding.

I look at the Goddess and she is smiling at me. "That's it Alexis. Inside you, you have the power of the Goddess herself – my power, divinity is in your blood Alexis. You can control it all."

"How," I ask.

"You will see in time," for today, you need to find the threads that will help to save your life." She isn't asking much. I have never used any of the threads. Despite what I am told, the power I have over the elements, is far from within my control. Fire shoots randomly from my hands when I lose it; my emotions cause storms. I can't see how any of that could be of use right now.

"You need to stop fighting for control, Alexis. It can't be forced. The power within you wants to be free. When you let go of the need to control it, it will respond to you. Just as it did when Brighid guided you." I think back to the day in my office when, Mum helped me to induce a vision. I did let go of the need to control and force it. When I did that, the power flowed naturally.

"You see you already know what to do my child. Now go and meet your destiny," she whispers as the temple fades, and I am again on the floor of a dark, damp cave.

The pain returns in earnest, and I want nothing more to return to the temple, where there is no pain, only peace. As I open my eyes, Sam approaches me and I back away until I hit the wall of the cave.

My entire body hurts so much I am struggling to remain conscious. I have too many broken bones to note. Sam kneels in front of me, grabbing a handful of my hair. I fight the urge to groan as my body screams in pain. "It didn't have to be this way, Lex. I could have made you happy, fulfilled your every desire, but you had to go and give yourself to that *prince*."

He pulls down the rag at my mouth and I begin screaming. I don't know where we are, but hopefully someone will hear me. Sam hits me so hard across the face I see stars as the pain of my already broken cheek bone erupts. His hand wraps around my throat, cutting off my scream. I struggle to free myself from his grip as my oxygen is shut off. "Shut up, bitch. We are going to have some fun."

He tears a scrap of material from my ruined dress before balling it up and pushing it into my mouth. He pulls the gag back up, preventing me from spitting it out.

Sam lifts me from the ground and stands me in front of him. I close my eyes and will my power to awaken. What was it the Goddess said. I need to find the threads to save my life. But what are they and how do I do that?

I breathe trying to remember how I felt in my office, when Mum helped me to tap into my power. My third sight abruptly opens. Suddenly I can see the threads. The threads of Lilith's magic block are tied in a messy knot. I begin untying them, focusing my attention on that rather than the man in front of me. I can still hear Sam ranting about what I am, and what he will do with me, but I push it aside and concentrate on loosening the strands of the knot.

It isn't easy and takes a few minutes before I make any headway. Sam is too far gone to even notice the faraway look on my face. His words are no longer having any effect. My entire being is focused on undoing Lilith's spell. Gradually one thread at a time I untangle the mess, breaking the spell apart.

I release the final thread and feel my magic return. Lilith's spell is broken. Sam hasn't even noticed. He pulls me out of the cave, and I look around for anything to identify where we are. Still on the island that is for sure.

"That's better," Sam says. "Now I can see your fear. Watch you tremble as I take what is mine." The sun is already coming up, night giving way to morning. I reach my mind out for Henri once again. It's my only chance. I know, the pain will pull me under any second. It has returned in full force, now I no longer have something to concentrate on. Undoing Lilith's spell used the remainder of my energy. There is nothing left to summon any other power to free myself. All that's left is the hope Henri will find me in time.

Sam is saying something to me, but I ignore him and focus on Henri. *"Henri, Sam has me, we are in the forest somewhere, they were keeping me in a cave, its set into a cliff face on the west side of the island."* I try to mind link with him. For a few minutes there is nothing, I just keep repeating the same words over and over.

Sam is using his knife to cut into my skin. None of the wounds are deep enough to kill, just enough to draw blood and cause more pain. The pull of darkness is getting strong, my body and mind want to succumb to the numb oblivion waiting for me. I want to return to the temple and peace I felt there. *"I'm so sorry Henri, I love you."* Is my last thought.

Just before I lose consciousness, I feel Henri in my head. *"Don't you dare give in, my love,"* I hear him say. It's almost a growl and I smile at the ferocity behind the thought.

Henri

The square erupts at my words. "Where is she?" Matias asks.

"I'm not sure," I say trying to remain calm. It won't help anyone, least of all my mate if I lose it now. "She has been blocking me all night."

"The girls are down at the dock," Ed says. "Ginny says she saw Alexis walk toward the beach, she thought she just needed a minute to herself."

Damn it, I should never have let her out of my sight. I curse my own stupidity. "Everyone to the dock," Ed shouts across the bar. We all take off at a run.

The women are already searching for her when we arrive. "I found some footprints," Ginny yells. Ed and I sprint to her. What I see turns my stomach. They aren't footprints, more like someone has been dragged through the sand.

"Fuck," I yell, startling everyone around me. "Someone has her." I break out in white hot rage. If Lilith has her, I will end her there and then. We were so sure, she had left the island, but who else could it be?

Realisation hits me square in the chest. Samuel! She had wanted to talk to him yesterday and I'd refused to let her. I should have known she would find a way to speak to him. Alexis is so kind and compassionate, she wants to see the best in everyone. She thought if she could talk to him, she'd make him see sense.

I could see his anger though. It's part of my own curse. The monster raging within me, can always see it in another. Samuel was too far gone to reason with. He would just hurt Alexis and I swore to never let anyone hurt her.

Now, I have failed her, again. I should have delt with him yesterday.

"Ginny, where does Samuel live?" I ask trying to remain at least outwardly calm.

She looks confused but answers me anyway. "The other side of town, in the forest." I take off at a run in the direction she points in. *Damn this island's magical protection.* If I could have apparated, I could have found her instantly.

Alexis, open your mind, please my love. Why can't I hear her? The others aren't far behind me, and everyone is calling her name.

I run for what feels like hours, until I reach a small hut in the forest. Pulling the door clean off its hinges, I enter, but immediately know she isn't here. Back outside the others have caught up and I shake my head at their expectant looks. "She isn't here."

Ginny looks like she is about to break down and I know the look on my own face mirrors hers. Ed takes her in his arms, attempting to reassure his mate that we will find her best friend.

"We'll find her babe, I promise," he coos.

"How Ed?" Ginny asks. "The island is protected, its mainly covered in dense forest. He could have taken her anywhere. What if we don't get there in time. What if we are already too late."

I close my eyes trying to subdue the rage. Losing control now will not get my mate back.

"She is a spinner, Gin. She can protect herself against a human," Ed says.

"I am sure she could, but I know her, and she won't want to harm Sam. He is like family. She loves him," she looks to me before clarifying, "he is the closest thing she has to a brother." Alexis and Samuel were clearly far closer than she ever let on.

Inside the rat's hut, my stomach rolls as I see photo after photo taken of Alexis from afar. He has been spying on us. I have been cut out of every picture. Even more alarming, there is evidence of a witch here. I can smell the acrid rotting scent left over by their dark magic. It's clear Lilith has been working with the *human*.

Knowing her powers, I can imagine how easy it would have been for her to manipulate him. In another world, I might have even felt sorry for him. If he hadn't just kidnapped my mate, that is.

I search the island for hours. From our cabin to the hospital, the forest to the beaches and even go to the Goddess's cove. I feel relief momentarily at the cove, thinking I sense her close by. "Please let me find her," I pray to the Goddess. "I have only just got her back. I can't lose her now."

"She is hurt but safe for now, child." The wind seems to whisper. I'm not sure if it is my imagination or the Goddess answering my plea.

Continuing my frantic search, there is no sign of her anywhere. It's like she just vanished into thin air.

"Are you sure, they couldn't have taken her from the island?" I ask Brighid for the millionth time. Ginny was right to panic, the island might be small, but the dense vegetation is making the search… difficult.

"I'm sure," she says again.

"Then where the fuck is she?" I roar. Brighid looks taken aback by my outburst and Matias goes to her side comforting his wife. I try to rain in my fury, reminding myself that I am not the only one who loves Alexis. "Brighid, I'm…"

"It's fine, Henri. I know." She comes over to me offering comfort, despite my outburst.

"Alexis is strong and more capable than you could imagine, Henri. She will find a way to save herself," Matias says, sounding like he is trying to convince himself. "She might not want to harm Sam, but her desire to survive will prevail."

I know she is strong and oh so powerful, but she doesn't understand her power yet. What if she can't figure out how to use it, to save herself?

The sun is starting to rise and with it, my sheer panic. I can't lose her now. This cannot be how our story ends. "It's not. We'll find her, Hen." Ed says, hearing my dark thoughts.

"*I'm so sorry Henri, I love you.*" I suddenly hear her thought. Thank the Goddess she is still alive – barely, but I can feel her pain through the link. Even in my mind she feels broken. I shudder thinking about what she could have been forced to endure over the last 12 hours. Today should be the happiest day of our lives, declaring our love in front of her family. "*Don't you dare give in, my love,*" I think back. "*Show me where you are.*" She does and I follow her thoughts.

"She's alive." I shout at the rest of the group, before setting off at a sprint towards the west side of the island. It seems to take hours to get to her, but I know it is more like minutes. My legs feel like they are trying to wade through treacle. Branches hit me, biting into my skin as I continue to push forward towards where I know, Alexis is laid on the damp forest floor. I barely notice the pain, focused solely on reaching my mate.

I reach the clearing beside the cave they were keeping her in and sure enough the acrid smell of dark magic taints the fresh morning air. Alexis is laid on the ground, her dress in tatters, she is covered in dirt and blood, all of which must be her own, the only blood on the rat is on his grubby hands – that can easily be remedied.

She is laid on her front, hands and feet bound, what looks to be a gag tied around the back of her head. Sure enough the piece of shit who dared to challenge me before, Samuel is stood above her. There seems to be no area of her body that isn't swollen and bruised – I don't dare imagine how many broken bones she has. How she endured such torture, I will never know.

My vision tunnels as the world around me turns red. I know my eyes are as black as obsidian. I am beyond caring. All I can think about is making him suffer as he has Alexis. Under a spell or not, I will not rest until his cold lifeless body lays at my feet. I will deal with Lilith in due course. It has been a long time since I let the monster take over, I usually fight for control. Not this morning though. He is free to do as he will.

My hands instinctively reach out and grab Samuel by the neck, determined to finish what I started weeks ago. I lift him from the ground and push him against a tree as I begin to squeeze the life out of him. I will show no mercy, this man deserves to die for laying a hand on my beautiful queen.

The monster is revelling at the feeling, of the life beneath my hands, slipping away. Samuel's eyes bulge in fear as he paws my hands, attempting to free himself. Stronger men than him, have attempted and failed to save themselves. This weak human does not stand a chance.

I vaguely hear protests behind me. They fall on deaf ears, the monster has full control and the only thing that will stop him, is feeling this rats cold, dead flesh in my hands.

Ed places a hand on my shoulder. He can see I am too far gone to listen to reason now. He has seen the monster in my eyes, he knows what's happening, so he simply says "Alexis" in my ear.

Her name reaches my consciousness and I drop the scum's lifeless body, watching as it crumbles to the floor, I don't care whether he is alive or not, in that moment I just need to see that she is. I turn my attention to Alexis. Ginny is kneeling at her head, silent tears streaking down her face as she strokes her friend's hair. I remove my shirt and use it to cover my mate's body.

As I near, Alexis stirs. Her beautiful green eyes flutter open, looking straight into my soul. They are swollen and bruised, but I can see her spirit is not broken, as I'd feared. Ginny produces a knife and cuts off her bindings and the gag.

"Henri," she creaks, once she can speak, it's the sweetest sound I have ever heard. I bend to pick her up, holding her close. "I'm here, my love," I say burying my face in her hair. Her usual honeysuckle and jasmine scent is mixed with that of blood, dirt, and dark magic. I hate it.

"Henri, I am so sorry. I should..." I silence her with a kiss.

"No, Alexis, I have got you, you're safe." Her eyes start to droop again. "Stay with me now, it's not time to sleep yet," I say, I'm afraid if she closes her eyes, they might not open again.

"Henri, we need to get her to the hospital," Brighid says approaching me, and placing a soothing hand on my arm. Her eyes are full of worry for her daughter.

I nod in agreement. Without a backwards glance at her attacker's body, I carry my mate back out of the forest. Daylight is coming quickly now, and, in the town, everyone is beginning to wake, blissfully unaware of what has happened. Elanor is in the square setting out chairs for the wedding. She turns to look at the trail of people emerging from the forest.

She drops the cloth in her hand and sprints towards us. "Alexis," she cries, "Oh sweet girl, what happened?" She asks looking around the gathered group.

"She is fine, Elanor," Brighid says, "but we need to get her to the hospital."

"She doesn't look fine, Brighid." Elanor replies. I am out of patience with the entire ordeal and set off walking again. Clearly Brighid is too as she easily catches up to me, leaving someone else to answer Elanor's questions.

We reach our destination quickly and Brighid shows us to a sterile room with a trolley in the centre. Reluctantly I lay Alexis down but keep holding onto her hand.

A swarm of people arrive and begin working on my mate. Someone tries to tell me it would be easier if I left them to it, but one look from me silences their protests. I will never leave her side again; the sooner people get used to that the better.

Standing beside her, I take in the full extent of her injuries for the first time. There is a bruise as big as my hand across her cheek which looks suspiciously broken, as are her ankle, arm, and several ribs from the look of it. A long gash across her jaw that is still bleeding and there is a huge lump on the back of her head. I could feel the wounds across her back as I carried her here. The remainder of her body is covered in scratches and scrapes.

Brighid, Ginny, and the healers expertly turn Alexis onto her side giving me a full view of the injuries on her back. Tears fill my eyes. The gashes are deep, and they were made by magic. Even with the best healers, these marks will leave scars. Lilith used her power to try and steal Alexis's. How she endured this assault, I will never know. Lesser beings would have crumbled.

I can tell my mate fought back. She didn't just lay down and let them take her. Although why she didn't use the fire laying just under her skin, is a mystery. No doubt she didn't want to hurt someone she cared for, even as he was torturing her.

Once her wounds are healed, Ginny and Brighid ask me to leave so they can clean her up. Ginny has fresh pyjamas in her arms. I am about to object when Ed appears. "Let them take care of her Hen, I need to speak with you." We step out of the room, and I turn to face him. "Hen, I," he begins but words fail him. There are none.

"She will be fine," I say, trying to convince myself more than him. Physically she will, at least, who knows what mental scars she will have.

Closing my eyes and taking a deep breath I go on. "You wanted to speak to me?"

"Yes," he says clearly feeling awkward. "Well, Matias has Samuel, he has locked him in the only cell on the island, there was no sign of Lilith." My rage begins to resurface.

"She was definitely there, the marks on Alexis's back were made by magic. Samuel is human." At the sound of his name my rage takes over and it's all I can do not to find the animal and kill him on the spot, human or not. The world begins to turn red, and I know my eyes are black again. I push it back, knowing a fast death would be too easy for him. When I am ready to deal with him, I will make him suffer, like he did Alexis.

"Matias wants to know, if he should face trial in Asgard, or if he should hand Sam over to the human authorities."

"It won't get that far," I think. Ed nods, acknowledging my thoughts.

"I thought as much," he replies aloud. "I will let Matias know to leave him where he is for now."

"Thank you," I say, before returning to my mate's side.

Alexis

When I open my eyes, I am surrounded by the worried faces of everyone I love, but there is only one that matters in this moment. "Henri," I breathe as his eyes meet mine. He is instantly by my side, pulling me into his arms. My body aches, but I don't complain, I just need him close to me. His solid form relaxes into me, and I hold on as if my life depends on it. I never want to leave his side again. I can only imagine what it would have done to Henri if I'd died.

I want to apologise to Henri for not listening to him, but he won't have it. I close my eyes again, feeling safe in Henri's strong arms. I was so reckless to go off alone with Sam. I knew he was angry, and I should have stopped to think before I went off after him. I shudder picturing what would have happened if Henri hadn't found me. "That's enough. Alexis," Henri chides, "you are here with me and safe now. For now, that's all that matters."

I close my eyes drifting back off to sleep.

When I come to again, I am alone with my one true love, we have a future I could never have imagined: I almost ruined that and for what? To stroke the ego of a deluded man?

Stupid. That's what I was, stupid.

Henri is quiet when I ask what happened to Sam. "Your Dad dealt with him," he says, clearly not wanting to discuss my attacker. I let it drop for now, I can see how hard he is trying to hold it together.

I slip back into my thoughts, hating myself for causing Henri so much pain. Still, I can't help wondering how my dear sweet friend turned into the monster, who just tried to kill me. It's then that I remember the Goddess and what she told me. How I used my power to untie the spell Lilith had cast. I can feel Henri in my thoughts, but he doesn't make a comment.

He sits in the chair beside my bed, holding my hand tightly.

"What were you thinking, Alexis?" he asks suddenly, catching me off guard.

"I... I don't know," I say defeated, I have been asking myself the same question over and over. "He was my friend Henri, I just wanted to make it right. Something must have happened to him while he was away. That was not the Sam I knew..." my words fade away; I can hear myself making excuses for Sam's behaviour. What I really need to say is, "Henri, I am so, so sorry."

"You have nothing to be sorry for, my love. I understand why you wanted to make things right," Henri sighs. I am too tired to argue. "There is just one thing I need to know, Alexis. Why didn't you use your power? You have so much crackling beneath your skin, you could easily have overpowered them." Shame washes over me and tears begin to fall.

"At first it just wouldn't come, by the time I was able to call upon it, I was too weak to do much. Then in the cave they kept me in, Lilith used a spell of some kind to block it. I lost consciousness at one point, and I saw the Goddess. She told me she needed me to come back, that I was needed to do something. She said, I needed to use my power to save myself. I needed to call on the threads of Lilith's spell to undo it. I did that, but by that point there was nothing left in me to fight. I just wanted to go back to the Goddess's temple – it was so peaceful there and there was no pain.

"When Sam brought me into the open, I felt it again but reaching my mind out to you was all I could manage. Even that was too much, and I lost my grip on consciousness.

"Lilith, she tried to get into my mind, to steal my powers. When I wouldn't let her, she…"

"I know, my love. I saw the marks."

"She had a knife, Henri. She called it a witch's blade. She said if she killed me with it, it would transfer my power to her. I think that is why she is so powerful. She kills spinners with that knife." My confession comes out in bursts, and I am sobbing when I finish. I can't bring myself to voice my other thoughts. *I think that knife was used to kill my parents.*

"It's been a long night; you need to rest." I think he is getting up to leave and I start to worry. I don't want to be away from him, now or ever again.

"Stay, please," I say quietly, feeling weak for needing his comfort. I should let him go and get some rest. His night must have been like torture too.

"I wasn't planning on leaving," he says sliding into bed behind me. The feeling of Henri's body pressed against mine helps me to relax, better than any healing ever could and I quickly fall asleep.

When I wake again Henri is already up. I can hear him talking to Mum just outside the room. It sounds like they are having a disagreement of some sort. They both go quiet, sensing me wake. "What are you arguing about?" I ask as they enter the room.

"We aren't arguing my love," Henri says. I look to Mum and her face tells a different story.

"Henri, your mate is the strongest person I know, you are a fool if you think you can keep anything from her," Mum says, calling Henri out on his lie.

I look to Mum for an answer, as it isn't forthcoming from my mate. "Lexi honey, we went to Sam's house last night when we were searching for you, it seems he wasn't acting alone. There were artefacts, potions, all manner of *things* that suggest a witch has been living there. I think he was working with Lilith."

Henri looks like he wishes he could set Mum on fire. I can feel his anger. I already knew they were working together, so I am not surprised by the comment. That isn't what Henri didn't want me to know. So, there is only one thing they could mean. "Was he under a spell?" I ask not knowing whether that would be better or worse. It would make sense; he was so different to the man I knew.

"We don't know, sweetheart."

Not for the first time, my world seems to fall apart around me.

I know my sweet friend would never do that to me, she must have done something. That *witch* turned him against me and now he is as good as dead. There is no way Henri is going to let him live. Kidnapping and torturing the mate of a crown prince is treason. It might not be Henri's hand that ends his life, but Sam won't survive this.

He has always been there for me, and yes, our relationship has been strained since he told me his true feelings. I always thought there would be a way back though. We started the hospital together and worked side by side for countless years. Even if our friendship was never the same, I'd hoped he could find love again and have a life.

This is my fault. I should never have left the party to talk to him alone. A sob escapes my mouth, followed by uncontrollable tears. Henri wraps his strong arms around me, holding me close. I am vaguely aware of Mum leaving the room, giving us space. We sit like this for hours as wave after wave of sorrow wash over me. The storm outside reflecting the storm inside me. I do as the Goddess said and surrender, letting go of my need for control.

"I am so sorry Alexis," Henri says eventually, I can hear the pain in his voice.

I pull back so that I can look in his eyes, I need him to know that nothing has changed between us, and I that he is in no way, responsible for what happened.

The responsibility for that rests solely on my shoulders. "You have nothing to be sorry for. I am sorry, for not listening to you. Your intuition told you Sam couldn't be trusted, and I ignored that.

"When mine told me what Lilith was, you never questioned me. I should have afforded you the same respect. I betrayed your trust, and I am truly sorry."

Tears start to fall anew, when I remember we should be celebrating the happiest day of our lives right now. "No more tears now, my love," Henri says gently.

"We should be getting married today," I sob.

A soft chuckle escapes his lips, I feel his amusement. "After everything you have been through, that is what's bothering you most?" he asks. "Stop worrying, it's all been taken care of. We will have the ceremony when you are feeling better."

"But we are leaving in two days," I say feeling confused.

"Ed has spoken to the palace. Considering last night's *events,* we will stay for a while longer. When you are up to it, our wedding will take place here in Serenity before we leave, as planned."

"Thank you," I squeak as new tears fall from my eyes.

There are no words that can ever express how much I love the man holding me.

Henri

Rage. It burns through my veins like fire.

Almost killing the vile creature, who dared to lay his filthy hands on my mate, was not enough to sate the monster inside me. It needs blood to be spilt - a lot of it, preferably slowly and painfully.

I feel it lingering just below the surface. Closer to taking over, than it has been for so long. A war is raging inside of me, and the monster is winning.

The only thing that stopped me tearing him limb from limb was the presence of Alexis. She is my anchor and reason for being. But even as I hold her in my arms, I know the only way to quell the burn, is to put an end to him and the ring master.

Lilith.

Even thinking her name leaves a bitter taste in my mouth.

When the monster is so close to the surface, I am grateful, Alexis doesn't have full access to my mind.

Yet.

She hasn't figured out that I am holding back.

Hiding part of myself, from my mate feels like a betrayal. But the alternative - letting Alexis see the darkness festering inside me - is not an option, she would hate me for sure.

I am selfish. I don't deserve the sweet creature in my arms, I know that. But I won't give her up.

Alexis' sobs died down eventually and she's been quietly coming to terms, with everything that's happened for a while. I can feel her resolve strengthening. We want the same thing but for different reasons.

I need to put an end to Sam and Lilith as they represent a risk to Alexis. My fierce mate, however, wants revenge on Lilith for her lost friend - the latest in a long line of losses the Endor clan have inflicted on her.

A small knock on the door brings us both out of our thoughts. "Come in," Alexis answers and Ginny pushes the door open - hand over her eyes.

Alexis laughs out loud, and it is the most wonderful sound, I have ever heard. I am starting to see why Ginny is the perfect match for Ed, her little joke, has broken any potential tension, before she is even in the room.

Ginny's smile fades quickly when she takes in my mate's appearance. It's obvious she's been crying and no matter how good the healers are, they can't take away the emotional pain, that's been inflicted on her.

"I need to go and speak with Ed, my love. I won't be gone long, then we can go home," I say, kissing her hair softly. I can see that she doesn't want me to leave, but I need to let some of the rage out before I lose control completely.

I move away quickly before I change my mind. I can't bear the thought of Alexis being out of my sight, but she is as safe as she can be, with Ginny in the room and her parents close by.

Closing the door, I mind link Ed. *"Meet me by Alexis' cabin."*

"OK," Ed replies. He doesn't ask any questions; he can sense my mood.

In less than five minutes I reach Alexis' small cabin on the beach. Ed is already there waiting for me, but this isn't the destination I had in mind.

We quickly trek through the forest and in less time than expected, emerge at Alexis' cove. The place where the Goddess told me Alexis was still alive. It's just as breath-taking as the first time Alexis showed it me. Even more so maybe. Alexis may think the Goddess has abandoned us, but she is still there. She came to Alexis's aid when she really needed it.

I thank the Goddess for allowing me to find her cove again.

"Wow, what is this place? I can feel the magic," Ed says.

"I'm not sure, Alexis brought me a few weeks ago. She comes here when she needs to be alone. I don't think anyone else on the island knows about it. I felt the Goddess here, when I was searching for Alexis last night. She promised me Alexis would be fine."

"I see, and we're here because you are close to losing it and don't want anyone on the island to know." It's not a question, Ed has been privy to my thoughts for longer than I care to remember. He can feel how close, the monster is to the surface.

Its anger burns in my veins, itching to be free. I hold onto the reins a little tighter, remembering how close I had come to tearing Samuel limb from limb, with Alexis's friends and family there to bear witness earlier on. I will not lose control like that again.

A grin suddenly appears on Ed's face. "I think, I know a way to help."

"No," I say, following his train of thought. He doesn't listen and before I can stop or block him, Ed throws a punch in my face, breaking my nose, then runs into the trees. "Come on Hen, being mated is making you lose your edge." My eyes water as blood begins to pour from my nose.

The arse knows exactly how to set the monster off. Red clouds my vision and I take off after him into the forest. It's not difficult to find him and he does nothing to hide his location from me.

I catch up to him in no time and we stand off, circling each other. The smug look on Ed's face makes me want to rip his head off. He smirks at the blood still oozing from my nose. "You just going to stand there with that stupid look on your face, *prince.*" I growl in response but make no move towards my best friend.

I simply wait, knowing I have to catch him off guard. He isn't as strong as me, but he is fast.

Ed breaks the stand-off first, running back to the beach. I know chasing him is pointless. If I take off after him again, we will spend all day chasing each other round the cove like two children. Strategy is needed here.

I climb a tree as quietly as possible and make my way through the canopy back to the beach. The sun is high in the sky, reflecting on the crystal-clear ocean. In other circumstances, I could sit here all day, basking in the sun, letting all my worries fade away. However, the need to get the rage out quickly and get back to Alexis, tears me away from the stunning view and I survey the ground. Ed is leaning nonchalantly against a tree, a few feet away from the one I'm hiding in.

I make my move, following instinct alone. I jump to the ground landing in the exact spot Ed was standing moments earlier. His laughter echoes around the cove. "Is that the best you've got? And here I was thinking you were a warrior. You're getting sloppy in your old age *prince.*" Ed shouts, knowing he is getting to me. I growl in frustration again. This makes him laugh harder.

"Something wrong Hen?" he asks without a care in the world.

"I will catch you Ed and when I do, I will kill you, you smug bastard." This actually makes him snort with laughter, but it has the desired effect. I climb another tree and use his distraction to get close. I jump and this time land right beside him, catching him off guard. I throw a punch of my own, hitting him square on the cheek. I hear a satisfying crack beneath my knuckles. That will teach him for breaking my nose and egging the monster on.

Ed recovers quickly and before I know it, we are wrestling on the sand. One moment I seem to have the upper hand, the next Ed - he learned long ago, how to use speed to his advantage, and he is a fearsome warrior. We each land more punches, beating each other as if we are enemies. Blood sprays over the white sand, pouring from wounds we inflict on each other. Ed's nose is now broken along with mine and bruises have blossomed beneath his eyes.

His plan is working though and before long, the rage subsides, somewhat. I feel the monster pull back, no longer fighting for control - for now at least. I have Ed pinned and he taps my leg twice, letting me know he is admitting defeat.

I let go pulling him up and hugging him tightly. For a while, we sit beside each other in the sand, watching the ocean. He absently rubs his broken cheek bone, wincing occasionally. I smile sardonically. I do feel slightly guilty for turning his face into a punch bag, but he had it coming. Who deliberately pisses off a monster?

"Thank you," I say earnestly.

"What I am here for, if not to be your stress relief?" Ed jokes. I shake my head at his awful joke. "No, seriously though, you're welcome."

We are quiet again for a moment, each lost in thought.

"You will have to tell her eventually, you know," Ed says, breaking the silence. "Alexis isn't stupid, she will figure out what you are hiding from her."

After everything we have been through already, I know Ed is right. There should be no more secrets between Alexis and me.

"I know," I sigh. "But how do you tell your mate, the other half of your soul that, you are cursed to share your body with a monster? A blood thirsty killer?"

"Hen, she has already been through so much and survived. Whatever you think her reaction will be, I can practically guarantee, you are wrong. Alexis won't care, she will understand but the longer you wait to tell her, angrier she will be when she learns the truth. Do you honestly want her to be angry with you? Her anger creates storms. I'm not sure you want that directed towards you," he says, only half joking.

Ed has a point though. Between the conjuring of storms and the fire at her fingertips, I know I never want to be on the receiving end of Alexis' wrath.

Chapter 14

Alexis

I am more shaken than I want to admit. It was so easy for Lilith to use someone I cared for, against me. I can feel Henri's fury, so I've been working hard to conceal my fear. I know it would only add fuel to the fire.

With one look at Ginny, all my carefully constructed walls, come crashing down. I let it all out as soon as I know Henri can't hear. Ginny sits in the chair by my bed and listens quietly, as I say the things I couldn't say to Henri.

"He almost raped and killed me," I say. "I just don't understand how, the Sam I knew could do something like that, Gin. He was always so sweet and considerate. How did the witch poison him so quickly?"

"I don't know Lex. There is no way Sam would have done it alone, but there must have been a seed of something there." I know she is right but that only makes me feel worse.

"It is my fault," I say matter of fact. "Lilith wouldn't have gone near him if it wasn't for me. Henri wouldn't want to kill him if I'd just listened and stayed away." Fresh tears spring to my eyes at this thought.

"How can you blame yourself?" Ginny asks. I look at her sceptically, does she really need to ask that question? She sighs and starts again.

"Lex, you are the kindest, most caring person, I have ever met. You did what you thought was right. You cannot take responsibility for the actions of others. Have you stopped to wonder, how Lilith got to Sam?" I hadn't, it had never occurred to me actually.

"No."

"Ed did. He asked around and Hugh told him that he'd seen Lilith and Sam looking very cosy before she suddenly disappeared. He saw them together, more than once.

"I know you don't want to think badly of Sam, but he wasn't the saint you make him out to be. He always knew what your feelings were and yet he pushed for more repeatedly. It was cruel of him to do that to you. Your boundaries were there to see. He chose to ignore them. Sam was always selfish; you just chose not to see it. He and Lilith were working together, and you know it.

Her words knock the wind out of me. It's just so hard to believe Sam is capable of hurting me like that - the names he called me.

I feel sick thinking about it. The way he looked at me. His hard cold touches. My skin crawls at the thought. I feel like I will never be clean again.

"Maybe you're right," I concede.

We are quiet for a while. I am trying hard to think about anything other than the fact that I was almost raped and murdered last night and what might have happened if Henri hadn't reached me in time. My body, mind, and soul are his and his alone. I would never have forgiven myself if Sam had taken my body. The thought of anyone other than Henri touching me in that way is unbearable.

We sense Henri and Ed approaching, just before we hear them. They are laughing at some joke, but I don't have the energy to poke around Henri's head to find out what it is. I manage to plaster a smile on my face before the door opens but it drops again as I take in the sight of my mate and his friend. "Oh, my Goddess, what happened to you two?"

Henri is more dishevelled than I have ever seen him. His hair is a mess, there is dirt on his clothes and face, but most worryingly, is the dry blood on his face and down his shirt. His nose appears to be broken and he is supporting two back eyes.

Ed doesn't look much better. From the look of his cheek, I would say that is also broken.

Henri senses my panic and rushes to my side. "We are fine my love," he says reassuringly.

"You don't look fine," I say. "You both look like you have been attacked." My imagination goes into overdrive, attempting to work out what could have happened to them. Were they attacked by Lilith? It's the only realistic option my brain can think of, but their laughter confuses me. There is no way Henri would be laughing if that had happened.

"I was," says Henri laughing, but stops quickly to explain when he sees my darkening face. "I am sorry we worried you, my love. I needed to let off some steam. Ed volunteered to help." I shake my head, finally understanding what happened.

"You were sparring?" I ask. Henri nods.

"Bloody idiots, the pair of you," says Ginny despairingly.

"But I'm your idiot," replies Ed, wrapping her up in his arms. Ginny laughs giddily.

"Come here," I tell Henri. He comes to sit beside me on the bed, and I place my hands over his face, to heal the brake. I have never felt the urge to heal someone before, but my palms prickle with the need to fix Henri's face.

He pushes them away. "No, my love, you need to rest. I will have someone else do it."

"Like holy hell you will," I say sternly. "If anyone is going to heal you, it will be me."

"Are you sure you can?" he asks.

"I am," I say with a nod. I can't explain how I know, but I do. My power is waking up, I can feel it rushing through my veins.

Placing my hands over Henri's broken nose, I pull the power to my fingertips. A white light emits from them and the bruises under Henri's eyes fade. His nose snaps back into place with a thwack. "Ouch," he says with the biggest smile on his face. Unfortunately, I can do nothing with the blood on his shirt and face. The shirt will need to be thrown and Henri will have to clean his face the old-fashioned way.

Once I finish with Henri, I turn my attention to Ed. He and Ginny are no longer there, I didn't notice them leave.

"You did it," he says. "How did you know…"

"The Goddess," I reply simply. His expression darkens.

"What about the Goddess, Alexis?" I sigh. I knew I'd have to tell him everything eventually but, I was hoping to keep the full conversation with her to myself for a while at least.

"When she came to me when I was in the cave. She told me to live, I needed to accept my power – all of it, my mother and my father's. I did. I wanted to live Henri. I wanted to come back to you."

"So, you *are* a healer, like your father?" He asks.

"Not exactly," I say. He looks at me questioningly. "I see all the threads, Henri."

"All of them?" he asks.

"Yes."

"Wow."

"I spoke to her too," Henri confesses. "I went looking for you at the cove. When I got there, I prayed to her, begging her to help me find you. She told me you were hurt but alive."

I don't say anything. She might have helped us today, but I am not ready to forgive two centuries of abandonment.

His strong arms wrap around me, pulling me close. "Let's get you home."

"I thought you'd never ask," I reply, sleepily.

I protest as Henri swoops down to pick me up. "For the love of Goddess woman, let me take care of you." I let it go, too tired to fight him, already knowing I won't win.

Back at the cabin, Henri sits me gently on the bed we have shared for the last few weeks and heads to the bathroom. I hear him turn on the shower before returning and scooping me back up.

Every fibre of my being screams to be put down, but I resist, allowing the man I love take care of me. I sense his need for this is greater than my desire to be independent.

We enter the small bathroom, which is already filling with steam. Henri sets me down gently on the vanity unit, looking me over to make sure I am truly healed. I take a look in the mirror, to see the damage for myself. The physical marks are all gone, but it will take more than a spinner's healing to fix what Sam broke inside me.

Satisfied by the lack of physical injuries, Henri begins peeling me out of my pyjamas. His touches are gentle and hesitant, like he is afraid I will break, or that his touches will remind me of what happened.

But the feeling of his warm fingers on my skin erases all memories of Sam. I sigh, letting him know with my thoughts, how much I need him right now. I sit patiently as he removes his own clothes before lifting me into the shower. He places me down under the running water and it feels like heaven.

I tip my face up to the water closing my eyes as the tension leaves my body. Henri steps in behind me and I lean back against his muscular body. His hands trace up my arms leaving fire in their wake.

I reach back to touch him, and he stills. "*No, it's OK. You don't have to,*" he thinks.

"I need to," I say aloud. "I need to know I'm still only yours." He remains silent, fishing in my mind until he is satisfied that I truly mean what I say. Once he has found his conformation, he continues his exploration of my body.

Featherlight touches, set my veins on fire, completely erasing the dirty feeling left there by Sam's cold hands. Henri turns me to face him and plants soft kisses down my jaw, I know he is trying to erase the mental scar left by Sam's knife. I reach up, lacing my fingers into his hair, pulling him until his lips meet mine.

The contact is not enough, though. The need to be closer to him overpowers me as I push my body against his. "Henri, I need you," I say again. He tries to pull away shaking his head.

"No, my love you need to rest, after everything you have been through at his hands..."

I almost scream, feeling the fire ready at my fingertips again. How can one man be so infuriating, why can't he see that rest is not what I need?

"No, Henri, I do not need to rest. I need you to take control of my body, the way only you can. I need to know that nothing has changed between us. I need to feel you inside me. I need to feel whole.

"What Sam did, trying to take me without even a thought for what I wanted – my skin crawls just thinking about it. I don't want that to be the last time someone touched me. I need you to be the last – the only person to ever – touch me in that way. Please, Henri. I need this. I need it now."

Henri

I stand motionless, taking in my mate's words and listening to the words she didn't say out loud. *I need you to make me forget.* I wasn't there to protect her when that *rat* laid his grubby hands on her, but I will spend the rest of my life trying to make up for that.

"Turn around, hands above your head," I say. Her eyes sparkle and delight dances across her face, before obeying my order. I move close behind her. I will never bind her hands again; it will forever remind me of finding her bound at the mercy of Samuel and Lilith.

She was made to be worshiped, not tied down. Still, I know how much she enjoys me pushing her boundaries and there is more than one way to achieve that.

Her breasts rise as her hands go overhead and it takes all my strength not to reach around and make her come with her pebbled peaks. "Against the wall," I whisper in her ear. A shudder runs down her spine as she obeys again. "Good girl. Keep your hands there, Alexis. If you move them, I will punish you."

"Hmm, maybe I should move them," she thinks, anticipating the flat of my hand on her perfect, round backside.

I chuckle, "There is more than one way to punish you and today is all about pleasure, no pain.

"I could keep you here all night, on the edge of ecstasy, but never allowing you to fall over that edge," I say darkly sliding my hand between her soaking folds. "Oh, so responsive, my love. You mustn't come until I give you permission."

I hear a sharp intake of breath and she turns her face to look at me. "Henri, I..." She can't bring herself to finish the sentence, but I hear it in her unguarded thoughts anyway.

"I know you can do it, Alexis."

She moans in response as I push her feet apart with my own and begin to circle her clit. Her legs almost buckle, and I wrap my free arm around her waist, holding her firmly in place. The moaning increases as her legs try to snap shut. I tsk in her ear and she opens them again. "Good girl," I breathe, moving my hand lower, finding her soaking entrance.

I slide three fingers inside, finding the magic spot quickly and rubbing the pad of my thumb over her swollen clit. Alexis begins to lose control rocking herself wantonly over my hand, attempting to increase the friction. "Henri, I'm so close, I can't hold it much longer," she moans.

"You may come," I say, and she lets go, her juices flowing freely over my hand. As much as I want to tell her she can't and keep this game up all night, I can't deny my queen anything today – there will be time for that later.

I give her a minute to catch her breath, before turning her to face me and lifting her into my arms. Long legs wrap around my waist as I position my throbbing cock at her entrance, sliding into the hilt. I still, letting her adjust to all of me inside her. Alexis wiggles her hips, letting me know what she wants. I lift her hips and allow her to fall back onto me. A moan escapes her lips, as her head tips back.

We move together – for seconds, minutes, hours? I am not sure; I just get lost in the feeling of being inextricably attached the woman in my arms and listening to her soft moans. The pleasure mounts as her walls begin to tighten around me. Her moans increase and I know I can't hold out much longer.

"Look at me," I command. Alexis opens her eyes, always so keen to follow orders - while I'm buried inside her at least. The look on her face is enough to drive me over the edge, as her walls begin to contract around me, milking every last drop of my own arousal.

We stay this way, joined together as the water cascades over our bodies, until our breathing slows. The bond healing the wounds inflicted on both of us over the last 24 hours.

"You are my world, Alexis. If anything had happened to you..."

"Hush now, no more of that. We are still here, together and for this moment that's all that matters," she responds, quelling the monster that has been too close to the surface since Samuel took her.

We both know that we have won this battle, but the war is far from over. When the time comes, we will face out enemies together. Alexis is right though, for now we should enjoy the remainder of our time on this paradise island.

I place her back on the ground and reach for the soap, lathering it up in my hands. They slide effortlessly over her silken skin and as they slip over her spinner's marks, I gasp as I feel the heat radiating from them.

Alexis looks at me shyly and follows my gaze to her stomach which is glowing under my touch. Ethereal light radiates from her, making her appear more deity than spinner. It's breath-taking.

White light emitted from her hands when she healed me - I've seen this before from the healers at court. She can wield fire, although I've never seen her use that power, I have felt it humming beneath her skin when she loses her temper. She can also control the elements – anger and sadness create epic down pours and impressive storms.

It hasn't slipped my notice that, she didn't use her power to protect herself when Samuel first attacked her last night, though I know she has plenty to use.

This though, is different from either of those things. It is power, but not one I've ever seen in a spinner, or any other earthly being for that matter. I try to hide my thoughts, not wishing to put anything else on her today. From the look on her face, I don't think it worked. I quirk up an eyebrow. "Do they do that often?" I ask.

"No," she shakes her head, nervously. "Only once or twice, and only then since you arrived," she answers, blushing slightly.

"Interesting, I felt mine tingle the day I arrived, I'd forgotten about it until now. I've never heard of spinners' marks doing that before though," I incline my head to where the other worldly light is still radiating from her.

"Oh, I thought it must be the mating bond," she says, confusion marring her beautiful face.

"I don't think so," I say hesitantly. I feel her mind go into overdrive as she tries to work out what this could mean. "We will figure it out when we get back to Asgard," I say trying to reassure her. "Stop over thinking it, my love."

She attempts to do as I ask, but I can still hear her worrying as I turn off the water and reach for a towel, to wrap her in. She heads to her closet to find clothes and leaves me to my own thoughts.

I am not worried. Intrigued, yes, but worried, definitely not. Our marks are a physical representation of our powers. Whatever is happening can't be anything bad.

Still, I thought I knew all there was to know about being a spinner and our power, I find it unnerving to think there is something I missed.

I've spent centuries studying our history, learning from our elders and seers. Either I overlooked something, or they withheld something from me. I'm not sure which is preferable.

Nevertheless, if Alexis and I are to overcome our enemies and rule together, I need to find out what this means. Another conversation with the Goddess may be required to get to the bottom of this one.

Just maybe though, this could help us.

Alexis

I wake early to find Henri watching me sleep – again. "Good morning," I say, a smile creeping onto my face.

"Good morning, my queen," he replies, with a dazzling smile of his own, lighting his handsome features.

"Were you watching me sleep?" I ask.

"I was," he answers, completely unabashed. "You make the sweetest little noises in your sleep." I blush right to the roots of my hair and attempt to cover my face with the sheet. "There is nothing to be embarrassed about, my love."

"That's easy for you to say," I pout, playfully hitting his chest.

His eyes darken and I realise my mistake. "Is it nice to hit me, Alexis?" Henri asks, there is a threat in his tone that I feel between my legs.

"No," I breathe. Before I know what is happening, Henri is hovering over me. He doesn't physically pin me, but the look on his face is daring me to move. I don't.

"No, it isn't." His eyes dance with lust. "Whatever am I going to do with you, my love?"

"Whatever you want. I am yours body, mind, and soul."

I wake once more to the sound of Henri opening cupboards in the kitchen. My limbs are deliciously sore, I love the feeling of knowing the reason for that, is currently making me tea. *Does life get any better than this*, I wonder.

"I'm only just getting started, my love," Henri calls from the kitchen. I don't think I will ever get used to him being inside my head.

Throwing back the covers, I pull on the closest item of clothing I can find - Henri's shirt - and pad into the kitchen where my prince hands me a steaming cup of English Breakfast Tea. I breathe in the intoxicating aroma of the tea, mixed with Henri.

He is watching me from the other side of the small space. "What?" I ask. A wide grin stretches across his face.

"You wearing my shirt, with your hair all mussed up like that, should be illegal." I reach up to try and flatten my wild locks. It's no use, only the shower can save it now.

Henri stalks towards me. "Stop," he says. "What I meant, Alexis, is you look sexy as hell and if you keep wearing that, we will never make it out of the bedroom."

"Oh," is all I can say. Henri leans down to kiss me but stops hearing a knock on the door. I groan in frustration and head to change, while my prince answers it. Finding some of my own clothes, I throw them on and pile my hair up on the top of my head.

I hear raised voices coming from the porch, but they go quiet as I walk out. Ginny and Ed are stood with Henri and the three of them look to be arguing. "What's wrong?" I ask, panic hitting me square in the face.

Henri reaches out to soothe me. "Nothing, my love," he says. I don't believe him and search his mind for the answer but come up short. He is hiding something from me.

"Ed and I are just nipping into town; Ginny will stay with you for a while." I feel like a child being managed, passed from one guardian to another. "You do know, I have lived here alone for quite a while now, you don't need to coddle me."

"We know that my love," Henri says. I narrow my eyes at his soothing tone, he is doing his best to keep something from me. I try to fish inside his thoughts, but he has sealed them off.

"No one is coddling you, Lex," Ginny says, "I just wanted to spend the afternoon with you." She looks pointedly at Henri before continuing, "without mother hen flapping around." She is lying, I can see it in the set of her mouth but stop arguing. None of them are going to budge.

Henri plants gentle kisses across my jaw, then leans his head on mine, breathing in deeply. I know he is taking in my scent. He turns away from me and heads up the beach towards the dirt track leading into town. He and Ed are putting on a good show. If I didn't know Henri better, it would look like they were just off for a walk together. However, I do know Henri and the tension in his shoulders, give him away. He is up to something, and I have a feeling I won't like what that something is.

I sit on the step trying to work out what's going on. I can't stand secrets and lies; they eat away at me. I know I am a hypocrite, given how long I kept my own secrets, but this is different.

Ginny goes to make tea, then comes to sit beside me. Her anger has abated now the men are out of sight and I lean on her for comfort lost in thought. The last few weeks have turned both of our simple lives on their heads. We are both facing the reality of leaving our home, heading towards a world we have kept out, for a long time.

It is hard for me, but it must also be hard for my best friend. It will take time for both of us to adjust to a segregated world again. So many people will be suspicious of us. Those at court especially. The ambassadors have spent long enough here now to appreciate our way of life, but for most, what we do here is considered odd at best.

As much as Henri wants to go back to Asgard and change so many things, we both know that is a huge challenge and it can't be done overnight. I close my eyes and try to stop dwelling on the future, speculation won't change anything.

My mind drifts to Lilith, wondering where she might be now. She could be hidden in the forest watching me at this very moment. It is so easy when Henri is with me to forget about what happened. To feel safe. But once he is gone, memories of the attack creep back in, seizing my chest.

It's more than the attack itself. I was prepared to die for Henri two centuries ago. What scares me most is, the thought of what my death would have done to him now. If Sam and Lilith had succeeded in killing me, they would have destroyed Henri at the same time.

All these years, I worried the curse would be the end of him, but now I see even without it, any pain I feel will hurt him too.

I am dragged from my thoughts as anger, red and hot shoots through me, I've never felt anything like it. It doesn't belong to me; it belongs to my mate. The world turns red for a moment and the need to kill something fills my being. Suddenly I realise where Henri and Ed went. I look at Ginny and her face tells me all I need to know.

"Gin, where have they gone."

Chapter 15

Alexis

Y ou already know, Lex. I tried to stop them but..." She looks like she wants to cry. She doesn't need to finish. There is no reasoning with Henri when he sets his mind to something. He has gone to see Sam.

"Ed told me he had to go with Henri to stop him if he goes too far." Ginny closes her eyes and when she opens them again, they are brimming with tears. I know how she feels, she is terrified for her mate.

Without so much as a word, I stand, going inside to hunt down some shoes.

I am halfway up the beach when Ginny catches up with me. "Where are you going?" she asks panic-stricken.

"Where do you think?" I answer never breaking stride. She grabs onto my arm, bringing my mad march to a halt.

"No, Alexis, we need to stay away." And here I was thinking I'd gone mad. "Ed told me when Henri really loses it, he is someone else, he would never want you to see him that way."

"Right now, Ginny, I don't care what he wants me to see. Henri is my mate, and we fight our battles together. I know the darkness that lives in him, but I will not allow him to commit murder for me."

I turn to walk again, and this time she doesn't try to stop me. Instead, she pulls out her phone and asks the person on the other end to meet us on the council steps. I don't stop to enquire to whom she is speaking.

The closer I get to Henri, the more I feel his rage. It is all consuming, threatening to choke me. How has he lived with this for so long. Within minutes I feel like I'm losing it, and Henri has lived with this for a century. It's Mum waiting when we arrive, a grim look on her face. "Take me to them," I say without a hint of the emotion I'm really feeling.

She leads the way, taking us into the basement of the building. If I didn't know we were still on the island I would have thought, we were somewhere else entirely. Hell maybe. It is so dark I can barely see my own hand in front of my face. The smell is overpowering. Damp and decay and something I can't put my finger on. I've never been down before. The need has never arisen. To think that this even exists here is crazy. Why would it be needed?

It must be Dad's doing. He seems like he is the world's gentlest vampire, but I know he has lived through more wars than I could ever imagine. This is his tiny insurance policy. He had the foresight to think we might need it one day. Two days ago, that moment finally arrived. I sense the magic in the air too. It is charmed to prevent escape. As the thought occurs to me, the threads of the spell spring to life reaching for me. It was created by a witch not a spinner and I could easily unbind it if I wanted to. I push them away mentally and the colours fade from view.

There is just one cell, and before I even see him, I know that is where I will find Henri.

"We can do this the easy way or the hard way, Samuel," I hear him say as we near the cell. "Either way, I will kill you for what you did, you just get to choose how slow and painful it is." Vomit rises in my throat at my mate's words. It is him, but not. The voice I hear carries a sinister edge; I've never heard from Henri before.

"Rot in hell," Sam replies.

"Wrong answer, *rat*. You meant a great deal to my mate, and I know your suffering would hurt her deeply. As much as it would give me a great deal of pleasure to torture you for hours like you did her. I have no desire to cause her any more pain. So, this is your last chance. Where is Lilith? What is she planning and what was your part in it?"

"Fuck you, *prince*," Sam sneers. I feel the exact nanosecond Henri's last thread of restraint snaps. Whether he wants to torture Sam for hours or not, he won't be able to hold back that long. I take as deep a breath, as the stagnant air will allow and turn the corner.

Ed stands close to the iron bars, looking on as Henri repeatedly punches a bloodied heap, that I know to be Sam, in the centre of the room. Ed hears our approach and turns to face me. We lock eyes for a moment before he looks beyond me to Ginny. His face goes from wary to furious in an instant, he never wanted his mate anywhere near this place. He doesn't say a word to either of us though.

Henri is too far gone to hear us approach. I hesitantly step inside the cell. Ed puts out an arm to stop me and flames erupt from my fingers, making him jump back. I stand close to the door and make my presence known. "Henri. One word is all it takes, and he turns his attention to me. He looks at me through cold eyes as black as night.

"Alexis leave, now," he says in a strange voice. Rage has taken over and the man before me is no longer my prince. I feel the order in his words, but it has no effect. I don't even have to fight to push it away, it bounces off me and I raise my eyebrows, looking Henri in his cold black eyes.

"No," I say defiantly. "Stop this now." It is my turn to make a command. I already know it won't stick for long, I just hope it will give Henri a moment to see what he is doing. He closes his eyes for a second, shaking his head like he is trying to dislodge something. When he opens them again, my mate is back in control. My plan worked.

Henri doesn't speak to me as runs past and bolts from the room.

I turn to follow Henri, but Ed blocks me. His hands are raised, clearly worried I'll set him alight, if he touches me again. "Give him some time, Alexis," he says. I nod my agreement and he looks relieved.

My attention turns to the groaning heap in the centre of the room. "Everyone out," I say. No one moves. "Now," I roar, putting the command back in my voice. The only people it has any real effect on are the spinners, Gin, and Ed but everyone else listens, nonetheless.

They begin to file out and leave me to face my attacker. The fear that has been present since I was kidnapped has left me and I stand tall looking at the dirty dishevelled heap on the ground.

I hadn't noticed Dad before, but he stands firm, clearly having no intention of leaving me alone with Sam. "You can stay, Alexis but I am staying with you. Henri would never forgive us, if we left you alone with him, again."

"OK, but everyone else leaves." Now my voice doesn't sound like my own. It is haunting and otherworldly as my power hums at my fingertips. The threads around me illuminate ready to do my bidding.

Dad turns his attention to the rest of the group and indicates for them to go. I pull a thread that is drawing towards me, and the iron bar door slams shut behind them.

That's new. I think to myself, momentarily distracted.

Once I'm sure the three of us are alone, I approach Sam. He is almost unrecognisable - he resembles someone in anaphylactic shock, with eyes so swollen he can barely open them. The rest of him doesn't look much better. I briefly wonder if that's what I looked like when he attacked me.

Even through my anger towards the man at my feet, my hands burn with the desire to heal him. I refrain, he doesn't deserve my care.

Cold eyes open minutely, and he snarls at me. "Bitch," Sam spits. Dad comes forward, but I push him back against the wall with another thread. This is my fight. After all the things Sam called me, as he attempted to rape me, his choice of word has no effect.

"I won't apologise for my mate's actions, nor will I heal the wounds he has inflicted on you, Sam." He closes his eyes and sinks back to the floor.

"But, if you start talking, I will ensure you have a fair trial, and no one will lay a hand on you again."

"I have nothing to say."

I use yet another thread to raise Sam off the floor and leave him dangling in mid-air with blood dripping onto the floor, forming a puddle. Sam groans but continues to stare me down, defiantly. "Sam, please don't do this. You are the closest thing I have ever had to a brother. I don't want to see you suffer. Let me help you."

"I said it to your *prince,* and I will say it to you. Fuck you, *princess.*

I sigh resigned to the fact he has lost all humanity. I did wonder if any lingering feelings for me, might make him reconsider. Then again, if whatever Henri has done to him over the last hour didn't work, I don't suppose I ever stood a chance of convincing him.

"Have it your way, Sam. We leave for Asgard in two weeks. When we go, you will come and face trial there. If you think of something to say before then, send for me. It might just help to plead your case."

I turn and walk out of the room, leaving Sam behind. "Leave him as he is," I instruct the guard outside the cell. He looks at me confusion clear on his face. "He isn't to be healed," I say, making my wishes clear.

It isn't like me to be so cold, however he needs to suffer. Not for the pain he caused me, but for the pain he is causing my mate. A fierce need to protect those I love has settled over me. I feel like I could tear the world apart to keep them safe.

Henri

I sprint across the island, towards Alexis' cove. The monster is still too close to the surface to go home. I can't face Alexis yet. I am disgusted by myself. I lost control as soon as I saw that creature and now my mate has seen what that looks like. Will she ever look at me the same again.

I am so far gone; I don't even stop to enjoy the beauty and serenity of this place. I can feel the Goddess's presence here again but the peace that usually settles over me when I cross the rocks protecting the cove is nowhere to be seen. My vision has not yet returned to normal, red tainting the edges. I can feel the poison in my veins still. It leaves a bitter taste in my mouth, and I wipe my arm across my lips, in an attempt to rid myself of it.

"Why did you allow me to become this?" I ask the Goddess. What sort of deity allows her child to be taken by the darkness? "You knew she was alive, and you didn't stop me. Alexis is so pure. She deserves better than the monster I have become." I fall to my knees in the sand, no longer able to stand. The pain eating me alive. Why did my life have to be so difficult. Why me? I know I am pitiful. Feeling sorry for myself like this, but at this moment in time I am struggling to care. Alexis deserves a better mate and my people a better leader.

"You are many things my child, but a monster isn't one of them," the Goddess answers. I look around to find the source of the voice, but there is nothing to see. I am beginning to think I imagined it when the voice speaks to me again. "There is darkness in you, like everyone else, but there is also light.

"I am so very sorry you have suffered as you have, but it needed to happen, to give you and Alexis the strength to face what comes next," she says, voice fading away.

"What do you mean, face what comes next? Have we not already faced enough. What more do you want from us?"

"You will soon see, Henri prince of spinners. There will be dark days ahead. But always remember, your mate is a beacon of light. She holds the spark to lead you both through that darkness."

"What does that mean?" I ask again, frustration rising. "You ask too much of us. We might be spinners, but do we not deserve some peace and happiness?"

Why can't she just give me a straight answer. Can she not see how close to losing it I am? How close I have been since the day Alexis left me? I just get her back and then she is almost dragged away from me again.

"I see it all child." The Goddess answers my unspoken questions. "In time you will see why it needed to happen. You and your queen are destined to bring about a change that will ask more of you than you can imagine right now. The hardships you have both faced so far needed to happen to prepare you for what is to come next. All will become clear in time.

"As for your happiness young prince, you do deserve it, as do all living beings on earth. However, all spinners and you more than any other have my divine power in them and it is your responsibility to maintain the balance and ensure the happiness of other creatures.

"You have seen what is possible here, away from prying eyes. You and Alexis must now, show the rest of the world what you already know in your hearts."

I don't have the opportunity to question her further, with her final words, I feel the Goddess's presence leave and I am again alone on my hands and knees on the sand.

I am so tired of the responsibility placed on me. My life has and will never be my own. I have known this since I was a small child. That doesn't stop me from wanting to remain here with Alexis and live out our days quietly on this tiny patch of paradise.

I almost smile imagining the life we could have. Raising a child or two. Watching them play on the warm sand without a care in the world. Alexis could stay with her family and continue to run the hospital. For a moment, I forget that we are meant to take over the throne of Asgard, allowing my parents to step down and live out the rest of their lives in peace.

For just a moment, I allow myself to forget everything that went before and what might come next. I just allow my imagination to conjure up a perfectly normal happy life with my mate by myside.

Too soon though, I know it's time to give up the fantasy. Alexis and I have a job to do. However, before that, I must once more beg for my mate's forgiveness.

Alexis

Stepping out into the air, I take a deep breath enjoying the fresh smell of the forest. It is so at odds with the pungent stench down in the basement of the town hall. The midday sun blinds me momentarily and I blink trying to adjust to the brightness.

Ed has his arms wrapped around a sobbing Ginny; I feel a pang of remorse for bringing her with me - not that she would have let me come alone. The set of Ed's face tells me they have been arguing. Ed's priority has always been Henri, but now he has Ginny, his priorities are shifting. He never wanted her to see what she just did.

When I am feeling up to it, I will speak to Ed and try to reassure him I can manage Henri now. He needs time to get to know his mate. Right now, though, I just need to be alone. I have nothing left to give anyone. The stress of the last few days has finally caught up with me and I need to escape.

Mum approaches me, concern etched on her face. I hold up my hands to stop her hugging me. "I'm fine," I say. "I'm going home. I need some space." She drops her arms and lets me go. I know Henri isn't at home, I can feel he went to the Goddess' cove. He will come back when he is ready.

I slowly wander out of town finally alone with my thoughts. Why would Henri try and keep something like this from me? He promised there would be no more secrets. Did he think my ordeal with Sam and Lilith would break me? That I couldn't stand by his side.

I am many things, but a damsel in distress in need of protecting isn't one of them. I will soon be ruling by his side. Does he think I'm going to sit on the sidelines while he deals with our enemies? Again, I need to have a conversation with my mate, but that too can wait.

Back at the cabin I strip out of my clothes. The stench of the morning seems to have seeped through them into my pores. Wrapping a towel around me, I go straight to the sea. Depositing the towel over a low hanging branch, I walk straight in up to my waist, looking up to the sun, revelling in the feeling of the rays on my upturned face. A swim is just what I need to help process my thoughts and clear my mind.

The water is warm and soothing on my skin and the repetitive action of moving arms in time with legs, is almost meditative. I swim out far enough that my feet can no longer feel the sand beneath me, and I tread water, turning in a circle for a few moments. Closing my eyes, I breathe deep, allowing, my head to bob below the surface. I dive down as far as I can, knowing the world at the bottom of the ocean, will lift my mood.

I open my eyes expecting to see the water around me teeming with life as usual. Small creatures going about their business, blissfully unaware of the troubles facing those of us on dry land.

Instead, I am in my Gran's cosy sitting room.

Gran is sat by the fire with her back to me. She turns and her face lights up. "Alexis," she beams. "I was hoping to see you today."

"You were?" I ask. I haven't seen my Gran since I left Asgard, I didn't even know whether she was still alive. It seems odd that she would even think about seeing me. How did I get here? Have I apparated or is this a vision? I'm not a seer as far as I know, although I don't know much. It doesn't feel like a vision though. I can feel the firm wooden floor under my feet and the heat of the fire warming my skin.

"Yes, dear girl, I was. It is time."

"Time for what?" I wonder.

"Time to learn who you are and what you must do." She answers mystically.

"Mormor, what are you talking about? How did I get here? I was swimming off the coast of Serenity. It's so nice to see you, but I must get back," I say in a panic. If Henri returns to find me gone, he will think I have run away again. I can't do that to him.

"You always did worry too much Alexis. Your prince won't even know you are gone. I will ensure you are back in time. He is busy with the Goddess at present." That can't be good. I start to worry for his wellbeing.

"What does she want with Henri?" I ask.

"That is between the Goddess and your mate. I am not privy to that information, Alexis. I need to speak with you though. So, focus for a moment. Do you remember the prophesy, I told you when you were small?" I nod remembering her attempting to imprint the words onto my memory. It is a long time since I heard it, but I still remember it word for word.

"Beware of the defenders, with power untold, their force shall end a world of old, when time comes, a soul unites, to save all beings, from endless night. The warrior, the protector, light and dark, a bond creates an eternal spark. This spark ignites a raging fire, to burn all evil upon a pyre," I recite. Gran nods, impressed.

"There is a reason you needed to know it, Alexis. Can you guess?" I shake my head no and she goes on. "The prophecy is about two spinners, one with power never before seen on earth and the warrior who stands by her side. They must bring about a new order, ending the rule of the Elders."

"The Elders?" I'm now thoroughly confused. "You've lost me, Mormor, the Elders don't rule. They guide. The king and queen rule. Henri's parents, and once we return to Asgard, Henri and I will take over." I have been away from court for a long time, but I'm sure that *small* detail hasn't changed in my absence.

"All is not as it seems, Alexis. The Elders hold far greater power than the king or queen. It might appear as though they are not the ones pulling the threads, but I can assure you they are."

"Mormor, what does any of that have to do with me?" I ask, trying to clear my head. I am clearly missing something. Gran looks at me with sparkling eyes.

"The Elder's power is second only to the Goddess' and one other. You." More riddles. My head is starting to hurt. First the Goddess and now Gran.

"The prophecy is about you, daughter."

"Me?" I say incredulously. "It can't be me; I don't have that kind of power." I say shaking my head.

"Don't you?" she asks. I begin shake my head no, but she raises her eyes at me. "You hide it well, dear. Better than I ever thought you would, but it is still there - waiting. You see the threads of the world equally, you can control the elements, there are other powers you have yet to discover at the tips of your fingers. It is all there; it has always been there."

"I'm not sure control is what I would call any of it, Mormor. Changes in my mood create storms. That's more of an outburst than control."

"The power of the Goddess herself runs in your blood, Alexis. Now it is time to rediscover that power and fulfil your destiny. Control will come with time and training. But you no longer have the privilege of hiding from your future. A war is coming, and the world needs you step up. Everyone is depending on you." Not for the first time I feel the weight of the entire world upon my shoulders. The Goddess, Gran, everyone is expecting way too much of me.

Gran smiles sadly as though she can hear my unspoken words.

"It is a lot to ask and have let the Goddess know what I think about her putting this on you. You have endured so much already, but you won't be alone," she says.

"The prophecy speaks of two people…"

"You already know who the other is, sweet girl."

"Henri," I breathe.

"Yes, Alexis. You and your dark prince have it within you to free the world from the tyranny of the Elders."

"How?" I ask. "I can barely control the fire in me. When I was in danger, I couldn't summon it. Then other times, it bursts out of me, when I least expect it."

"And therein lies the problem, Alexis. You must stop trying so hard to contain it. You have affinity for all the elements within you, earth, wind, and water, fire, as well. Dominion over life and death too, thanks to your father. You can spin all the threads of the earth.

"You are a true daughter of the Goddess, my darling brave girl. You are more than an ordinary spinner and when you learn to follow your instinct, your intuition, you will be unstoppable."

I try to make sense of everything I have been told, but my head is spinning. How can I possibly be a daughter of the Goddess? She has spent 250 years, resolutely ignoring me and now she expects me to save the world. There is so much I don't understand and even more I need to know.

"The Goddess, I saw her a few days ago. I was attacked and she told me, I needed to accept my power to save myself. Why wouldn't she tell me about this?" I ask.

Gran looks at me with sad eyes. "Your destiny is yours alone to discover, Alexis."

"Then why am I here?"

"To win the war, you must remember who you are, who you were born to be."

"What do you mean Mormor? Who am I?" She looks sad again and shakes her head.

"I wish I had time to tell you everything now," she says, "but alas it is time to return to your body. All will become clear soon. I love you, Alexis."

Before I can even form a question, I feel myself being pulled away. Gran turns back to the fire, I reach out for her, but strong hands pull me back.

"Wait, no," I scream as my face breaks the surface of the water. Familiar arms wrap around my waist, pulling me deftly from the ocean, onto the sand.

"Alexis, I am so sorry," Henri cries, full of shame. "I will do anything, but please don't leave me." I look at him confusion etched over my features. Tears stream down his handsome face and I reach up to wipe them away.

"What do you mean, Henri? I would never..." I see into his mind and realise what he means. He came onto the beach, saw me face down in the water and thought I was ending it.

"No," I gasp, "it's not what it looks like. I went for a swim, and something happened. I'm not sure if it was a vision or maybe I apparated, but I opened my eyes under the water and found myself in my Gran's sitting room." I use my thoughts to show him what happened, and he relaxes slightly, before tensing again. There will be time to discuss what my conversation with Gran meant and what the Goddess has told Henri, but for now, there are other issues we need to discuss.

"What you saw in that cell, my love..." I place one finger over his lips, silencing him.

"There is no need for apologies or explanations, I would have done the same in your shoes." He looks relieved until I start to talk again. "But, my prince, we fight our battles together. We are a team now, I don't need protecting, I need to be by your side, where I belong. I will never run from you or a fight again.

"The prophecy, Gran taught it me when I was young. I didn't understand its significance then. I'm not sure I still do fully, but one thing I do know is it is about the two of us. Whatever we face, we face it together. Neither one of us can do what must be done alone.

"I don't really understand what Gran meant about the Elders and the Goddess either, but Dad said somethig to me a few weeks ago, that I finally understand. If we are alone our enemies win. The only way forward is together. Promise me, you won't go off on your own again. No matter what happens."

He nods in agreement, but I feel the hesitation in his mind. "What is it," I ask.

Henri's eyes close momentarily as he begins to speak. I don't need him to say the words out loud, I can see them in his mind, but his confession comes all the same. "Alexis, my queen, my heart, there are things you don't yet know about me. Things I have done." He takes a deep breath before continuing.

"When I lost you, I went looking for answers. I cut down any being that got in my way. Destruction like that, has a price, even when it is evil you are destroying. Every life I took, I paid for with a piece of my soul, our soul. You saw my eyes. They reflect the monster I have become. Its rage…" He hangs his head in shame. Unable to meet my eyes.

I reach out to touch his face, raising it until his eyes to meet mine. I didn't flinch when I saw the obsidian depths before, I won't when I see the pain in his piercing blue eyes now. I will never shy away from Henri's pain. I meant what I said, we are a team, and we face both the good and bad together.

"Look at me, Henri," I say forcefully. "None of that matters to me. There is light and dark within us all. I didn't need to see your eyes to know the price you paid for my mistakes…" He tries to interrupt me, and I place a finger over his lips again, letting him know I am not finished.

"But, from now on, there will be no secrets between us. You cannot hide from me, I see you Henri, all of you. The good and bad, light, and dark. We fight together, and if Gran is right, we have a hell of a fight before us.

"This is bigger than Sam and Lilith. Bigger than The Witches of Endor, even. If the prophecy is to be believed, it is up to the two of us, to take down an institution as old as the earth herself."

I don't understand most of what Gran told me, but I have a feeling deep within me that whatever happened while I was face down in the water was not a dream. The goddess needs our help to take down the Elders. Why she needs the help of her creations to take down more of the same, I am unsure. Surely her power is far greater than ours, but now is not the time to question her. It is time for action.

I have known all my life that the segregation and discrimination in this world is beyond wrong. I have now seen for myself that there is another way to live.

I finally understand why my life had to be this way. I needed to leave Asgard and find Serenity. Not just to visit the island, but to live among the residents here; to see for myself the possibilities when all creatures of the earth live and work side by side. I wonder if this is how it was meant to be when the Goddess created the world. Did the Elders become so power hungry that they created the division and if so, why? And more to the point, why did their creator – the Goddess – not stop them?

As painful as it has been for both of us, I needed to leave Henri. It made me stronger than I could ever have been if I'd never left and helped me to fully understand what life can be like. If I'd never left, my life would have been comfortable, I would have no drive to change anything.

Equality is not a word many spinners are familiar with, but it is a word we live by in Serenity. It is now my job, with Henri beside me, to bring this equality to the rest of the world.

Henri

What Alexis is suggesting is suicide. We cannot just walk back into Asgard and take down the Elders, they are immortal. Not in the way that she and I are. We stop ageing in our 20's and might live for thousands of years, but there are still ways to kill a spinner. No one knows this better than Alexis who lost her family far too soon.

But the Elders cannot be killed. They exist in a realm somewhere between earth and the heavens, acting as our link to the Great Almighty.

I have never enjoyed dealing with them, as out of touch with the modern world as they are. But to even contemplate taking them down is madness. I try to explain this to my stubborn mate, but she won't even entertain me.

"Henri, don't you see. We have shown here…" she indicates to the island around us, "what can happen when all creatures come together. The Elders won't stand for it though. Why?" She doesn't want an answer from me, she already has her own. "Because they are afraid to lose their power." She finishes triumphantly.

"I know all too well what people will do for power." I feel the pain in her words, and it shoots through me like a knife. She has been shown time and time again just that. First losing her parents and more recently almost losing her own life. My arms instinctively wrap around her, pulling her close. I will never let anyone hurt my queen again.

"Alexis, my love, I'm not saying I don't agree, just that…" She looks at me sternly, silencing my argument.

"Just that what, Henri? Spinners are already at the top of the hierarchy, so we can live with things the way they are. Maybe you and your parents can, but I can't. Don't you see, no other creatures would stand a chance going up against The Elders, but maybe we; you and I, do.

"I will no longer live in a world where any creature is thought of as less than another. This is *our* battle to fight. But know this Henri, whether you fight by my side, is your choice. You can turn away if that is what you want to do, but I will – no, can – no longer sit by and watch the suffering our Elders have created. With or without you I will go against them."

I eye her warily. When she speaks so passionately, she reminds me of a lion. There is great power there, the true embodiment of a leader, but she is wild, untameable and will do anything she can to protect her loved ones, her pride. Which in recent weeks appears to have grown considerably from the people of this tiny island to the whole world. It's a huge weight to carry and I would never allow her to do so alone.

"No Alexis, I can't live with that, my love." I shake my head in shame. I don't want to be a tyrant, allowing other creatures to suffer so my own kind may thrive, but I'm not sure what she is asking, is even possible. Prophecy or not.

"It is," she says, answering my unspoken thought.

"O.K," I concede. His face brightens and then falls hearing my next thought. "But we will not go in blind. We will return to Asgard and prepare. We need information and allies – a plan." Her eyes narrow, but she nods in agreement.

"Thank you," she says.

"Anything for you, my queen."

Anything? She thinks, her thoughts turning lustful. "Anything," I reply. Alexis moves closer straddling my lap, it hadn't escaped my notice, that she was completely naked, while we had this conversation, and I can see in her mind that she is now planning to use that to her advantage.

She leans down to kiss me, passionately, as my hands explore her body. "Too many clothes," she says against my mouth.

"No just the right amount," I reply with a grin, running my hands across her soft as silk skin. She rolls her eyes at me. In an instant, our positions are reversed. I lift her off my lap, placing her down on the sand.

"Did you just roll your eyes at me, my love?" she lowers her eyes and nods once. "What happens when you do that?" I ask.

Her breath catches but she doesn't answer me. "I expect and answer, Alexis."

"I'm punished," she says, quietly.

"Yes, you are. And why is that?" I ask again, moving my body lower, taking the hardened peak of her nipple in my mouth. I bite down just enough to elicit as gasp when she fails to answer my question.

"Because it's not nice." I smile against her skin, feeling her enjoyment of me taking control.

"No, it isn't nice." I say, lifting my head to look into her eyes. "Alexis, if this gets too much and you want me to stop, promise you will tell me." I want to push her, but she needs to know, she is the one in control. After the attack, I don't want to push her too far.

She nods, but I need to hear her say it. "Tell me," I demand.

"I promise, if I want you to stop, I will tell you."

"Good girl." I reach my hand down between her legs and find her arousal dripping already. "Oh, my love, you are so responsive."

Chapter 16

Alexis

L ex, we're going to be late." Ginny yells at me from the other room.

"I'm almost ready," I shout back. I have been ready for a while; I'm just taking a moment to look around my old bedroom. This room was a haven to me when I first arrived in Serenity. It seems fitting to spend a last moment here. We leave for Asgard in two days, there is just the matter of the wedding to get through first.

The whitewashed walls haven't changed in a century. Mum and Dad left it as it was when I lived here, to let me know that it was always mine to come back to, if I wanted. There have been nights where, Dad has given me one too many of my favourite rum cocktails at a BBQ and had to put me to bed here.

This home is so full of love. I was broken the first night I stayed here and somehow Mum and Dad put me back together again. Keeping me safe until I could be with my mate. Not that they had known it at the time, none of us could have guessed how things would turn out.

Grief had been my constant companion until just a few weeks ago, but looking around it is no longer anywhere to be seen. Trying times lie ahead, I know that, but today all I feel is love and happiness. I hold onto the feeling, trying to commit it to memory, hoping it will sustain me when life gets hard.

I stand and look in the full-length mirror, barely recognising myself. Ginny pulled my hair into elaborate braids around my head, with the lengths falling into my natural wave. I look like a Norse Goddess. At one time I'd have been horrified to wear my hair like this. Wanting to put as much space between myself and Asgard as possible, but rather than scaring me, I allow it to bring me strength.

Gran would be so happy to see me embrace the Goddess in this way. The women of the Beaumont family always wore their hair like this. We are warriors and need to look the part. My makeup has been kept minimal, just enough to highlight my green eyes and ruby red lips. I smile at the woman looking at me and she smiles in return.

Rather than a tiara, I am wearing a silver handfasting head chain, which was made on the island especially for me. The intricate trinity knot at its centre representing the interconnectedness of all things; love, unity, and eternal life. Either side of this are love knots featuring two interwoven hearts symbolising the unbreakable bond I share with Henri.

My dress is again traditional. The simple neckline highlights my breasts perfectly and the V back dips to my waist where the skirt kicks out allowing me to walk freely. Wide straps sit just off the shoulder and loose flowing sleeves create a wing like effect. The entire dress is covered in ivory lace. Tiny vines with colourful flower buds run up the skirt and across the bodice. An almost exact representation of my spinners marks below. The bouquet of flowers currently resting on the nightstand matches them also.

Mum has given me a tiny silver locket dangling from an elegant chain. It contrasts with my traditional Norse dress, but I love it for that reason. It's an acknowledgement of Mum and Dad, the people who got me this far. There is a small photo of the three of us together at Dad's bar inside. I will never take it off. I don't ever want to forget what it represents.

A solid silver cuff winds up my arm in three spirals signifying my power over the three life forces; water, fire, and earth.

Someone clears their throat behind me, and I turn to see Dad looking at me with tears in his eyes. "Alexis, you look... Wow." I blush at the complement, but know what he means, the girls have made me look otherworldly. "You would make the Goddess herself envious looking like that. I am so, so proud of you, Alexis." He clears his throat of the emotion lodged there.

"Are you ready to go, sweetheart," he asks when he has composed himself.

"Yes," I say brightly. "I've never been more ready for anything." I take his outstretched arm and we head down the hall together.

Excited squeals of delight, greet us as we turn the corner into the sitting room. Everyone I love – other than Henri – is gathered to accompany me to the square. Ginny hugs me tightly, then steps back smoothing down my dress. She looks stunning, her emerald-green floor length gown sparkles in the early afternoon sun, accentuating her womanly figure. She has left her hair down and it falls in a golden curtain down her back.

Mum is next to hug me and tears fill my eyes as she nears. She deftly wipes a stray one away before it falls. "Alexis, your Dad and I are so proud of you," she says, tears filling her own eyes. She is dressed in a simple emerald maxi dress. I nod, momentarily too overcome with emotion to speak. I take a deep breath and ask for a moment alone with Mum and Dad.

Everyone files out and I turn to speak to my guardians. "I just wanted to thank you both properly for... well everything," I say, over the lump forming in my throat. "I don't know where I would be without the two of you and I hope you know that you will always be my Mum and Dad, no matter how far away I am."

We stand in a circle holding hands, in full awareness that this maybe the last time we share a moment alone in the place I have called home, for most of my life.

"We love you, more than words could ever express, firefly," my Dad says.

"I love you both too."

No more words are necessary.

Opting to walk to the square in my sandals, I carry my ivory satin wedding shoes in my hand, rather than dirty them. Using the other hand, I use spinner's threads to hold my dress off the ground.

Henri and I are to be married on the steps of the council building – the place our mating bond was re-awakened.

A tent has been set up out of view of the square, allowing me a moment to gather myself before I walk down the aisle. Mum has taken her seat with the other guests leaving Ginny and Dad to help me into my shoes and fuss over my dress.

"There, perfect," Gin says with one final adjustment. I nod in agreement and take Dad's arm ready to face my future.

Ginny leads the procession, with two small flower girls dropping jasmine petals from baskets down the sides of the aisle – the smell is divine. Dad and I follow. Butterflies erupt in my stomach, as I am hit by the enormity of what I am about to do. Silly really, given I have already given myself to Henri, heart, body, mind, and soul.

Everything fades into the background as my eyes lock again with my mate. Suddenly, Dad is holding my back as I attempt to rush to his side. We have been apart no more than a few hours, but already I yearn to be closer to him.

Falling into step with my dad, I rake my eyes over Henri's perfect from. He too is outfitted in dress representing traditional Asgardian attire. A deep royal blue cotton tunic elaborately embroidered with the same pattern as his spinner's marks, falls just above his knees. The long sleeves are capped off with black and brown leather cuffs, which match the belt at his waist. His outfit takes me back to 1700s Asgard and the way he looked when I first met him. The only things missing are his long-braided hair and beard. I always saw him as a warrior and in this moment, he is the true embodiment of one.

Henri

I'm restless as I wait at the end of the aisle for Alexis. We have only been apart for a few hours, having both refused to spend the night away from each other, but a few hours are more than enough. I have stayed out of her thoughts, not wanting to spoil the surprise.

I feel her as she approaches the aisle and even though, I hadn't planned to, I turn and meet her gaze. I can feel her urge to be close to me. It makes me smile to know we feel the same way.

The slow pace of the procession does give me the opportunity to take her in. I didn't think it would be possible for her to look more beautiful, but somehow, she does. She is utterly breath-taking. The Goddess incarnate.

That dress should be illegal.

I can see every curve of her flawless body and yet she oozes elegance. Her red hair, though braded in places has been left to fall down her back in waves, just how I like it.

It feels like an eternity, watching her walk towards me and I have to hold myself back from running to meet her. Alexis and Matias come to a stop beside me, he takes her hand, placing it into mine, my marks tingle in recognition as our skin meets. One glance at Alexis and I know she feels it too.

Matias steps away and we turn to face Hugh, who is acting as our celebrant. "We are gathered here today," he begins. Everything else falls away and there is only Alexis and I, as we look into each other's eyes.

I feel a flutter of nerves as the moment for our vows arrives.

"Alexis, my queen, my heart, my soul. I loved you from the first moment I saw you. I didn't know then what the future would bring, but I always knew you held my soul.

"I promise to love you without condition, to honour and worship you each and every day of our life. To laugh when you're happy and hold you when you are sad. Our kind aren't at liberty to choose our mate, but if we could I would still choose you."

Tears fill her eyes and drop silently down her cheeks. I wipe them away with my thumb as she begins her own vows to me.

"Henri, I am unconditionally and irrevocably in love with you. You are my best friend, my lover, my soul mate. When we were born our soul was split in two, half lives within me and half within you. I am sorry it has taken so long to get to where we are now, but I vow to spend eternity making it up to you.

"I promise to walk with you every step of our life, that no matter where our journey leads, I will be there by your side.

"I will be there when the darkness threatens to overwhelm you, my prince. I will shine a light to show the way through your blackest night. The Goddess created us to be together as one, which we will remain from this day on."

Her poetic vows to me, do exactly as she says, shining a light on even the darkest corners of my broken soul. For the first time in forever, I believe there might still be some good within me.

Hugh ties the elaborate handfasting cord around our joined hands and the crowd gasps, as they begin to glow brighter than the moon on a clear winter's night. The cord is made of nine knots all representing love and eternity. Six cords of ivory, emerald and ruby have been woven into a continuous thread. Tiny ruby rose buds adorn the cord. At its centre is a single triquetra knot. It represents our past, present and future. None of which I ever want to forget.

The feeling of being forever joined to the magnificent woman in front of me reaches the depths of my being, as every fibre of my past present and future merges with hers. There will never be a secret between us now, I will feel her joy and pain as she feels mine.

The light subsides and the cord, no longer silk ribbon and rope has imprinted across our joined hands.

"Henri and Alexis, the Goddess has blessed your union. Henri, you may now kiss your mate."

Epilogue

The woman sat hidden among the thick trees surrounding the small town, waiting for an opportunity to strike. She'd been there all day, as the *happy couple* celebrated their wedding. Even the woman had to admit that the spinners had looked spectacular as they had tied the knot. Jealousy and rage almost made her leave her hiding place and stick her knife through the spoiled bitch's heart.

It should have been her stood before the prince, but the little spinner put a stop to that.

Not that she wanted happily ever after, just the perks that come with being wed to the future king. The power that came with it. The power the *Elders* had promised. How could those worthless fools call themselves all powerful when they hadn't even seen this coming? Watching the couple as they laughed and smiled with their guests, was almost as revolting, as watching them declare their love.

Love. Love is weak, it makes you vulnerable. The woman didn't want or need love. Nevertheless, once she had completed her task, her master's would reward her with power beyond her coven's wildest dreams.

She could adapt, she'd learned how over the years. There was more than one way to achieve a goal.

Now wasn't the time to finish the job though. For now, retrieving her puppet would have to do. Working with a human was beyond demeaning, but the woman would work with what she had. Everyone else on the island were too loyal to the prince and his new princess. The human though, she could feel his jealousy. He wanted the princess for himself. It was easy to twist his feelings into hate and use him for her own ends.

Only the idiot got himself caught. He was supposed to lure her away and stick a knife through her heart. But no, the fool had to play with her. *Did his mother never tell him not to play with his food.* The woman would not make the same mistake twice. Next time she would be the one to finish the job and then rid herself of the boy.

The boy was the spinner's weakness. She had already used that to her advantage, she could do that again.

When she looked inside the boy, she could see his love for the spinner who would never love him the same in return. The spinner loved him, yes. But she only ever had eyes for the prince. Her love was that of a sister. Families – the curse of the good – could be used to manipulate. When the time came, the boy would be her bargaining chip. First though she had to get to him.

Shaking herself from her thoughts, the woman refocused on where she could feel his energy. Witches like her feed from hate and jealousy, greed, and anger. It gave them power. It made her sick to think she had resorted to feeding from a lowly human, her last source of energy was so decadent. The rage bubbling inside his veins, was exquisite, the woman couldn't remember the last time she'd felt so powerful, so alive. It made her mouth water, just thinking about it.

Finding his *mate* put an end to that, though. Looking at him now, made her stomach turn, joy came off him in waves. His rage was still there, but barely. Even that had changed, it could no longer be a source of sustenance to her. She didn't understand why, but the change of its focus, give it a sickly-sweet taste, she couldn't stomach.

Coming to this island had almost drained her completely, everyone here was always so *happy*. She had been lucky to stumble across the broken-hearted human. His bitterness was strong, even for a human, it was just enough to refuel her. Still, it wasn't enough for her to find the spinner and kill her alone. She'd still needed the boy and he had made such a mess. So, he would have to do, for now. His rage was greater than before and it would be enough fuel to get them both off the island.

She could feel he was being kept below the building at the other side of the square. She had only been inside once, but it wasn't big, there wouldn't be an issue locating her target. The only problem she could foresee, was whatever magic was being used to contain him. Her worry was unfounded though, even from here she could feel the magic wasn't cast by a spinner. It wouldn't take her long to break through.

Night had long since fallen when the party eventually began to die down. She'd endured hours watching as the prince and his spinner danced and laughed with their guests. They were there until the end. Things couldn't be that good in the bedroom if they would rather spend their wedding night with other people. She smirked at this thought. That pathetic creature could not give the warrior prince what he needed.

The woman heard the last guests as they said their goodbyes, wobbly from too much alcohol heading for their beds.

She could feel there was no one else around, but the woman stuck to the shadows regardless. It wouldn't do to kill someone and raise an alarm before she was clear of the island. She'd spent weeks scouring for an escape route and knew she would only get one opportunity to take it and even for that she needed the boy.

Inside the building was almost pitch dark, it made little difference to her though, she would just follow her target's energy. She could feel him below her and set off in search of a route down. She found the stairs which were magically concealed. The woman easily broke the spell and set off again to find the human.

Coming to a stop at the gate of a small cell she took a moment to survey him. The man resembled a wounded animal, curled up in the middle of the floor. Injuries – no doubt bestowed on him by the prince – were just starting to heal. Looking beyond him, the woman could see that the cell itself wasn't protected by magic.

Clearly the man's captors didn't think it was necessary, a weak human couldn't break out of the cell. He wouldn't have the power. It must never have occurred to them, someone might want to break in. *Fools.*

"Get up," the woman boomed. The man's eyes shot open, and he scrambled back in panic, no doubt afraid someone had come to finish him off. The spell cast over him by the woman, had long since worn off allowing the seed of hate she sowed, to wither. It was still inside him, she could feel that much, but other emotions were creeping back in. The man felt as sorry for himself as he looked.

"I said, get up," the woman repeated. This time the man got to his feet. He was weak from the endless hours curled up in his cell and it took him a while to steady himself.

The woman raised her hands and directed them at the iron bars, enclosing the human inside. The bars began to shake before falling to the ground. Stepping over them the woman seized the man, pulling him along after her.

Narrowing his eyes, the human finally recognised the woman, and his features relax.

"Lilith," he breathed. "What happened to me?"

"Nothing to worry about my sweet boy," the woman answered in a soothing tone. "I have you now, you are safe."

Acknowledgements

I must start by thanking my mum, Joanne Coles for always supporting me and encouraging me to follow my dreams. Without her constant feedback and honesty, this book would never have been possible.

Thank you to my daughter Lily for always reminding me it is OK to be myself unapologetically and giving me a reason to show up daily. And to my boys who are a constant source of joy in my life.

To my husband, David. Thank you for looking after me, ensuring I eat, drink, move around, and sleep when I am at the bottom of a 'writing rabbit hole.'

I would like to thank my friend, Natasha Herrington. She might not know it, but her lovely words after reading a draft of this book, pushed me to finish and publish it.

Finally, thank you to everyone in my life – past and present – for your support (or lack of in some cases) you all shaped me into the person I am today.

 About The Author Rochelle Tattersall Rochelle began writing at a young age working in public relations and advertising, creating copy for clients. That ended abruptly with the Covid-19 pandemic, and she started writing for her own enjoyment. This led to some amazing opportunities, writing blog posts for her university, where she is a student nurse. Rochelle even became one of just seven student editors for the Nursing Times, a major publication in the nursing industry.

Finding the need for something new, Rochelle decided to try her hand at creative writing and her debut novel, The Spinners Tale is a result of this. She has always dreamed of writing books and characters that readers would fall in love with as much as her. With The Spinners Tale, she hopes to have achieved just that.

Rochelle lives in Halifax, West Yorkshire and has three children, so when she isn't writing or on clinical placements, you can usually find her in a play gym! Rochelle's other interests include, chocolate, drinking copious amounts of tea, being a prolific romance reader, walking and yoga.